# ANGRY BIRDS™ COMICS

## WELCOME TO THE FLOCK

Cover Artwork by Paco Rodriquez
Cover Colors by Digikore Studios

Original Series Edits by David Hedgecock
Collection Edits by Justin Eisinger & Alonzo Simon
Collection Production by Chris Mowry

ROVIO BOOKS
Mikael Hed, Rovio CEO
Laura Nevanlinna, Publishing Director
Mikko Põllä, Creative Director
Jukka Heiskanen, Editor-in-Chief, Comics
Juha Mäkinen, Editor, Comics
Jan Schulte-Tigges, Art Director, Comics
Jean-Michel Boesch, Senior Graphic Supervisor
Henrik Sarimo, Graphic Designer
Nathan Cosby, Freelance Editor

Thanks to Jukka Heiskanen, Juha Mäkinen, and the Rovio team for their hard work and invaluable assistance.

ISBN: 978-1-63140-090-2

17 16 15 14 1 2 3 4

IDW®
www.IDWPUBLISHING.com
IDW founded by Ted Adams, Alex Garner, Kris Oprisko, and Robbie Robbins

Ted Adams, CEO & Publisher
Greg Goldstein, President & COO
Robbie Robbins, EVP/Sr. Graphic Artist
Chris Ryall, Chief Creative Officer/Editor-in-Chief
Matthew Ruzicka, CPA, Chief Financial Officer
Alan Payne, VP of Sales
Dirk Wood, VP of Marketing
Lorelei Bunjes, VP of Digital Services
Jeff Webber, VP of Digital Publishing & Business Development

Facebook: facebook.com/idwpublishing
Twitter: @idwpublishing
YouTube: youtube.com/idwpublishing
Instagram: instagram.com/idwpublishing
deviantART: idwpublishing.deviantart.com
Pinterest: pinterest.com/idwpublishing/idw-staff-faves



Originally published in ANGRY BIRDS COMICS issues #1-4.

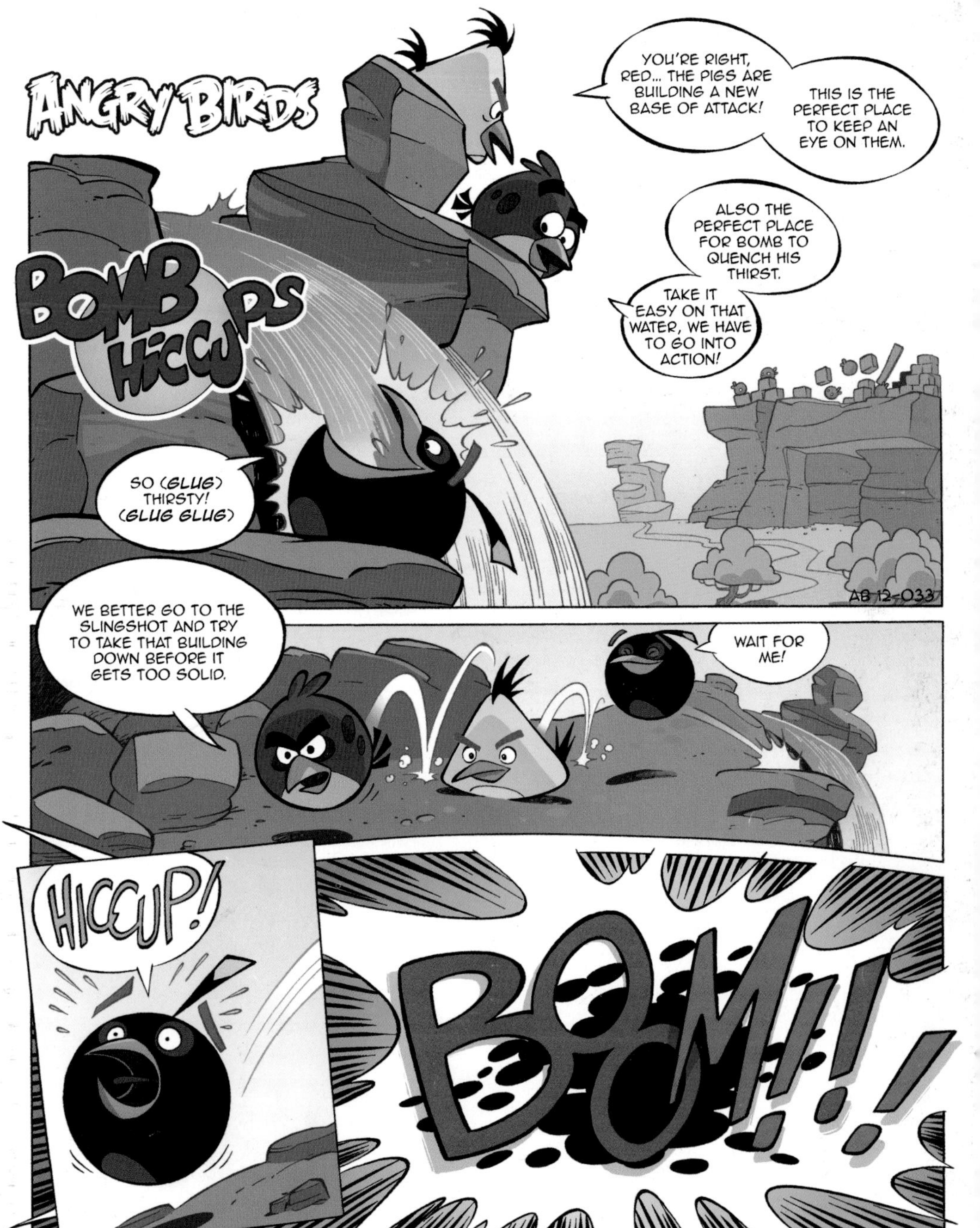
ANGRY BIRDS
BOMB HICCUPS
YOU'RE RIGHT, RED... THE PIGS ARE BUILDING A NEW BASE OF ATTACK!
THIS IS THE PERFECT PLACE TO KEEP AN EYE ON THEM.
ALSO THE PERFECT PLACE FOR BOMB TO QUENCH HIS THIRST.
TAKE IT EASY ON THAT WATER, WE HAVE TO GO INTO ACTION!
SO (GLUG) THIRSTY! (GLUG GLUG)
AB 12-033
WE BETTER GO TO THE SLINGSHOT AND TRY TO TAKE THAT BUILDING DOWN BEFORE IT GETS TOO SOLID.
WAIT FOR ME!
HICCUP!
BOOM!!!

WRITTEN BY: JEFF PARKER • ART BY: PACO RODRIQUES • COLORS BY: JULIE GORE • LETTERS BY: ROVIO COMICS

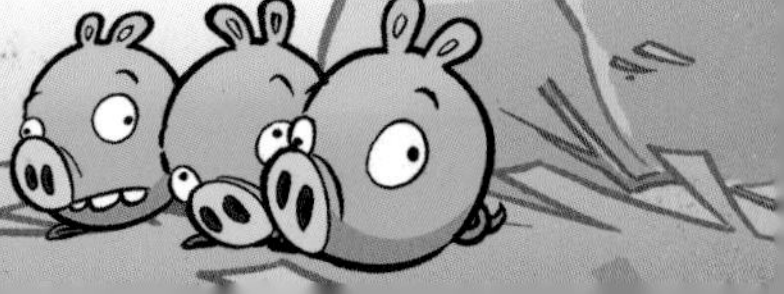

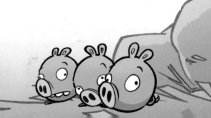

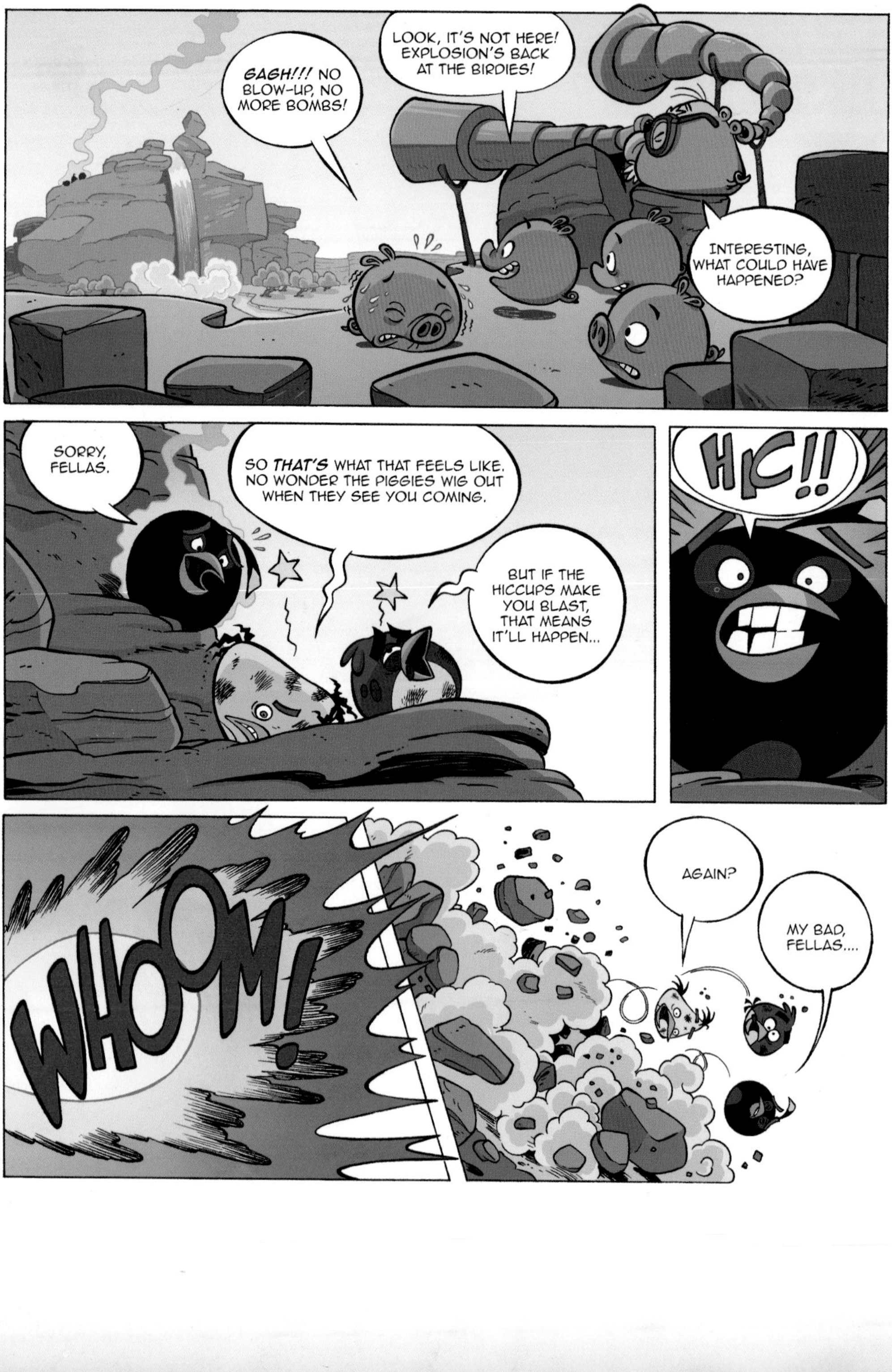
GAGH!!! NO BLOW-UP, NO MORE BOMBS!
LOOK, IT'S NOT HERE! EXPLOSION'S BACK AT THE BIRDIES!
INTERESTING, WHAT COULD HAVE HAPPENED?
SORRY, FELLAS.
SO THAT'S WHAT THAT FEELS LIKE. NO WONDER THE PIGGIES WIG OUT WHEN THEY SEE YOU COMING.
BUT IF THE HICCUPS MAKE YOU BLAST, THAT MEANS IT'LL HAPPEN...
HIC!!
WHOOM!
AGAIN?
MY BAD, FELLAS....

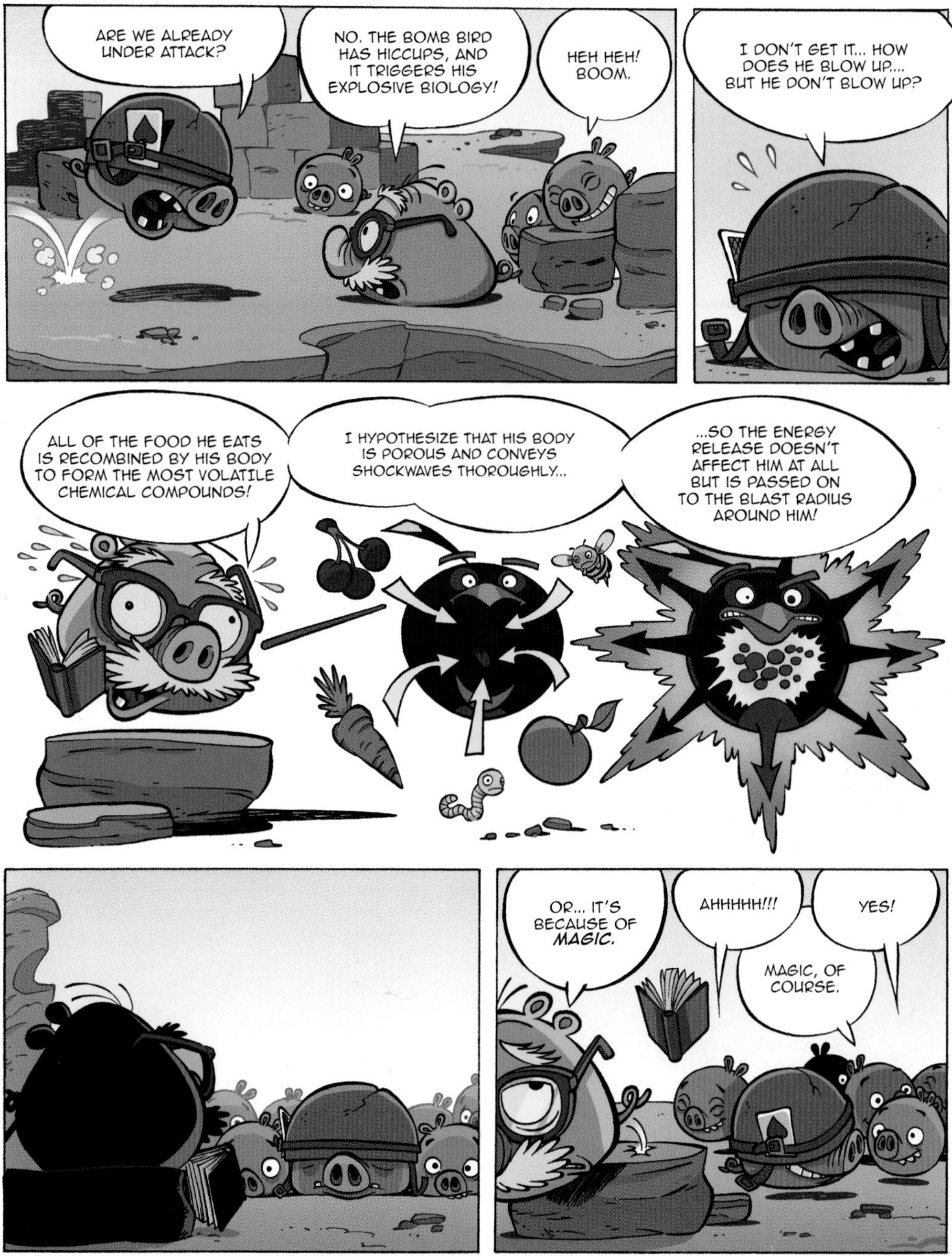
ARE WE ALREADY UNDER ATTACK?
NO. THE BOMB BIRD HAS HICCUPS, AND IT TRIGGERS HIS EXPLOSIVE BIOLOGY!
HEH HEH! BOOM.
I DON'T GET IT... HOW DOES HE BLOW UP.... BUT HE DON'T BLOW UP?
ALL OF THE FOOD HE EATS IS RECOMBINED BY HIS BODY TO FORM THE MOST VOLATILE CHEMICAL COMPOUNDS!
I HYPOTHESIZE THAT HIS BODY IS POROUS AND CONVEYS SHOCKWAVES THOROUGHLY...
...SO THE ENERGY RELEASE DOESN'T AFFECT HIM AT ALL BUT IS PASSED ON TO THE BLAST RADIUS AROUND HIM!
OR... IT'S BECAUSE OF *MAGIC.*
AHHHHH!!!
YES!
MAGIC, OF COURSE.
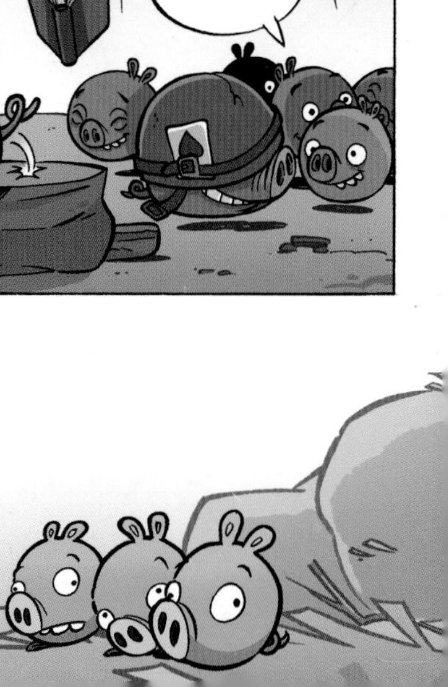

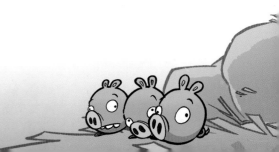

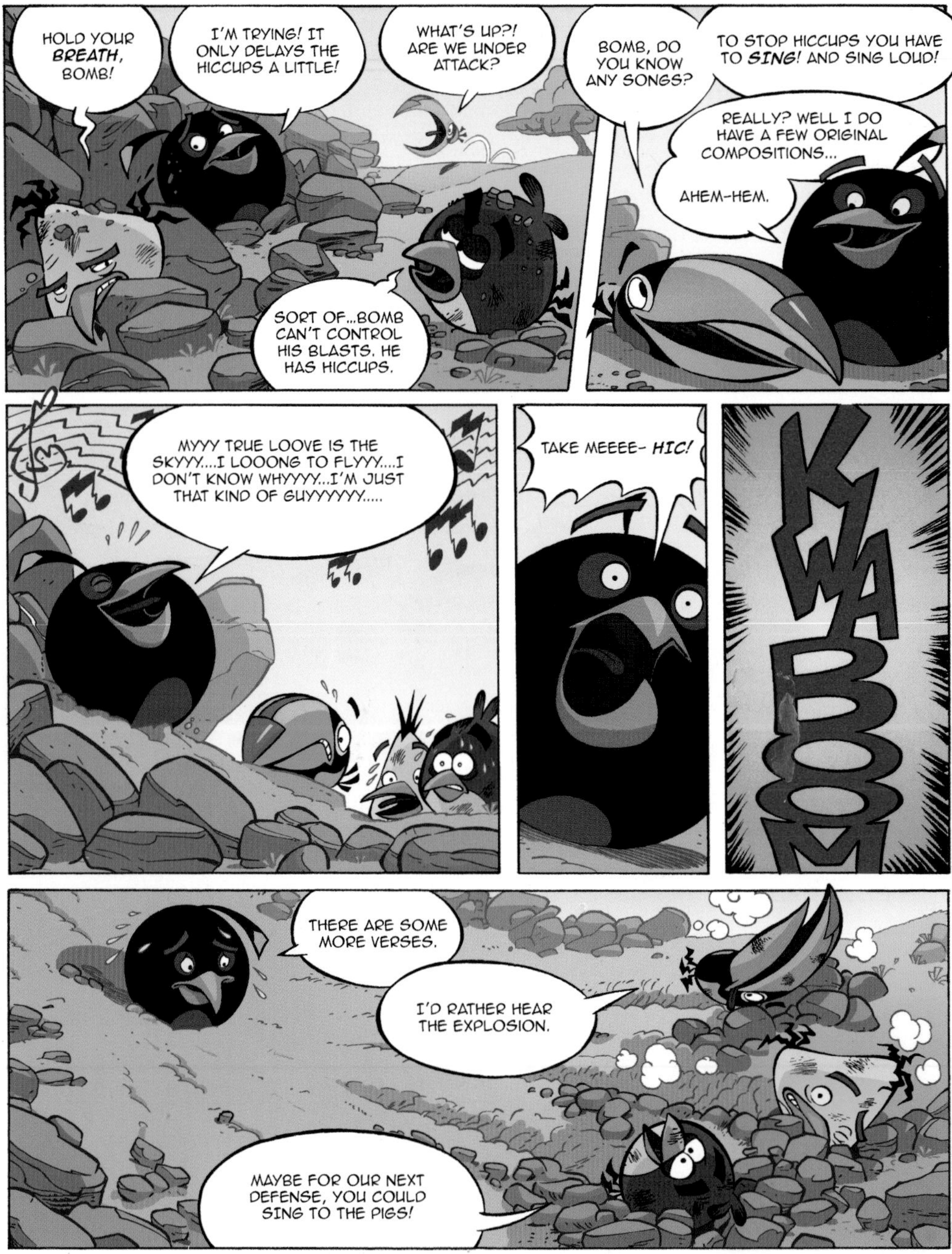
HOLD YOUR BREATH, BOMB!
I'M TRYING! IT ONLY DELAYS THE HICCUPS A LITTLE!
WHAT'S UP?! ARE WE UNDER ATTACK?
SORT OF...BOMB CAN'T CONTROL HIS BLASTS. HE HAS HICCUPS.
BOMB, DO YOU KNOW ANY SONGS?
TO STOP HICCUPS YOU HAVE TO SING! AND SING LOUD!
REALLY? WELL I DO HAVE A FEW ORIGINAL COMPOSITIONS...
AHEM-HEM.
MYYY TRUE LOOVE IS THE SKYYY....I LOOONG TO FLYYY....I DON'T KNOW WHYYYY...I'M JUST THAT KIND OF GUYYYYYY.....
TAKE MEEEE- HIC!
KWABOOM
THERE ARE SOME MORE VERSES.
I'D RATHER HEAR THE EXPLOSION.
MAYBE FOR OUR NEXT DEFENSE, YOU COULD SING TO THE PIGS!

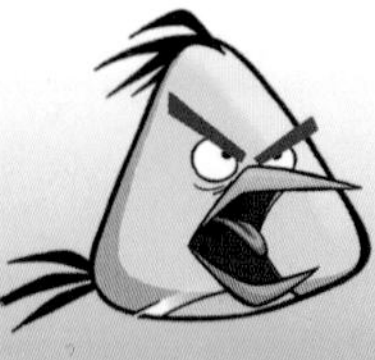

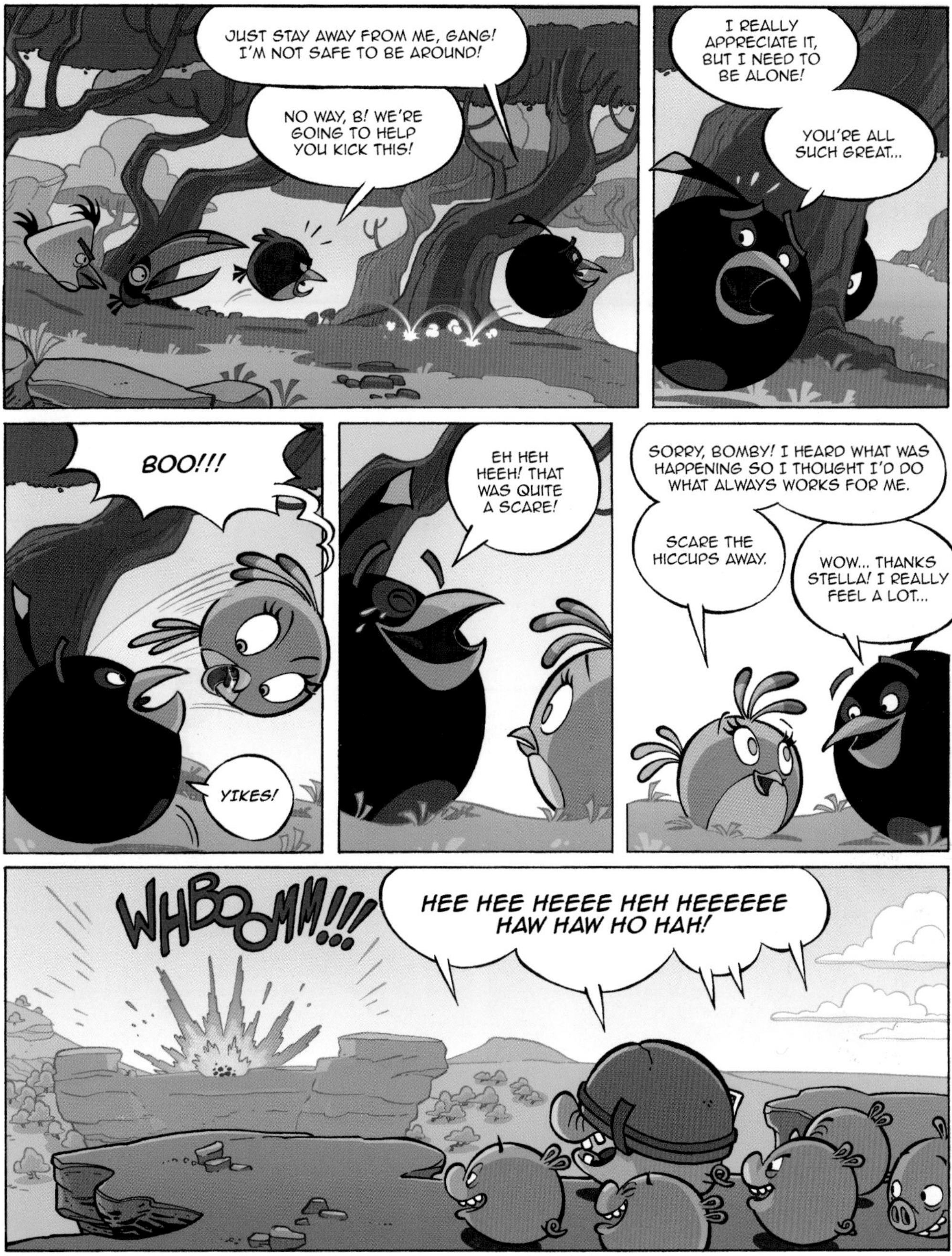
JUST STAY AWAY FROM ME, GANG! I'M NOT SAFE TO BE AROUND!
NO WAY, B! WE'RE GOING TO HELP YOU KICK THIS!
I REALLY APPRECIATE IT, BUT I NEED TO BE ALONE!
YOU'RE ALL SUCH GREAT...
BOO!!!
YIKES!
EH HEH HEEH! THAT WAS QUITE A SCARE!
SORRY, BOMBY! I HEARD WHAT WAS HAPPENING SO I THOUGHT I'D DO WHAT ALWAYS WORKS FOR ME.
SCARE THE HICCUPS AWAY.
WOW... THANKS STELLA! I REALLY FEEL A LOT...
WHBOOMM!!!
HEE HEE HEEEE HEH HEEEEEE HAW HAW HO HAH!

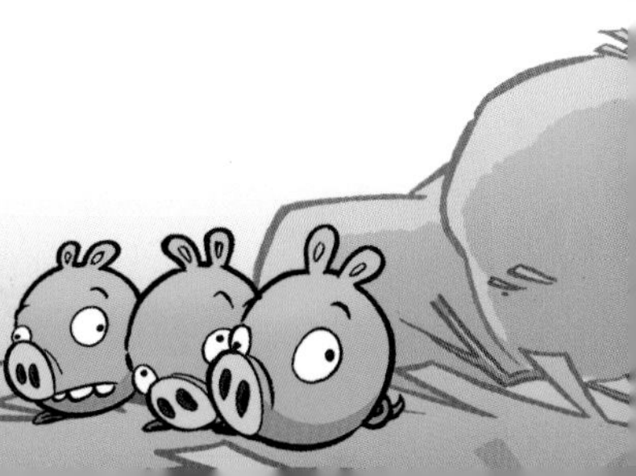

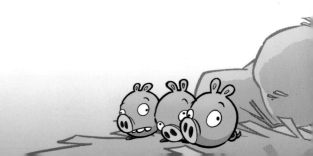

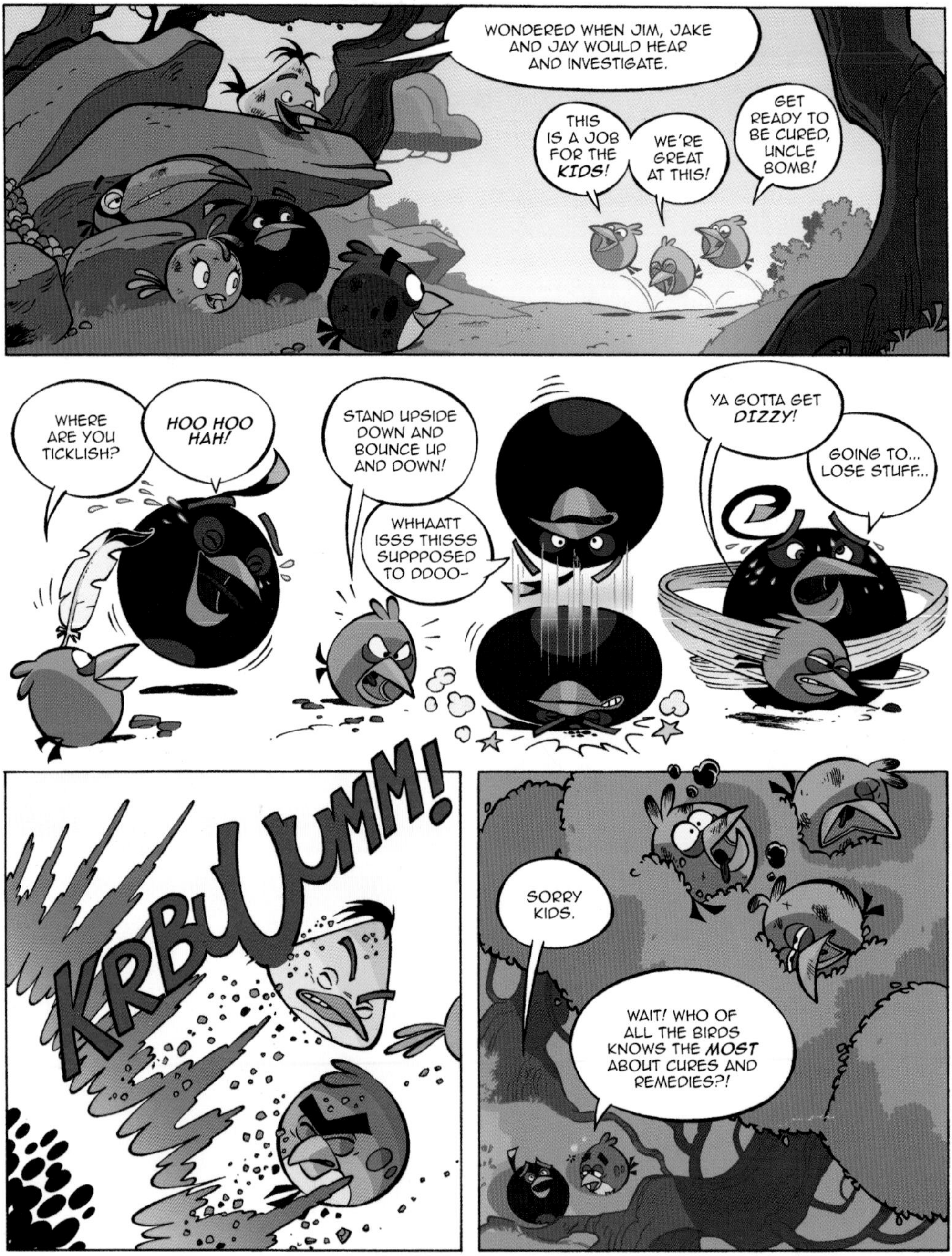
WONDERED WHEN JIM, JAKE AND JAY WOULD HEAR AND INVESTIGATE.
THIS IS A JOB FOR THE KIDS!
WE'RE GREAT AT THIS!
GET READY TO BE CURED, UNCLE BOMB!
WHERE ARE YOU TICKLISH?
HOO HOO HAH!
STAND UPSIDE DOWN AND BOUNCE UP AND DOWN!
WHHAATT ISSS THISSS SUPPPOSED TO DDOO-
YA GOTTA GET DIZZY!
GOING TO... LOSE STUFF...
KRBUUMM!
SORRY KIDS.
WAIT! WHO OF ALL THE BIRDS KNOWS THE MOST ABOUT CURES AND REMEDIES?!

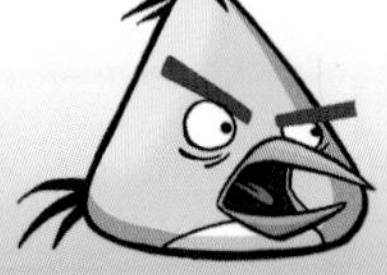

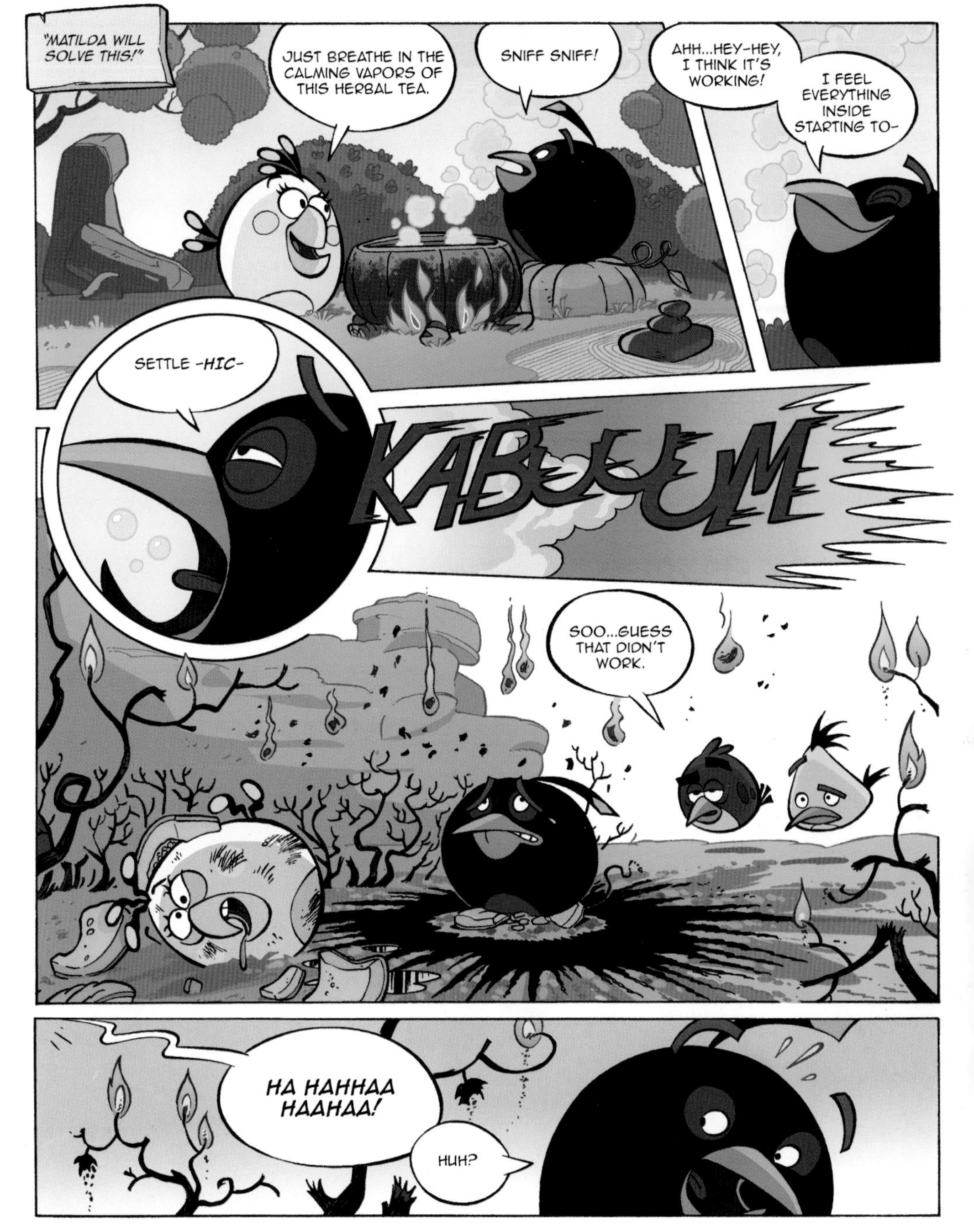
"MATILDA WILL SOLVE THIS!"
JUST BREATHE IN THE CALMING VAPORS OF THIS HERBAL TEA.
SNIFF SNIFF!
AHH...HEY-HEY, I THINK IT'S WORKING!
I FEEL EVERYTHING INSIDE STARTING TO-
SETTLE -HIC-
KABOOOOM
SOO...GUESS THAT DIDN'T WORK.
HA HAHHAA HAAHAA!
HUH?

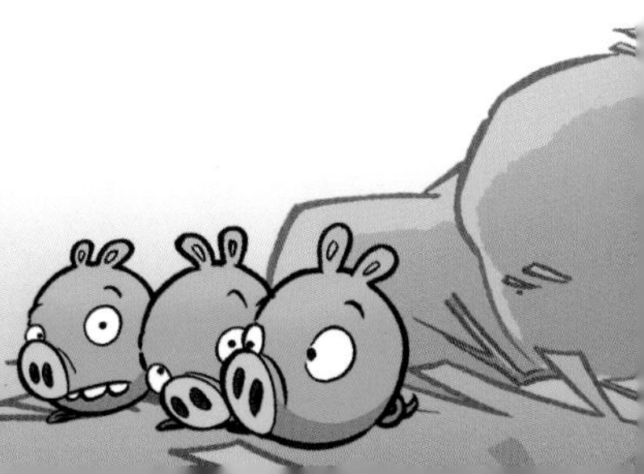

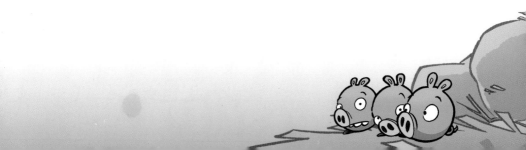

SO GLAD WE COULD ENTERTAIN YOU!
HAW HAW HEE HEH HEEEE! SNORT!
THAT DOES IT!!
WUH-OH.
I'VE HAD IT! IF I'M JUST GOING TO DETONATE RANDOMLY, I'M GOING TO DO IT AROUND THOSE PIGS!
NORMALLY I'D SAY WAIT UNTIL I'VE WORKED UP A PLAN, BUT THIS ACTUALLY SOUNDS PRETTY GOOD TO ME.
GO BOMB!
WHAT ARE THEY DOING NOW?
I CAN'T TELL...

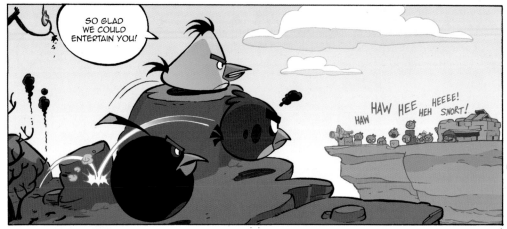

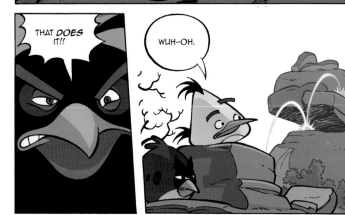

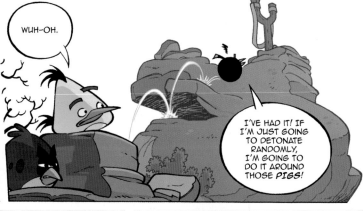

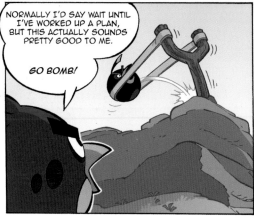

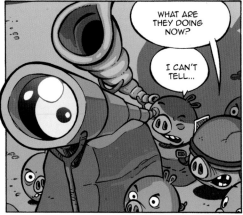

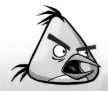

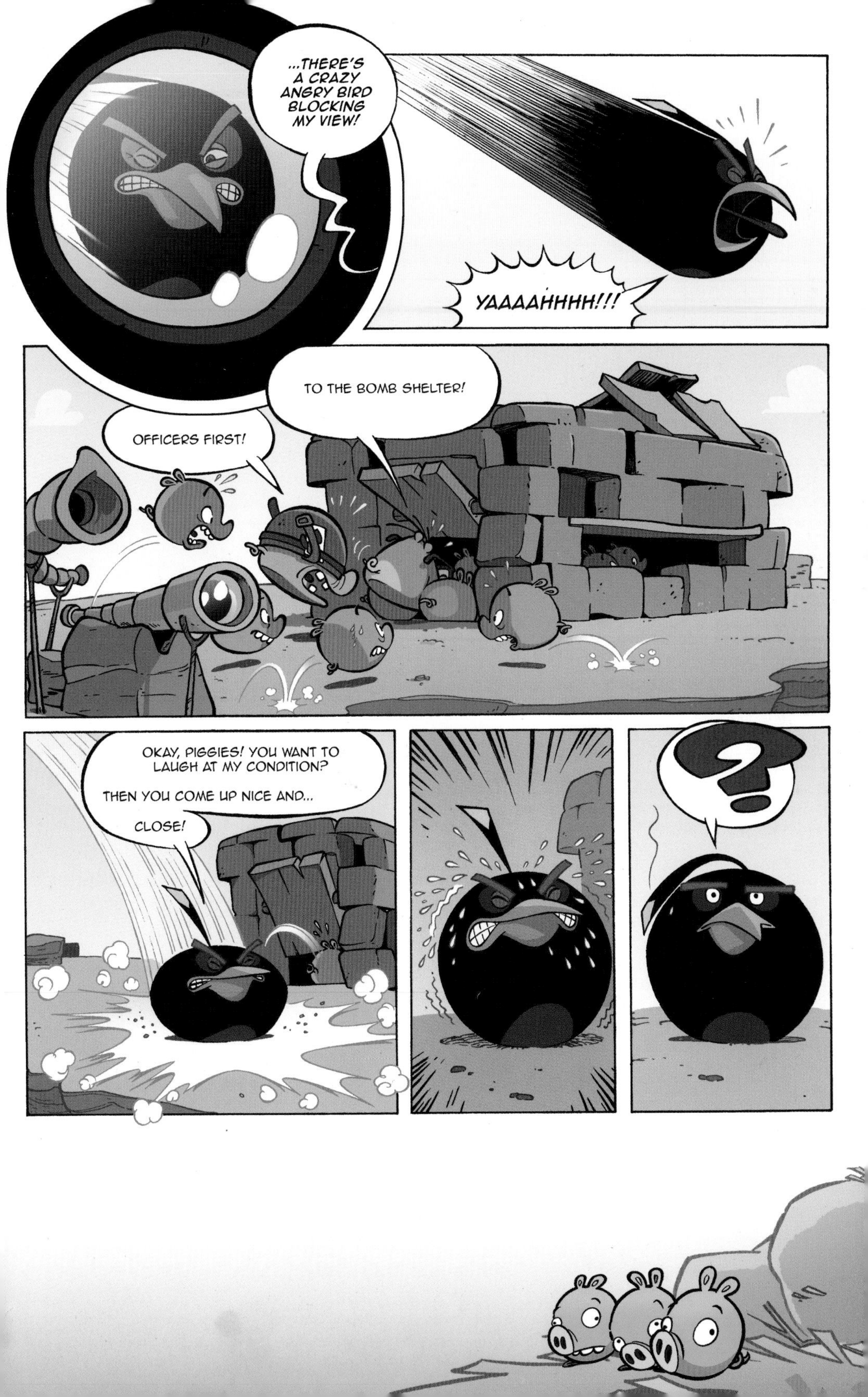
...THERE'S A CRAZY ANGRY BIRD BLOCKING MY VIEW!
YAAAAHHHH!!!
TO THE BOMB SHELTER!
OFFICERS FIRST!
OKAY, PIGGIES! YOU WANT TO LAUGH AT MY CONDITION?
THEN YOU COME UP NICE AND...
CLOSE!
?

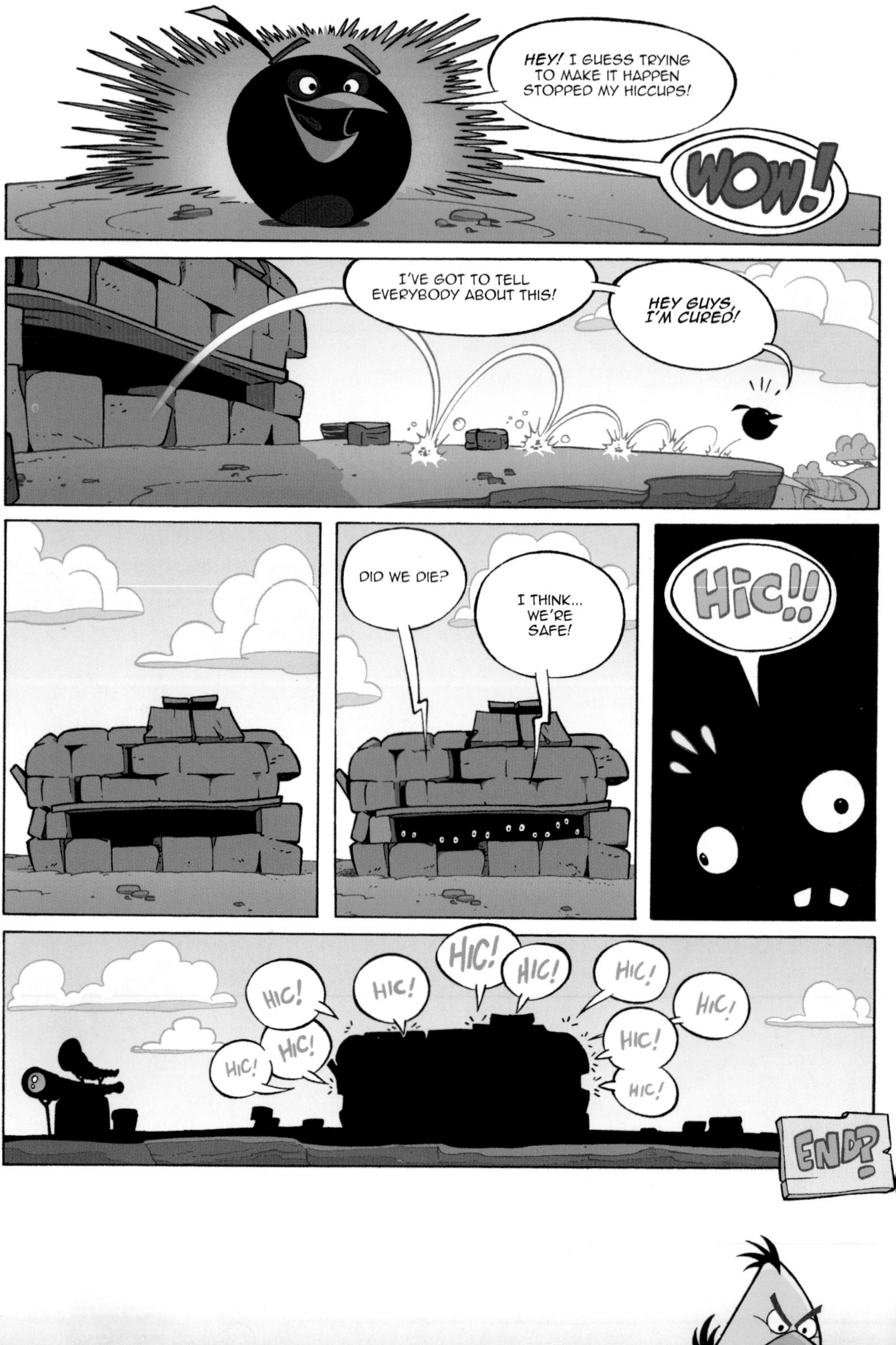
HEY! I GUESS TRYING TO MAKE IT HAPPEN STOPPED MY HICCUPS!
WOW!
I'VE GOT TO TELL EVERYBODY ABOUT THIS!
HEY GUYS, I'M CURED!
DID WE DIE?
I THINK... WE'RE SAFE!
HIC!!
HIC!
HIC!
HIC!
HIC!
HIC!
HIC!
HIC!
HIC!
HIC!
HIC!
END?

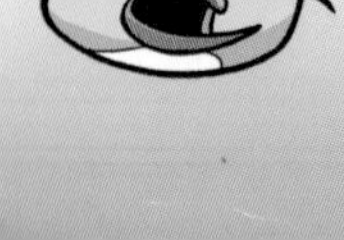

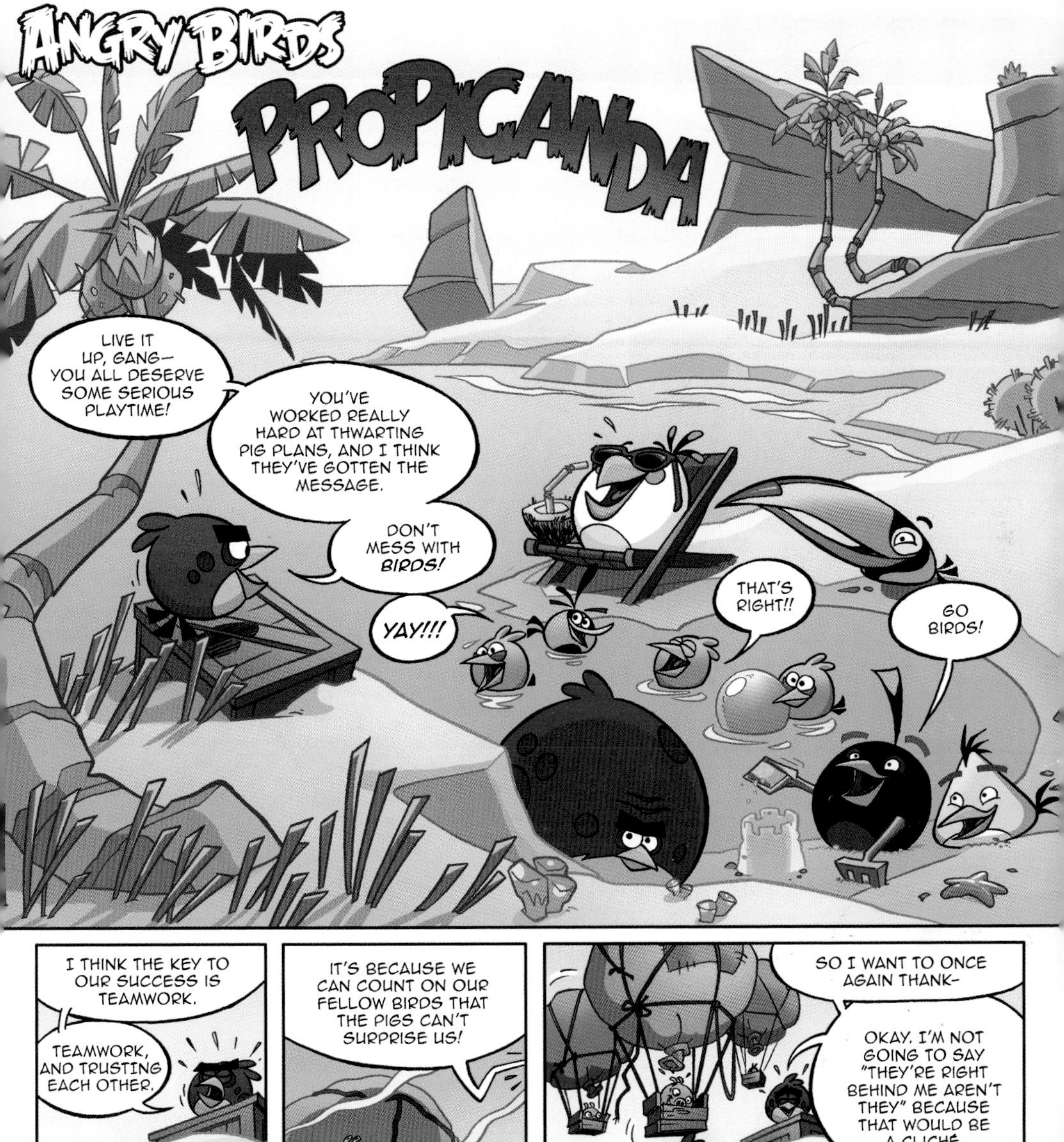
ANGRY BIRDS
PROPICANDA
LIVE IT UP, GANG— YOU ALL DESERVE SOME SERIOUS PLAYTIME!
YOU'VE WORKED REALLY HARD AT THWARTING PIG PLANS, AND I THINK THEY'VE GOTTEN THE MESSAGE.
DON'T MESS WITH *BIRDS!*
YAY!!!
THAT'S RIGHT!!
GO BIRDS!

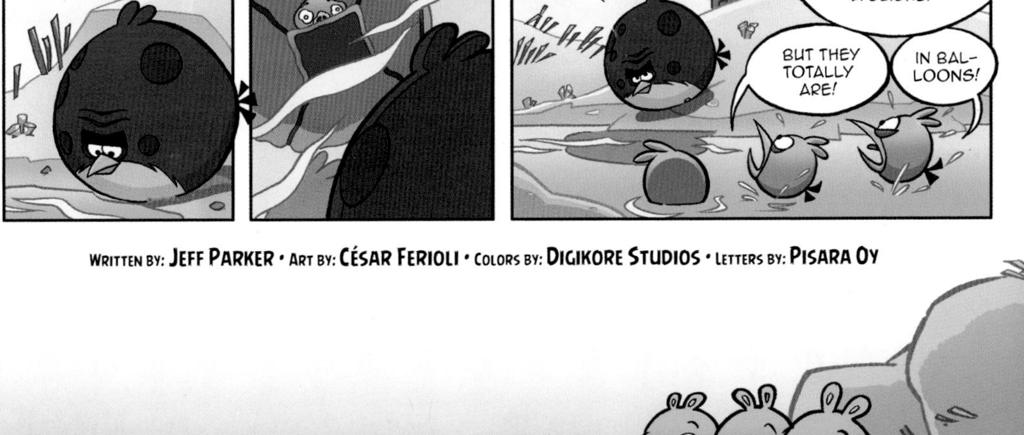
I THINK THE KEY TO OUR SUCCESS IS TEAMWORK.
TEAMWORK, AND TRUSTING EACH OTHER.
IT'S BECAUSE WE CAN COUNT ON OUR FELLOW BIRDS THAT THE PIGS CAN'T SURPRISE US!
SO I WANT TO ONCE AGAIN THANK-
OKAY. I'M NOT GOING TO SAY "THEY'RE RIGHT BEHIND ME AREN'T THEY" BECAUSE THAT WOULD BE A CLICHÉ.
BUT THEY TOTALLY ARE!
IN BAL-LOONS!

WRITTEN BY: **JEFF PARKER** • ART BY: **CÉSAR FERIOLI** • COLORS BY: **DIGIKORE STUDIOS** • LETTERS BY: **PISARA OY**

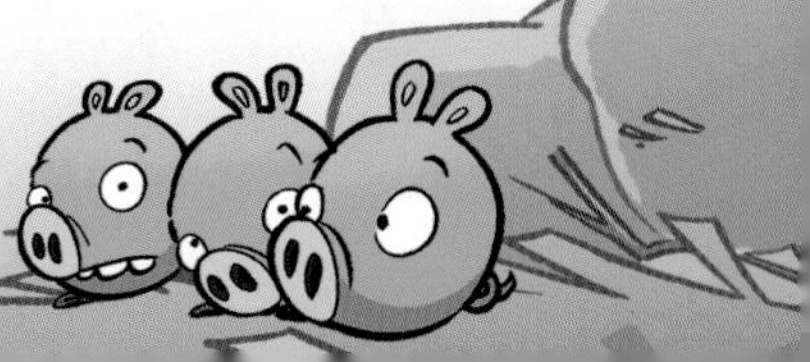

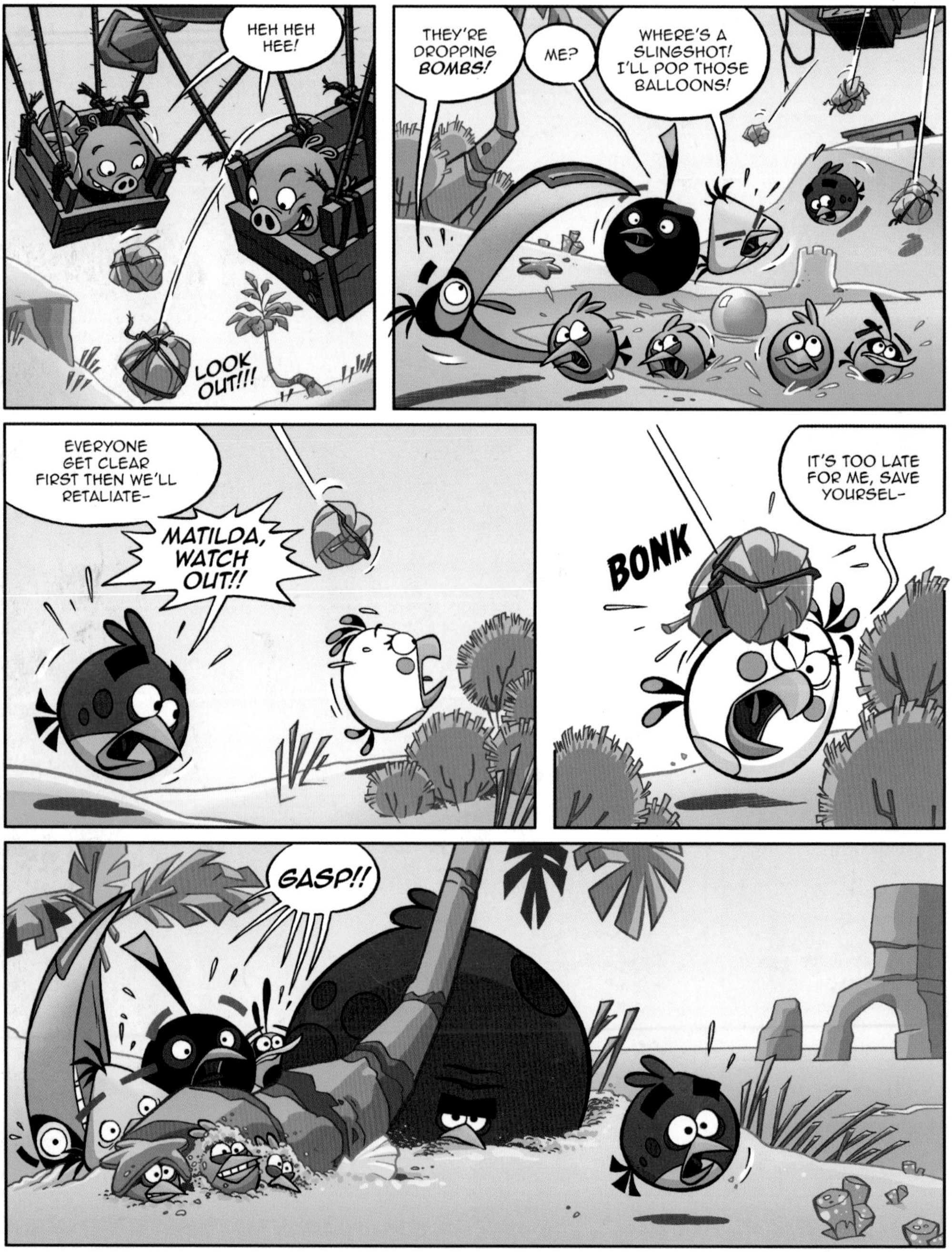
HEH HEH HEE!
LOOK OUT!!!
THEY'RE DROPPING *BOMBS!*
ME?
WHERE'S A SLINGSHOT! I'LL POP THOSE BALLOONS!
EVERYONE GET CLEAR FIRST THEN WE'LL RETALIATE-
MATILDA, WATCH OUT!!
BONK
IT'S TOO LATE FOR ME, SAVE YOURSEL-
GASP!!

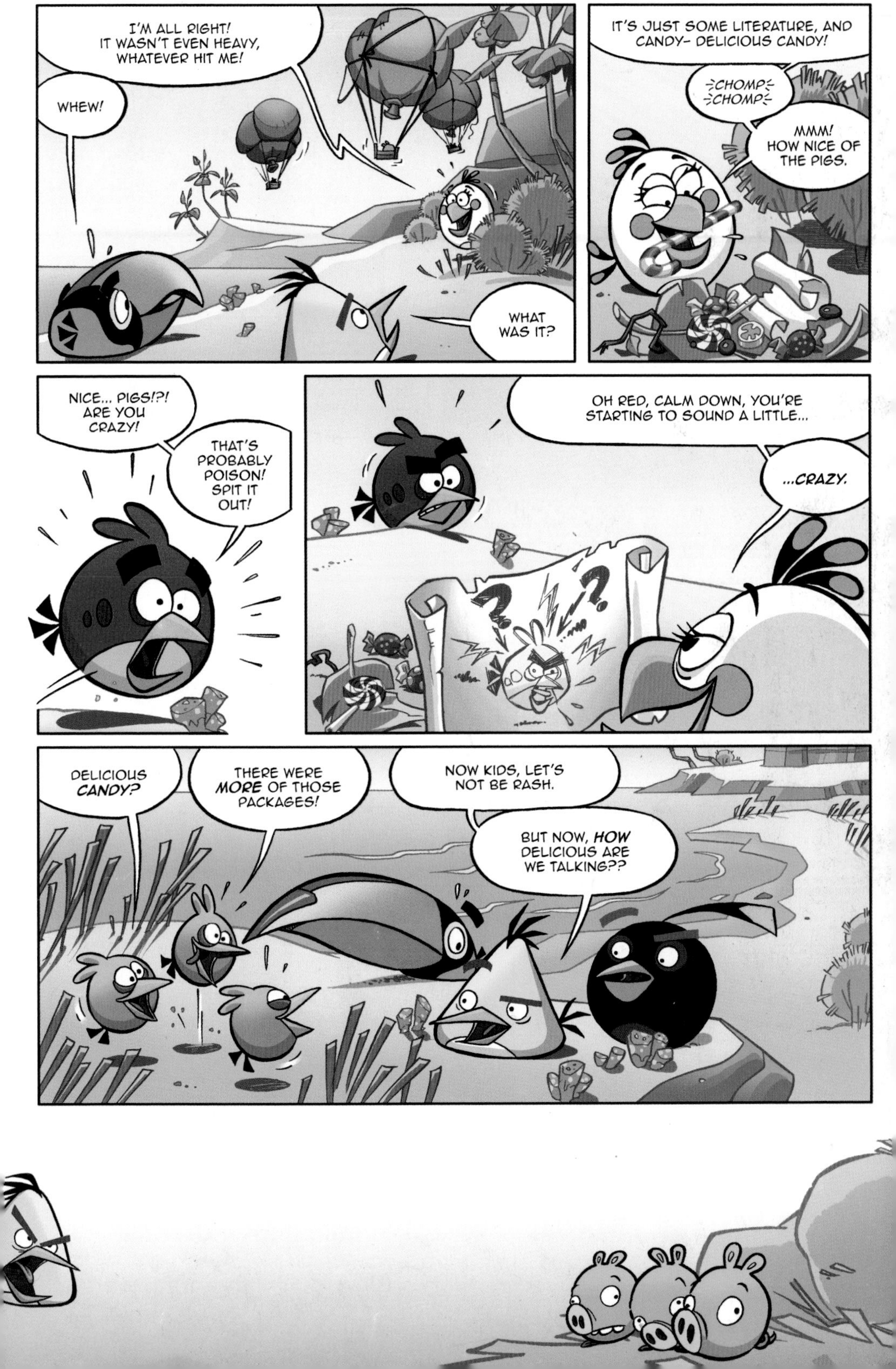
I'M ALL RIGHT! IT WASN'T EVEN HEAVY, WHATEVER HIT ME!
WHEW!
WHAT WAS IT?
IT'S JUST SOME LITERATURE, AND CANDY- DELICIOUS CANDY!
CHOMP CHOMP
MMM! HOW NICE OF THE PIGS.
NICE... PIGS!?! ARE YOU CRAZY!
THAT'S PROBABLY POISON! SPIT IT OUT!
OH RED, CALM DOWN, YOU'RE STARTING TO SOUND A LITTLE...
...CRAZY.
DELICIOUS CANDY?
THERE WERE MORE OF THOSE PACKAGES!
NOW KIDS, LET'S NOT BE RASH.
BUT NOW, HOW DELICIOUS ARE WE TALKING??

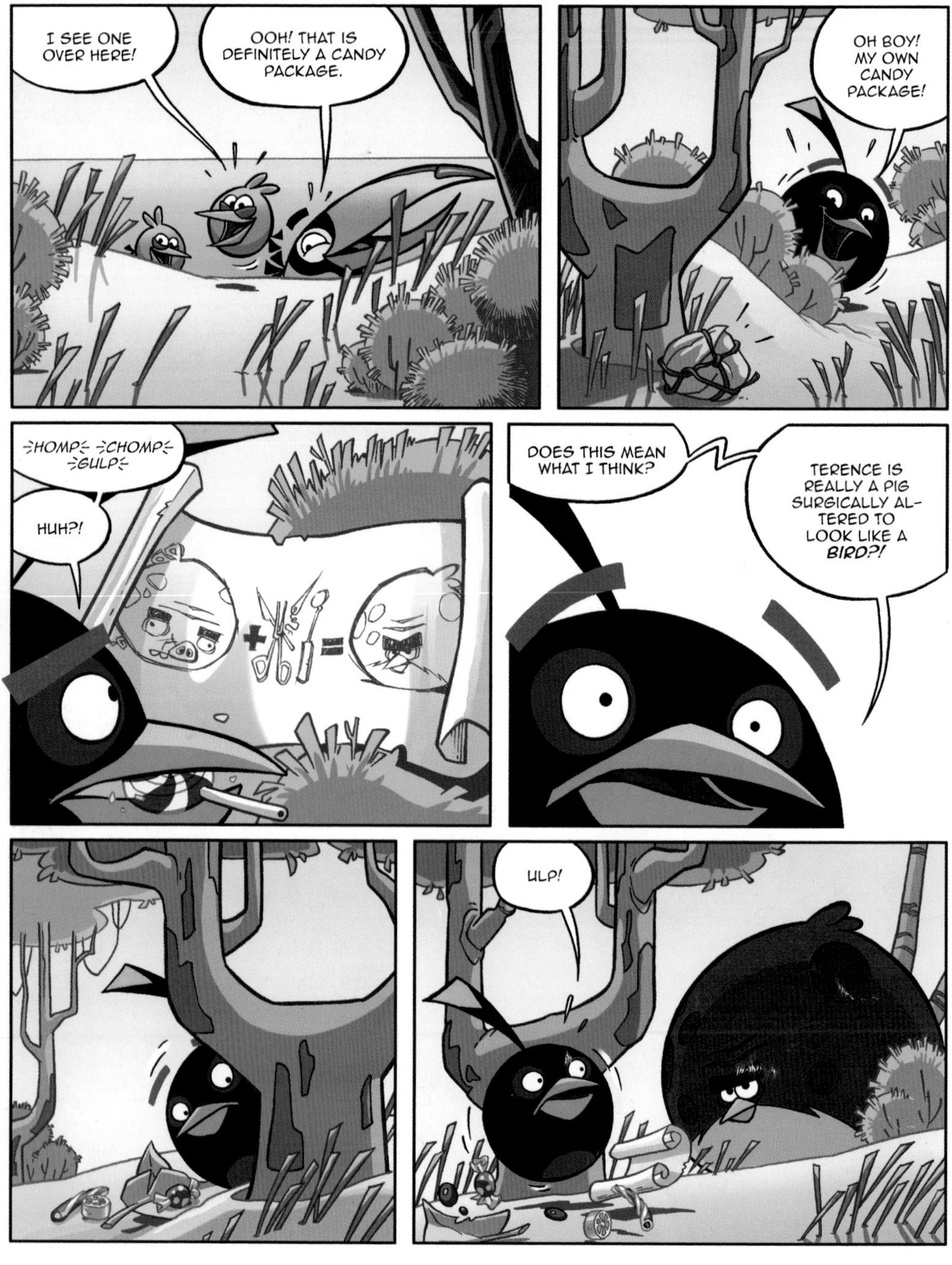
I SEE ONE OVER HERE!
OOH! THAT IS DEFINITELY A CANDY PACKAGE.
OH BOY! MY OWN CANDY PACKAGE!
HOMP CHOMP GULP
HUH?!
DOES THIS MEAN WHAT I THINK?
TERENCE IS REALLY A PIG SURGICALLY AL-TERED TO LOOK LIKE A *BIRD?!*
ULP!

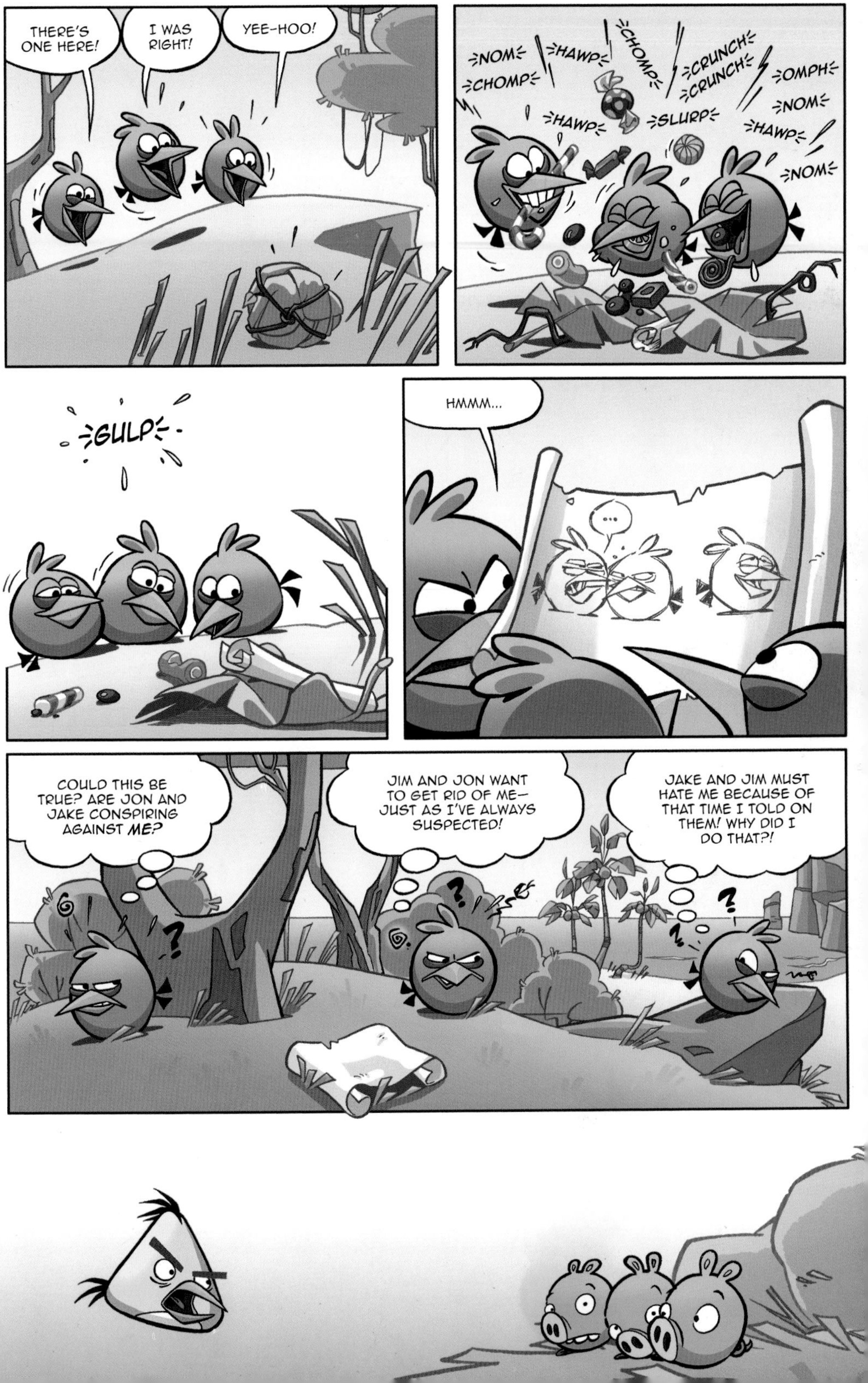
THERE'S ONE HERE!
I WAS RIGHT!
YEE-HOO!
NOM
CHOMP
HAWP
CHOMP
HAWP
CRUNCH
CRUNCH
SLURP
OMPH
NOM
HAWP
NOM
GULP
HMMM...
...
COULD THIS BE TRUE? ARE JON AND JAKE CONSPIRING AGAINST *ME?*
JIM AND JON WANT TO GET RID OF ME— JUST AS I'VE ALWAYS SUSPECTED!
JAKE AND JIM MUST HATE ME BECAUSE OF THAT TIME I TOLD ON THEM! WHY DID I DO THAT?!

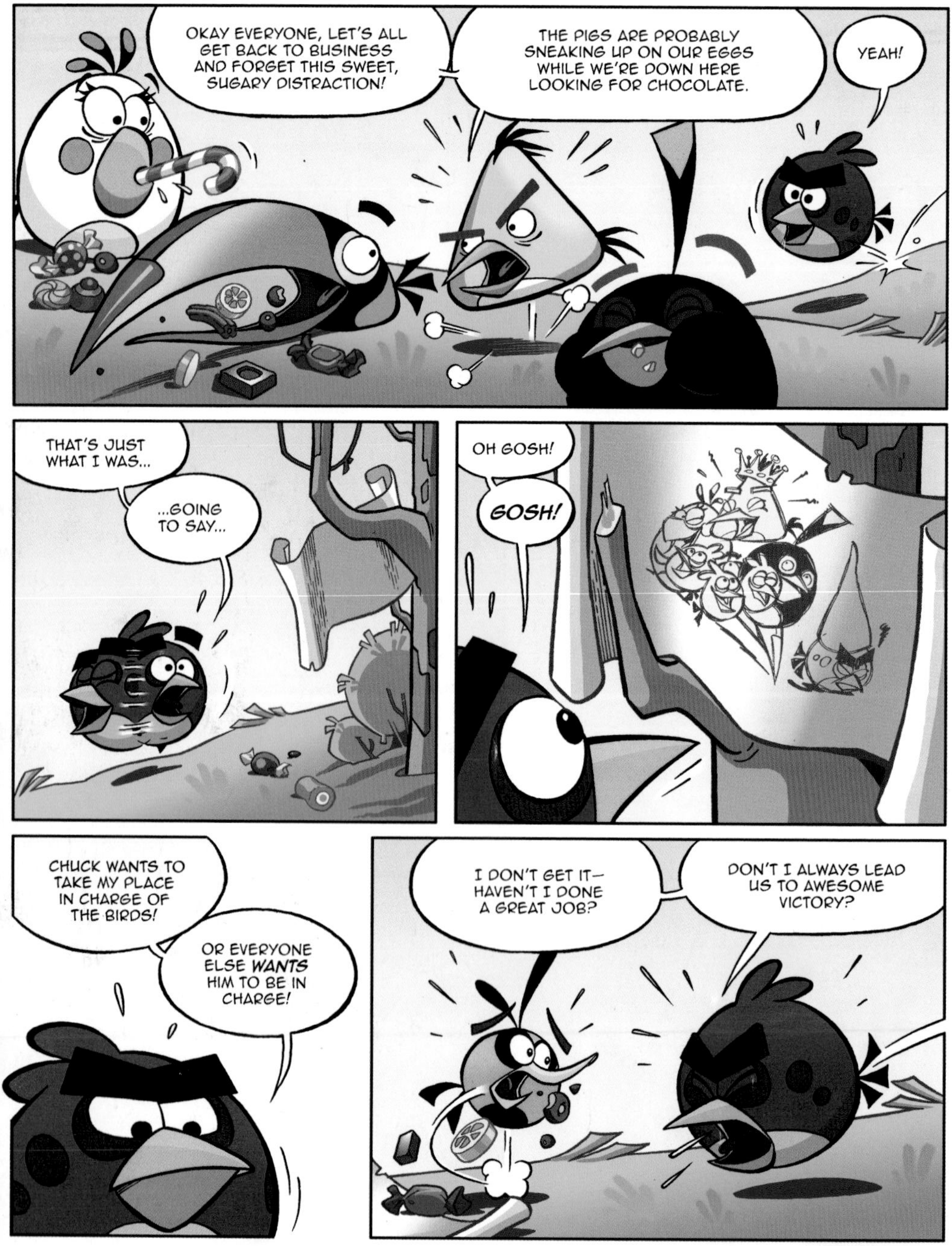
OKAY EVERYONE, LET'S ALL GET BACK TO BUSINESS AND FORGET THIS SWEET, SUGARY DISTRACTION!
THE PIGS ARE PROBABLY SNEAKING UP ON OUR EGGS WHILE WE'RE DOWN HERE LOOKING FOR CHOCOLATE.
YEAH!
THAT'S JUST WHAT I WAS...
...GOING TO SAY...
OH GOSH!
GOSH!
CHUCK WANTS TO TAKE MY PLACE IN CHARGE OF THE BIRDS!
OR EVERYONE ELSE WANTS HIM TO BE IN CHARGE!
I DON'T GET IT— HAVEN'T I DONE A GREAT JOB?
DON'T I ALWAYS LEAD US TO AWESOME VICTORY?

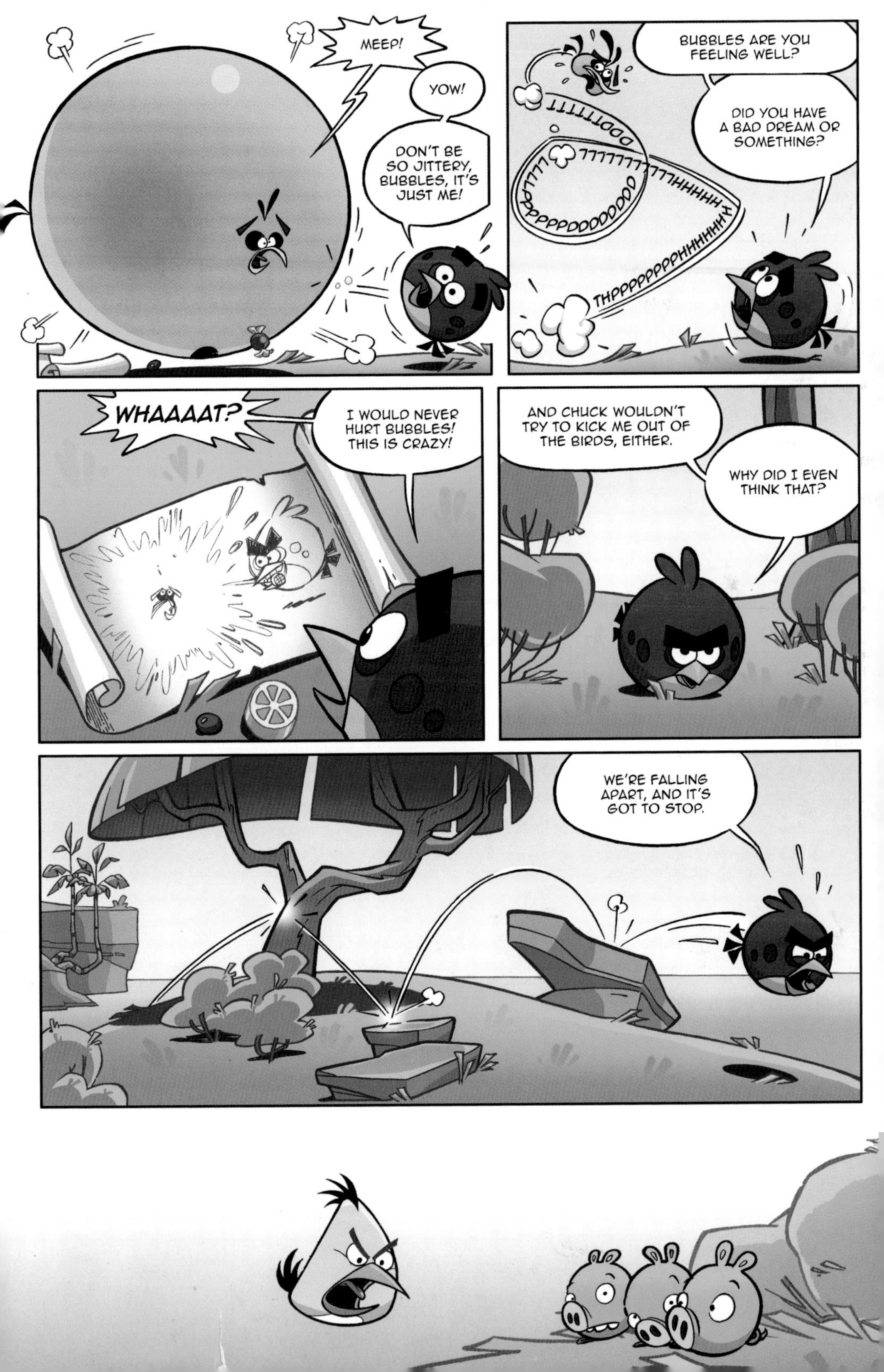
MEEP!
YOW!
DON'T BE SO JITTERY, BUBBLES, IT'S JUST ME!
BUBBLES ARE YOU FEELING WELL?
DID YOU HAVE A BAD DREAM OR SOMETHING?
WHAAAAT?
I WOULD NEVER HURT BUBBLES! THIS IS CRAZY!
AND CHUCK WOULDN'T TRY TO KICK ME OUT OF THE BIRDS, EITHER.
WHY DID I EVEN THINK THAT?
WE'RE FALLING APART, AND IT'S GOT TO STOP.

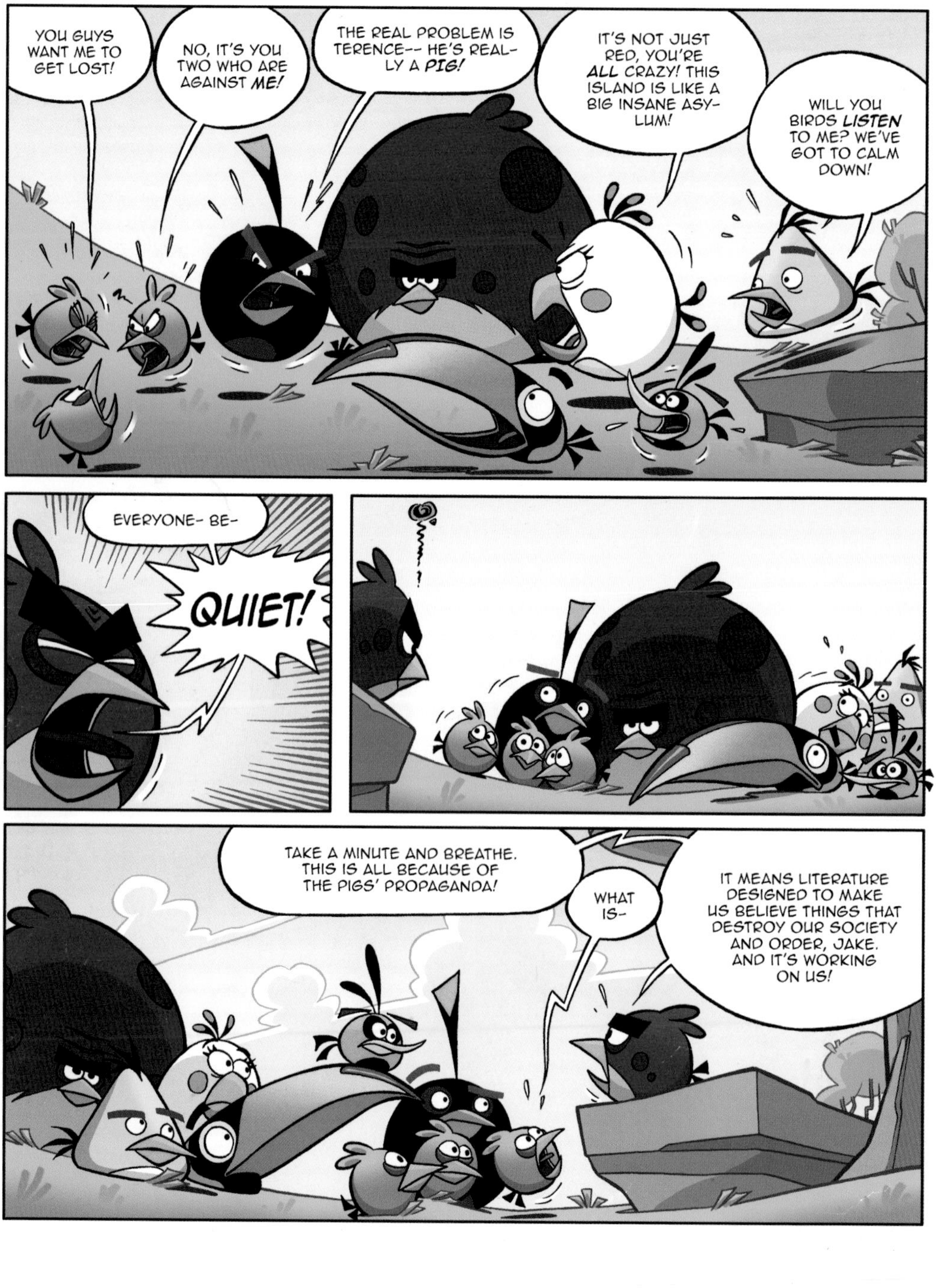
YOU GUYS WANT ME TO GET LOST!
NO, IT'S YOU TWO WHO ARE AGAINST ME!
THE REAL PROBLEM IS TERENCE-- HE'S REALLY A PIG!
IT'S NOT JUST RED, YOU'RE ALL CRAZY! THIS ISLAND IS LIKE A BIG INSANE ASYLUM!
WILL YOU BIRDS LISTEN TO ME? WE'VE GOT TO CALM DOWN!
EVERYONE- BE-
QUIET!
TAKE A MINUTE AND BREATHE. THIS IS ALL BECAUSE OF THE PIGS' PROPAGANDA!
WHAT IS-
IT MEANS LITERATURE DESIGNED TO MAKE US BELIEVE THINGS THAT DESTROY OUR SOCIETY AND ORDER, JAKE. AND IT'S WORKING ON US!

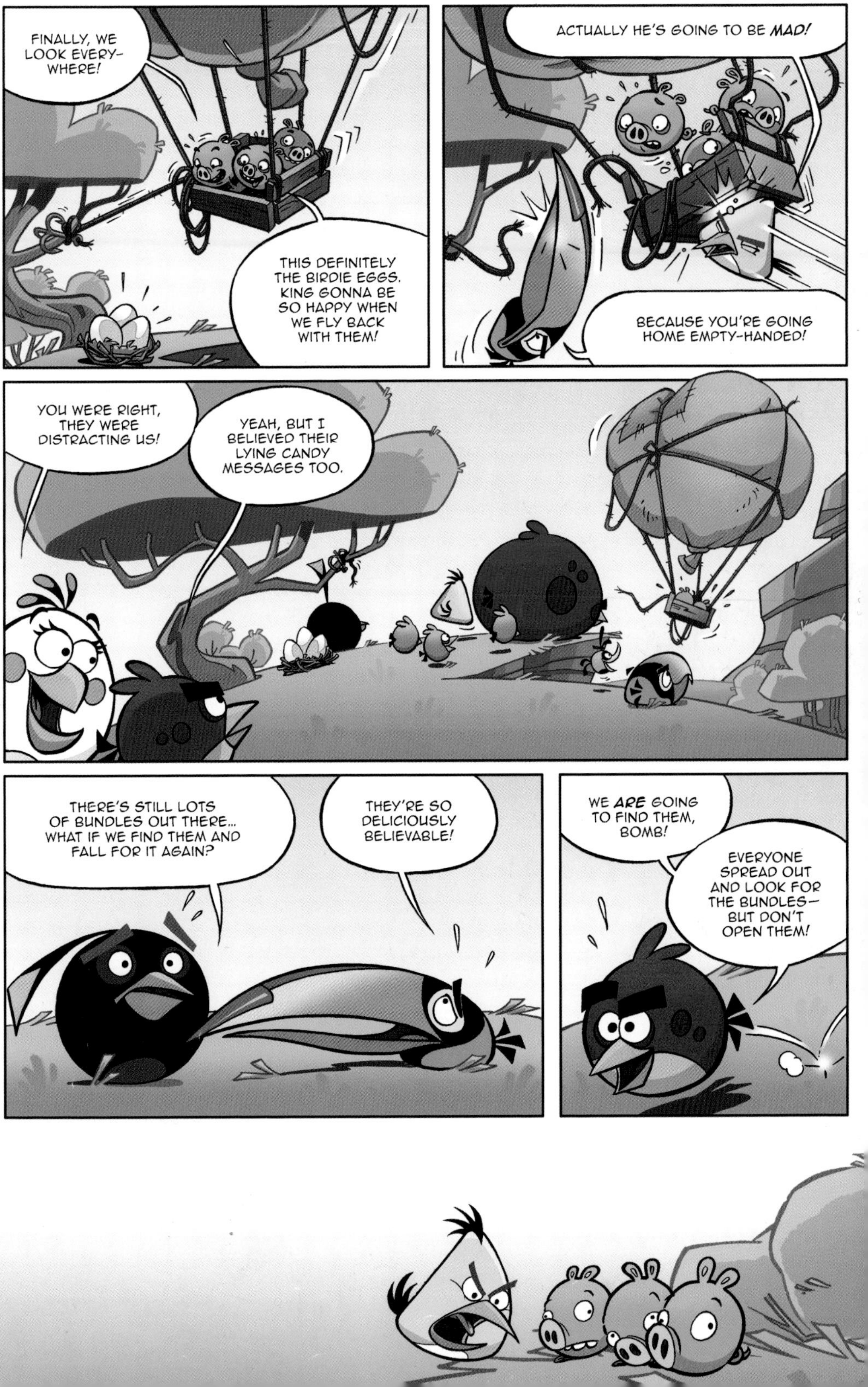

FINALLY, WE LOOK EVERY-WHERE!
THIS DEFINITELY THE BIRDIE EGGS. KING GONNA BE SO HAPPY WHEN WE FLY BACK WITH THEM!
ACTUALLY HE'S GOING TO BE *MAD!*
BECAUSE YOU'RE GOING HOME EMPTY-HANDED!
YOU WERE RIGHT, THEY WERE DISTRACTING US!
YEAH, BUT I BELIEVED THEIR LYING CANDY MESSAGES TOO.
THERE'S STILL LOTS OF BUNDLES OUT THERE... WHAT IF WE FIND THEM AND FALL FOR IT AGAIN?
THEY'RE SO DELICIOUSLY BELIEVABLE!
WE ***ARE*** GOING TO FIND THEM, BOMB!
EVERYONE SPREAD OUT AND LOOK FOR THE BUNDLES—BUT DON'T OPEN THEM!

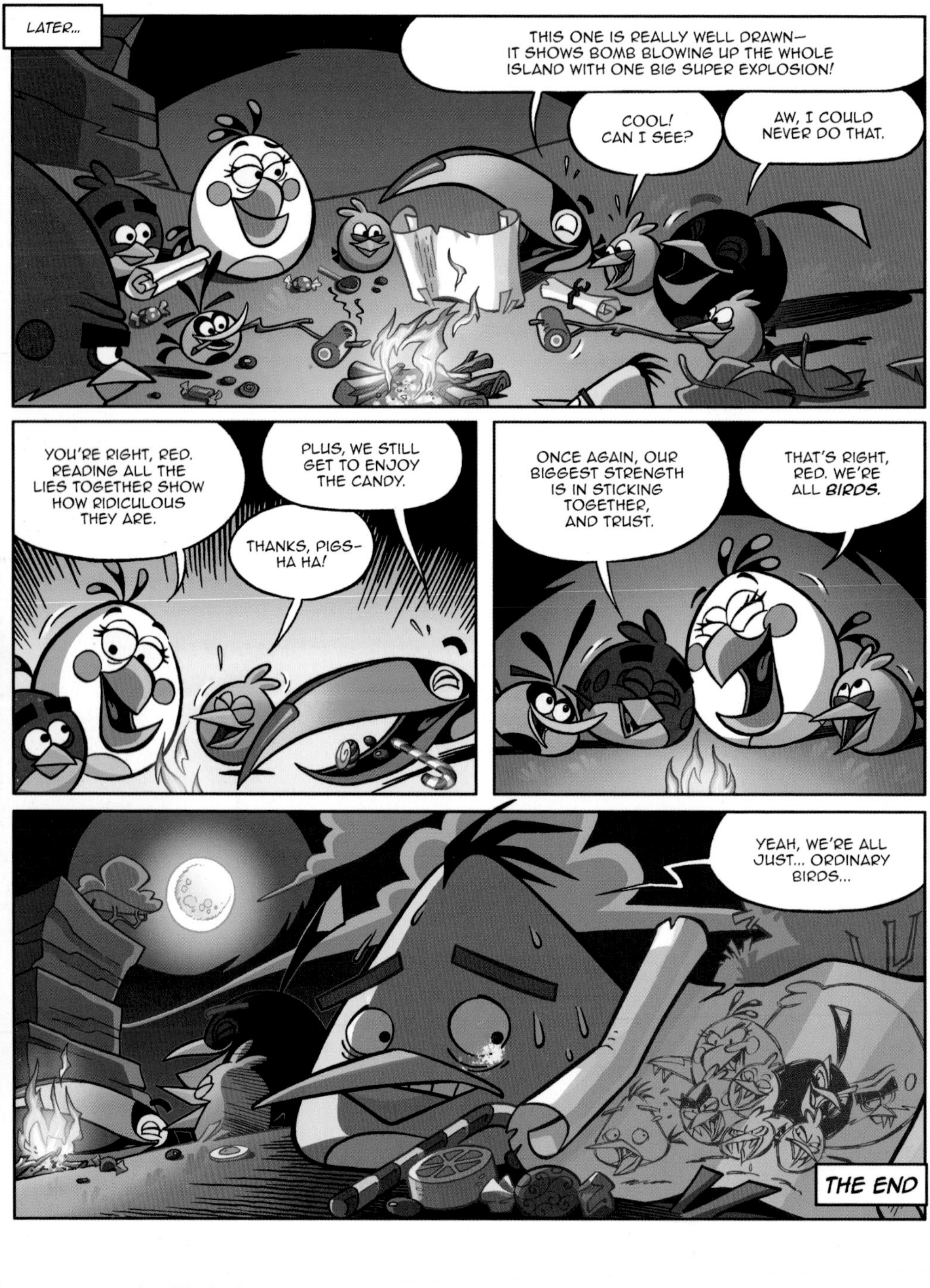
LATER...
THIS ONE IS REALLY WELL DRAWN—IT SHOWS BOMB BLOWING UP THE WHOLE ISLAND WITH ONE BIG SUPER EXPLOSION!
COOL! CAN I SEE?
AW, I COULD NEVER DO THAT.
YOU'RE RIGHT, RED. READING ALL THE LIES TOGETHER SHOW HOW RIDICULOUS THEY ARE.
PLUS, WE STILL GET TO ENJOY THE CANDY.
THANKS, PIGS-HA HA!
ONCE AGAIN, OUR BIGGEST STRENGTH IS IN STICKING TOGETHER, AND TRUST.
THAT'S RIGHT, RED. WE'RE ALL ***BIRDS.***
YEAH, WE'RE ALL JUST... ORDINARY BIRDS...
THE END

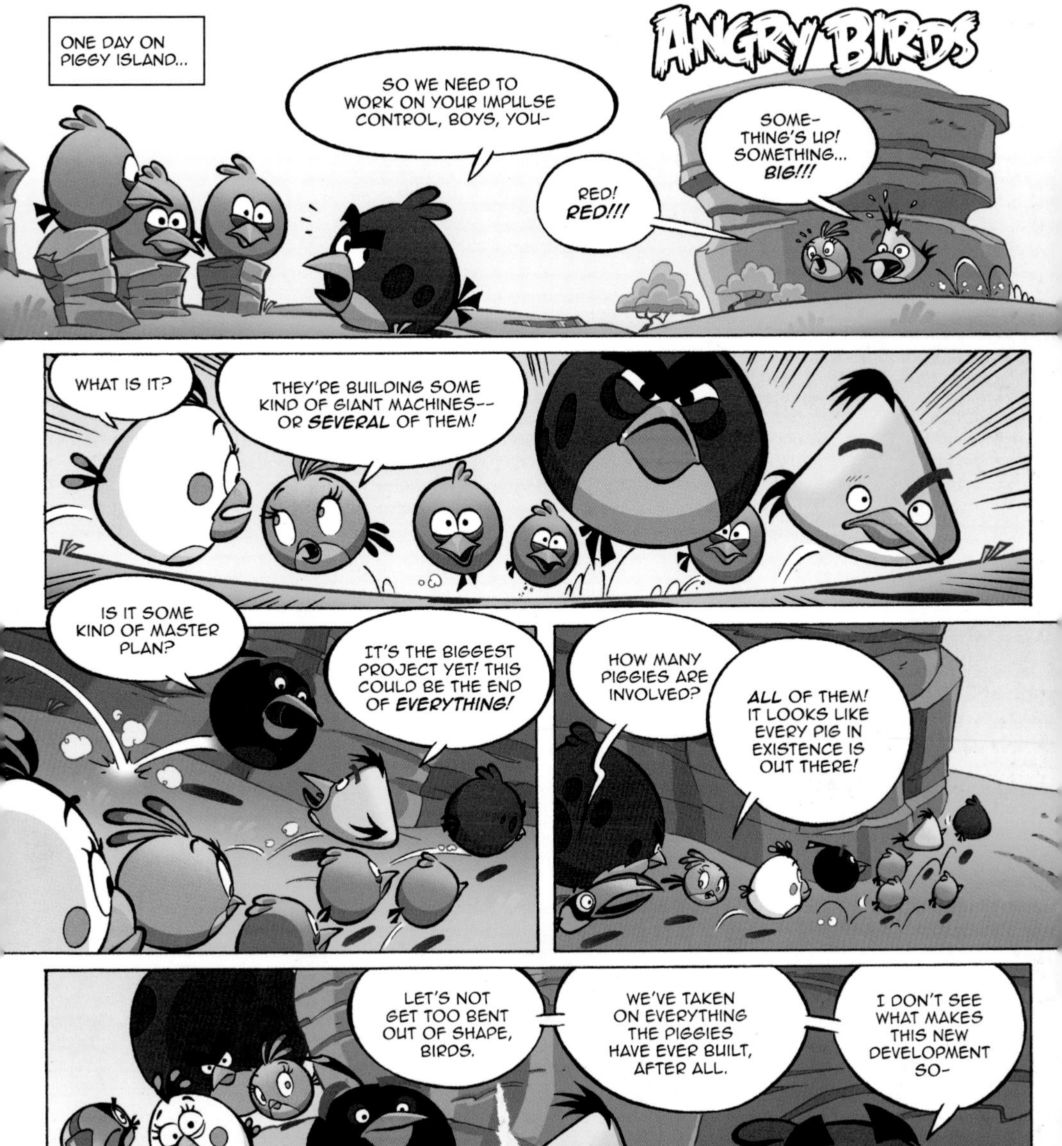
ONE DAY ON PIGGY ISLAND...
ANGRY BIRDS
SO WE NEED TO WORK ON YOUR IMPULSE CONTROL, BOYS, YOU-
RED! RED!!!
SOME-THING'S UP! SOMETHING... BIG!!!
WHAT IS IT?
THEY'RE BUILDING SOME KIND OF GIANT MACHINES-- OR SEVERAL OF THEM!
IS IT SOME KIND OF MASTER PLAN?
IT'S THE BIGGEST PROJECT YET! THIS COULD BE THE END OF EVERYTHING!
HOW MANY PIGGIES ARE INVOLVED?
ALL OF THEM! IT LOOKS LIKE EVERY PIG IN EXISTENCE IS OUT THERE!
LET'S NOT GET TOO BENT OUT OF SHAPE, BIRDS.
WE'VE TAKEN ON EVERYTHING THE PIGGIES HAVE EVER BUILT, AFTER ALL.
I DON'T SEE WHAT MAKES THIS NEW DEVELOPMENT SO-

WRITTEN BY: JEFF PARKER • ART BY: PACO RODRIQUES • COLORS BY: DIGIKORE STUDIOS • LETTERS BY: PISARA OY

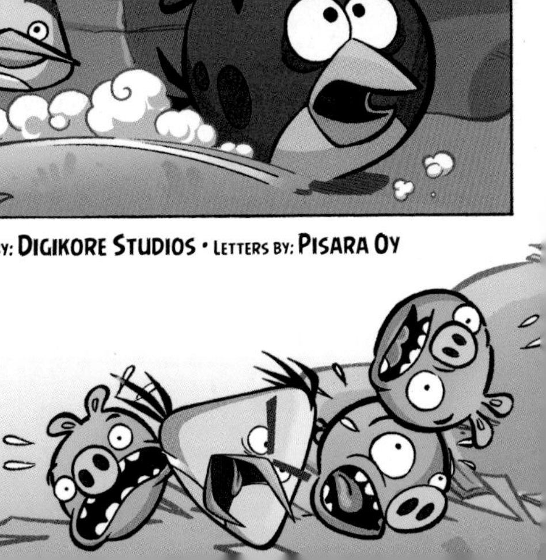

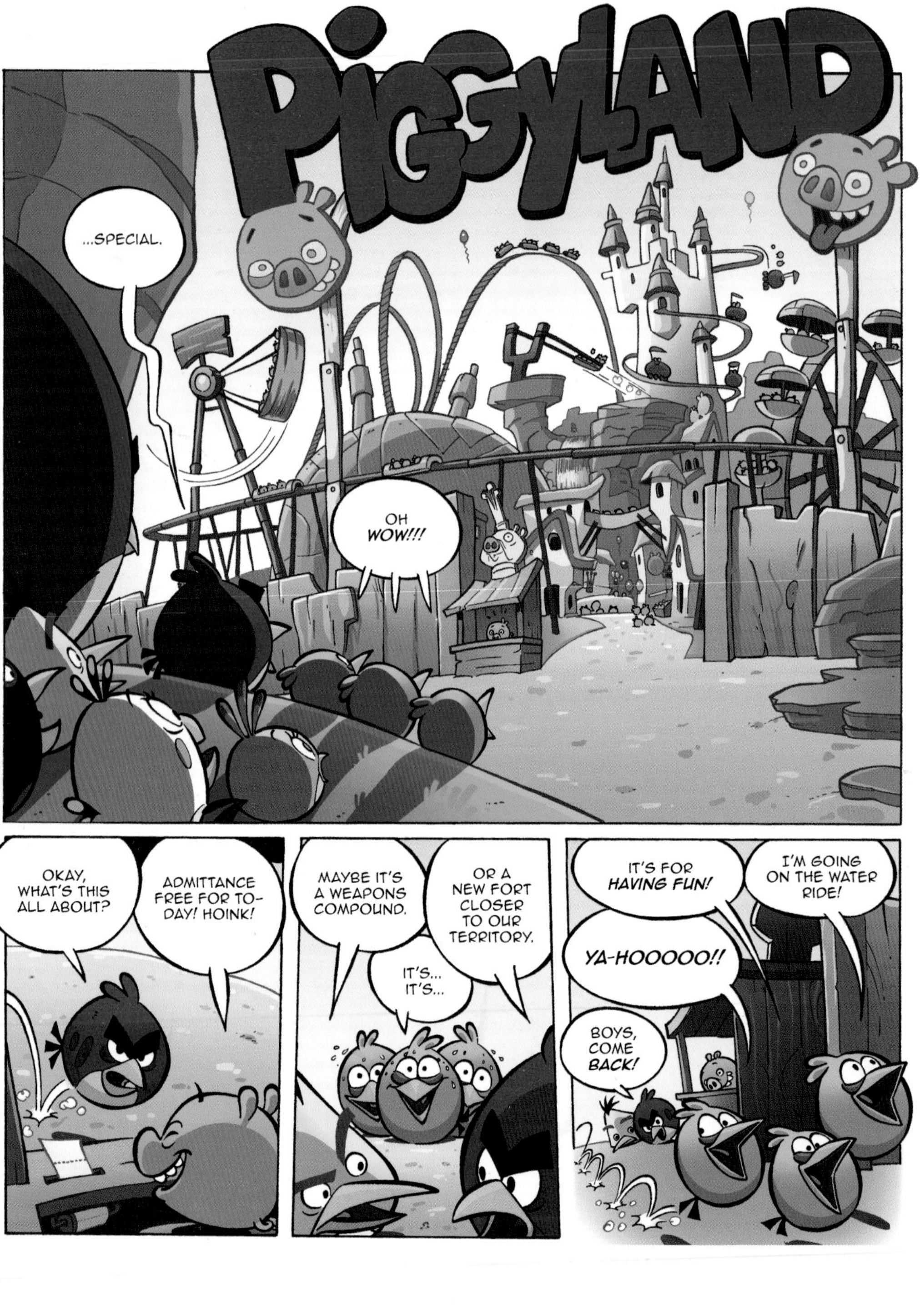
PIGGYLAND
...SPECIAL.
OH WOW!!!
OKAY, WHAT'S THIS ALL ABOUT?
ADMITTANCE FREE FOR TO-DAY! HOINK!
MAYBE IT'S A WEAPONS COMPOUND.
OR A NEW FORT CLOSER TO OUR TERRITORY.
IT'S... IT'S...
IT'S FOR HAVING FUN!
I'M GOING ON THE WATER RIDE!
YA-HOOOOO!!
BOYS, COME BACK!

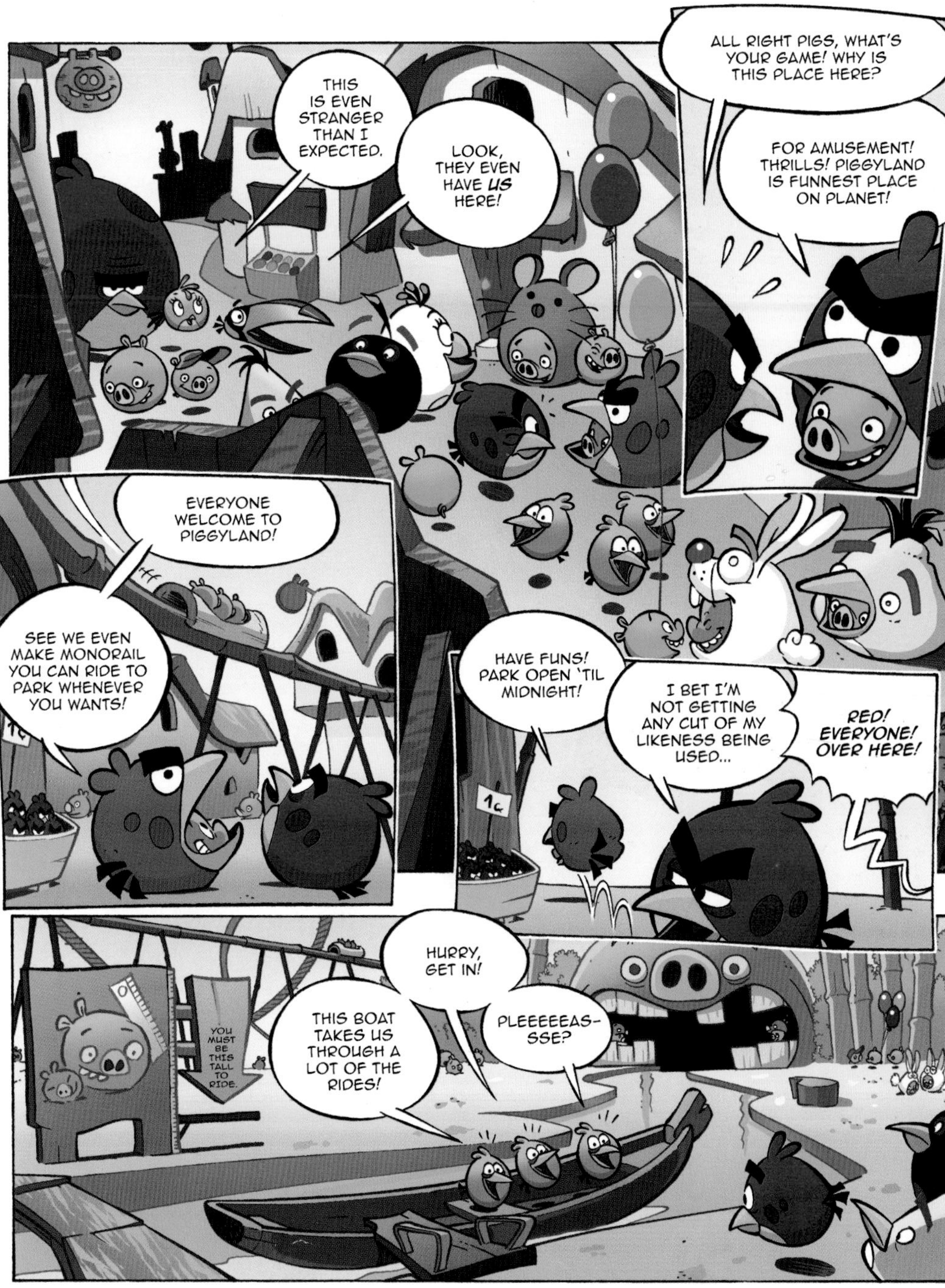
THIS IS EVEN STRANGER THAN I EXPECTED.
LOOK, THEY EVEN HAVE *US* HERE!
ALL RIGHT PIGS, WHAT'S YOUR GAME! WHY IS THIS PLACE HERE?
FOR AMUSEMENT! THRILLS! PIGGYLAND IS FUNNEST PLACE ON PLANET!
EVERYONE WELCOME TO PIGGYLAND!
SEE WE EVEN MAKE MONORAIL YOU CAN RIDE TO PARK WHENEVER YOU WANTS!
HAVE FUNS! PARK OPEN 'TIL MIDNIGHT!
I BET I'M NOT GETTING ANY CUT OF MY LIKENESS BEING USED...
*RED! EVERYONE! OVER HERE!*
YOU MUST BE THIS TALL TO RIDE.
HURRY, GET IN!
THIS BOAT TAKES US THROUGH A LOT OF THE RIDES!
PLEEEEEAS-SSE?

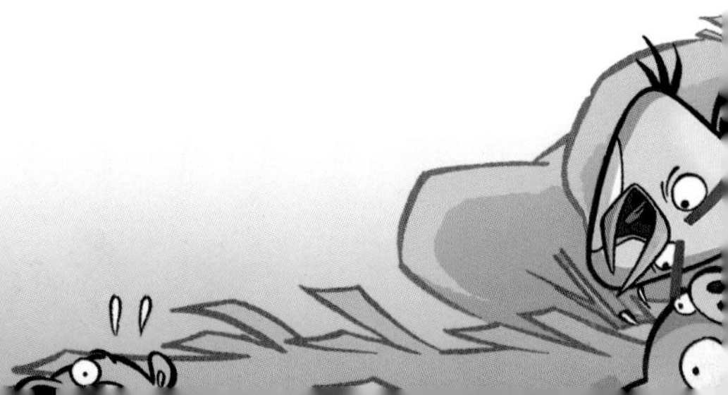

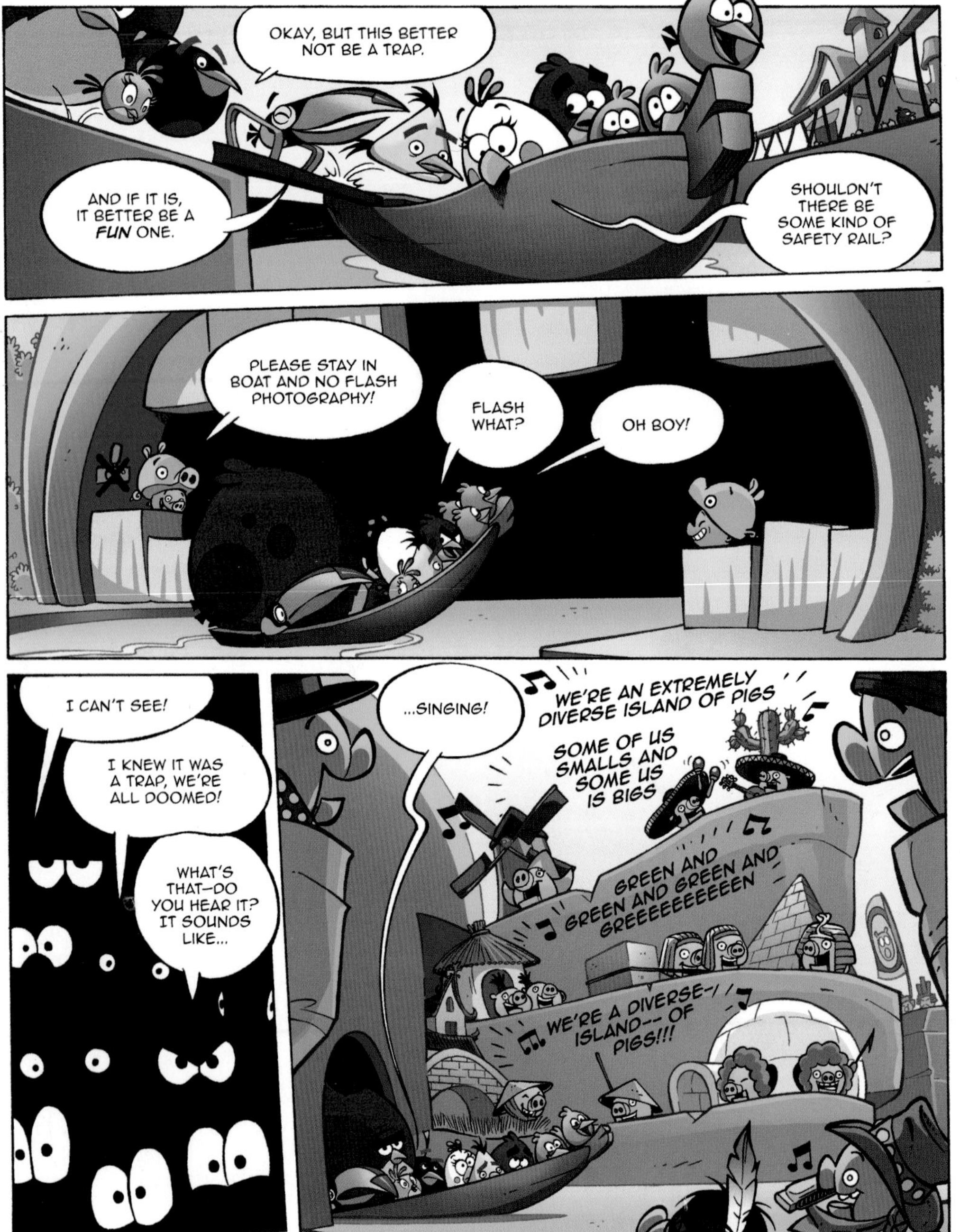
OKAY, BUT THIS BETTER NOT BE A TRAP.
AND IF IT IS, IT BETTER BE A *FUN* ONE.
SHOULDN'T THERE BE SOME KIND OF SAFETY RAIL?
PLEASE STAY IN BOAT AND NO FLASH PHOTOGRAPHY!
FLASH WHAT?
OH BOY!
I CAN'T SEE!
I KNEW IT WAS A TRAP, WE'RE ALL DOOMED!
WHAT'S THAT—DO YOU HEAR IT? IT SOUNDS LIKE...
...SINGING!
WE'RE AN EXTREMELY DIVERSE ISLAND OF PIGS
SOME OF US SMALLS AND SOME US IS BIGS
GREEN AND GREEN AND GREEN AND GREEEEEEEEEEN
WE'RE A DIVERSE-ISLAND-- OF PIGS!!!

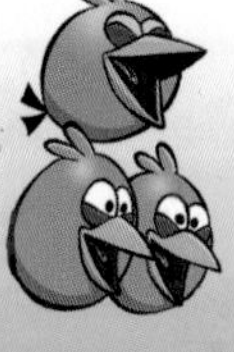

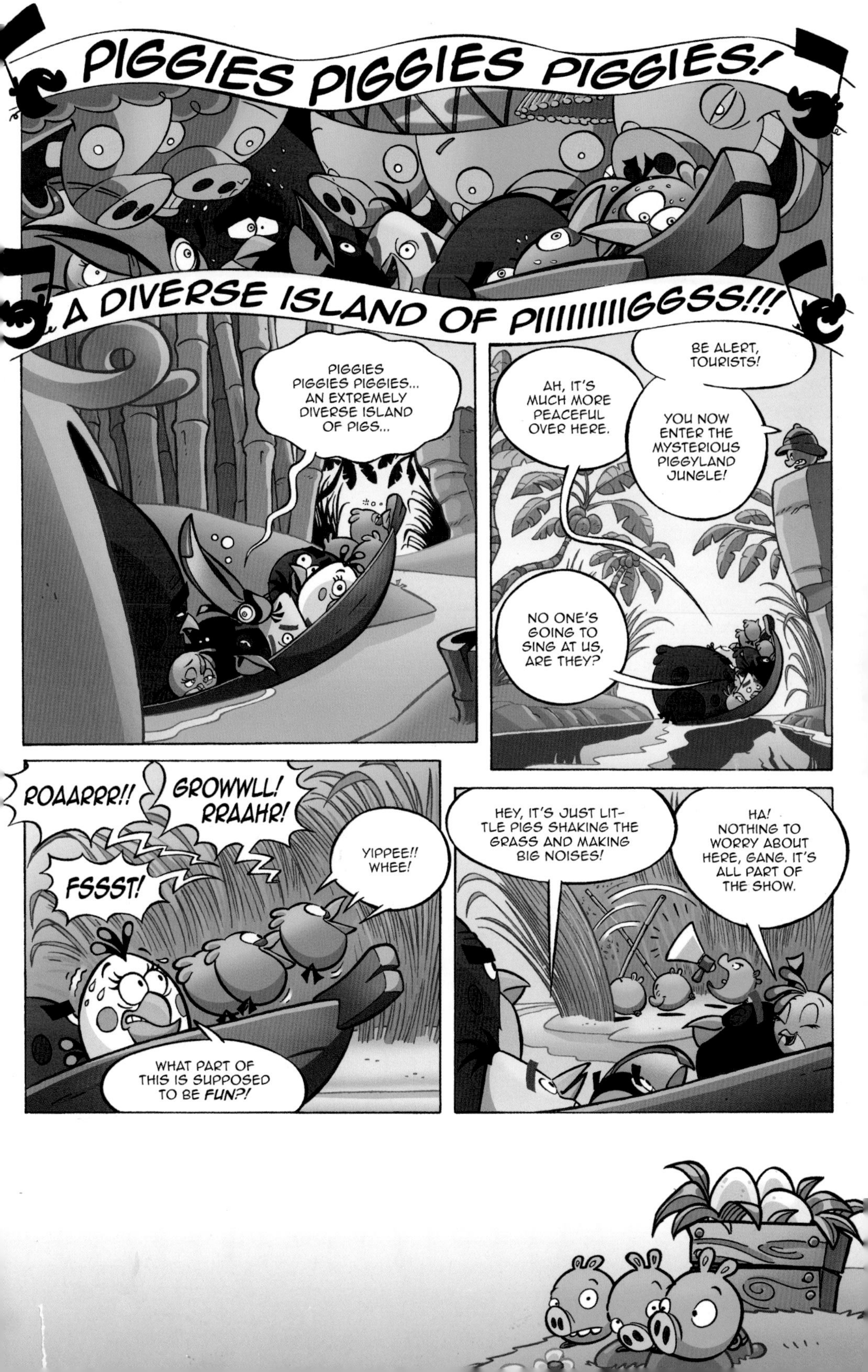
PIGGIES PIGGIES PIGGIES!
A DIVERSE ISLAND OF PIIIIIIIIGGSS!!!
PIGGIES PIGGIES PIGGIES... AN EXTREMELY DIVERSE ISLAND OF PIGS...
BE ALERT, TOURISTS!
AH, IT'S MUCH MORE PEACEFUL OVER HERE.
YOU NOW ENTER THE MYSTERIOUS PIGGYLAND JUNGLE!
NO ONE'S GOING TO SING AT US, ARE THEY?
ROAARRR!!
GROWWLL! RRAAHR!
FSSST!
YIPPEE!! WHEE!
WHAT PART OF THIS IS SUPPOSED TO BE *FUN*?!
HEY, IT'S JUST LIT-TLE PIGS SHAKING THE GRASS AND MAKING BIG NOISES!
HA! NOTHING TO WORRY ABOUT HERE, GANG. IT'S ALL PART OF THE SHOW.

DO NOT DISTURB THE RESIDENTS OF THE FOREST!
SSSSNK
WHOOOSH
AHHHH!!!
SSNNK
WZEWWW
SHEWWW
SHUNK
I THINK OUR BOAT'S TAKING ON WATER NOW...
BUT LOOK-- JUNGLE ANIMALS!
CAN WE TALK TO THEM? HELLO, DO YOU SPEAK BIRD?
FOOOOOSHHHH
WHEE-HEEE!
FINALLY A BATH THAT'S FUN!
YEAH, THAT WAS SOME FUN, ALL RIGHT.
NOW THE BOAT IS *DEFINITELY* TAKING ON WATER.

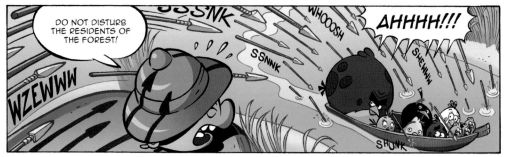

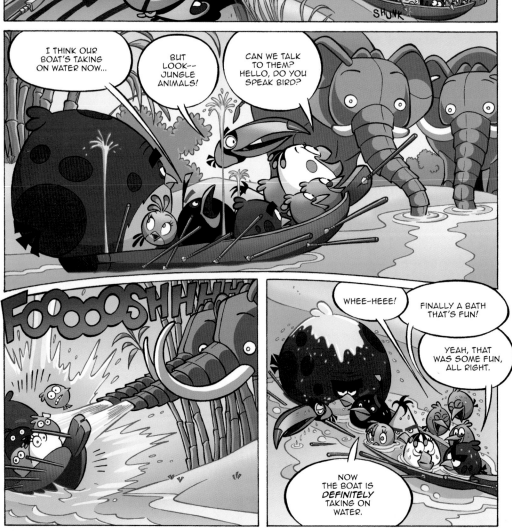

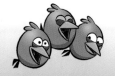

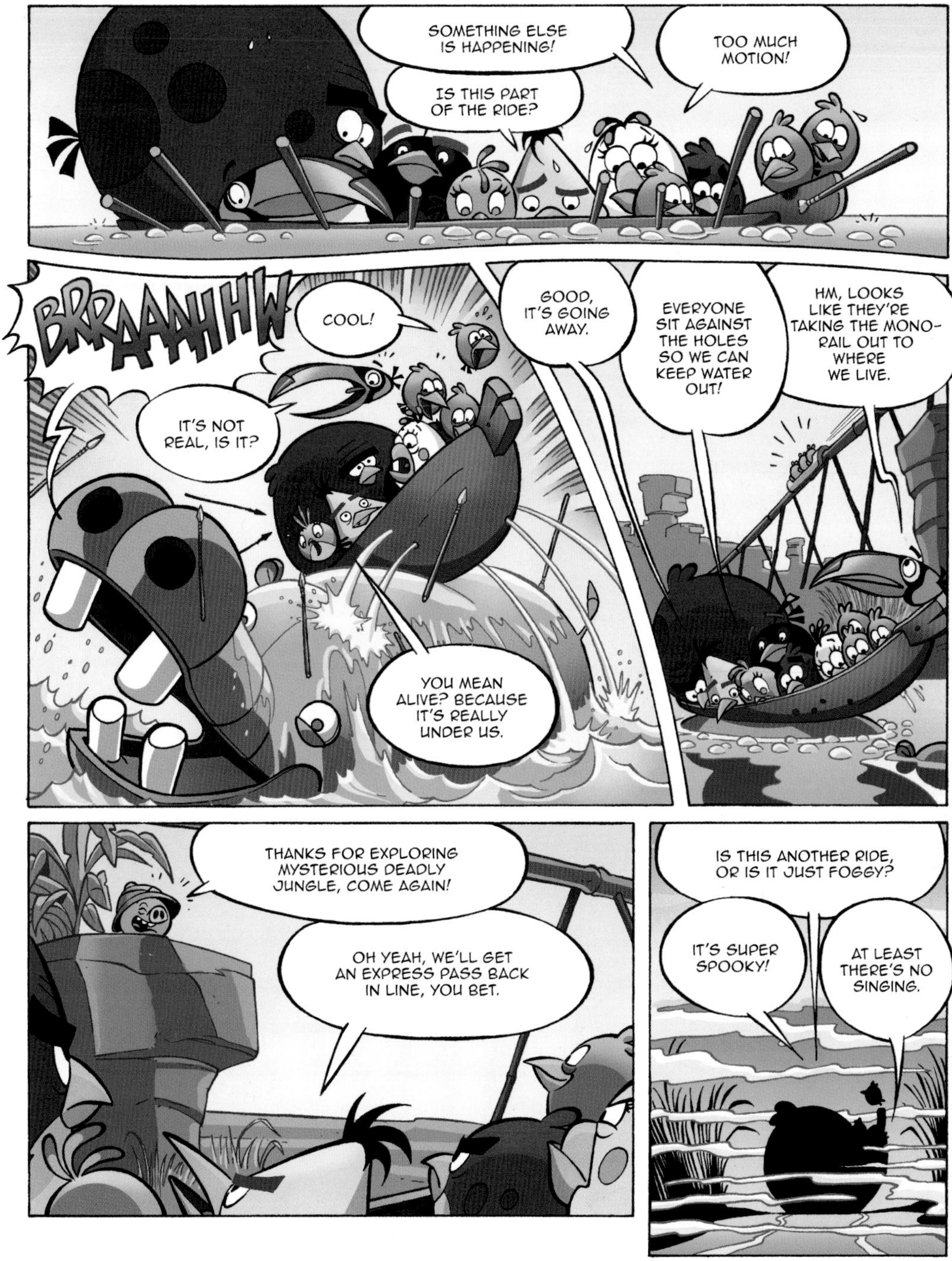
SOMETHING ELSE IS HAPPENING!
IS THIS PART OF THE RIDE?
TOO MUCH MOTION!
BRRAAAHHW
COOL!
IT'S NOT REAL, IS IT?
YOU MEAN ALIVE? BECAUSE IT'S REALLY UNDER US.
GOOD, IT'S GOING AWAY.
EVERYONE SIT AGAINST THE HOLES SO WE CAN KEEP WATER OUT!
HM, LOOKS LIKE THEY'RE TAKING THE MONO-RAIL OUT TO WHERE WE LIVE.
THANKS FOR EXPLORING MYSTERIOUS DEADLY JUNGLE, COME AGAIN!
OH YEAH, WE'LL GET AN EXPRESS PASS BACK IN LINE, YOU BET.
IS THIS ANOTHER RIDE, OR IS IT JUST FOGGY?
IT'S SUPER SPOOKY!
AT LEAST THERE'S NO SINGING.

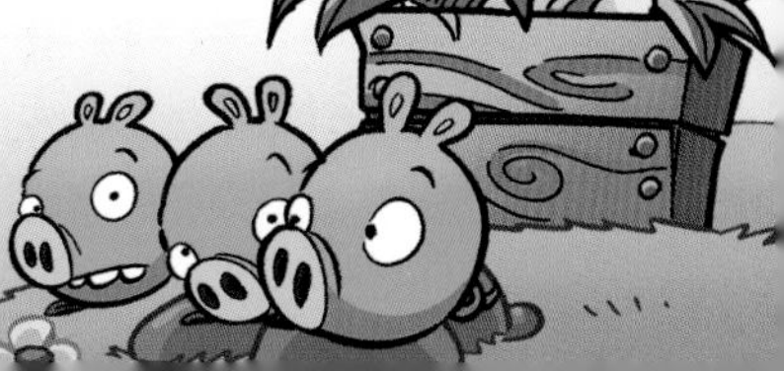

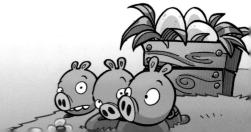

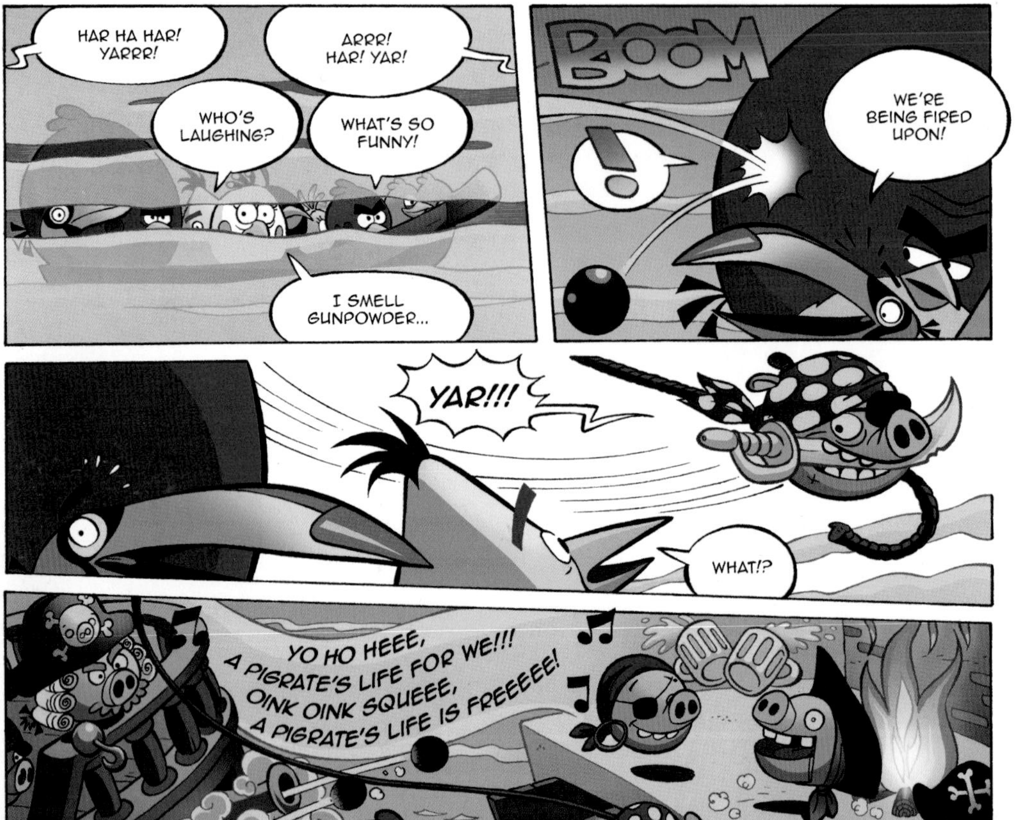
HAR HA HAR! YARRR!
ARRR! HAR! YAR!
WHO'S LAUGHING?
WHAT'S SO FUNNY!
I SMELL GUNPOWDER...
BOOM
!
WE'RE BEING FIRED UPON!
YAR!!!
WHAT!?
YO HO HEEE,
A PIGRATE'S LIFE FOR WE!!!
OINK OINK SQUEEE,
A PIGRATE'S LIFE IS FREEEEE!
NO, THEY'RE SINGING AGAIN!!

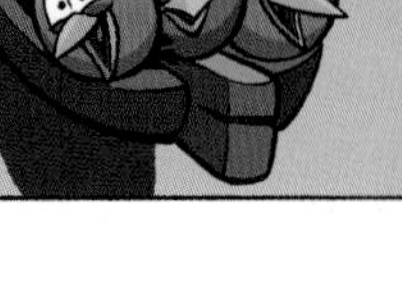

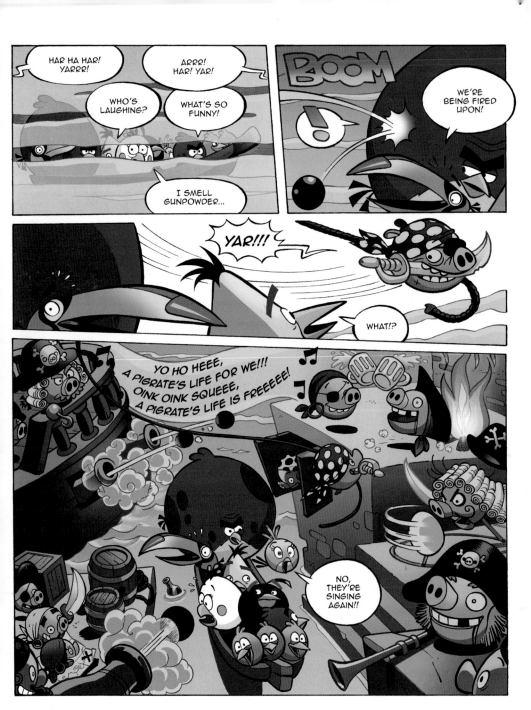

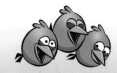

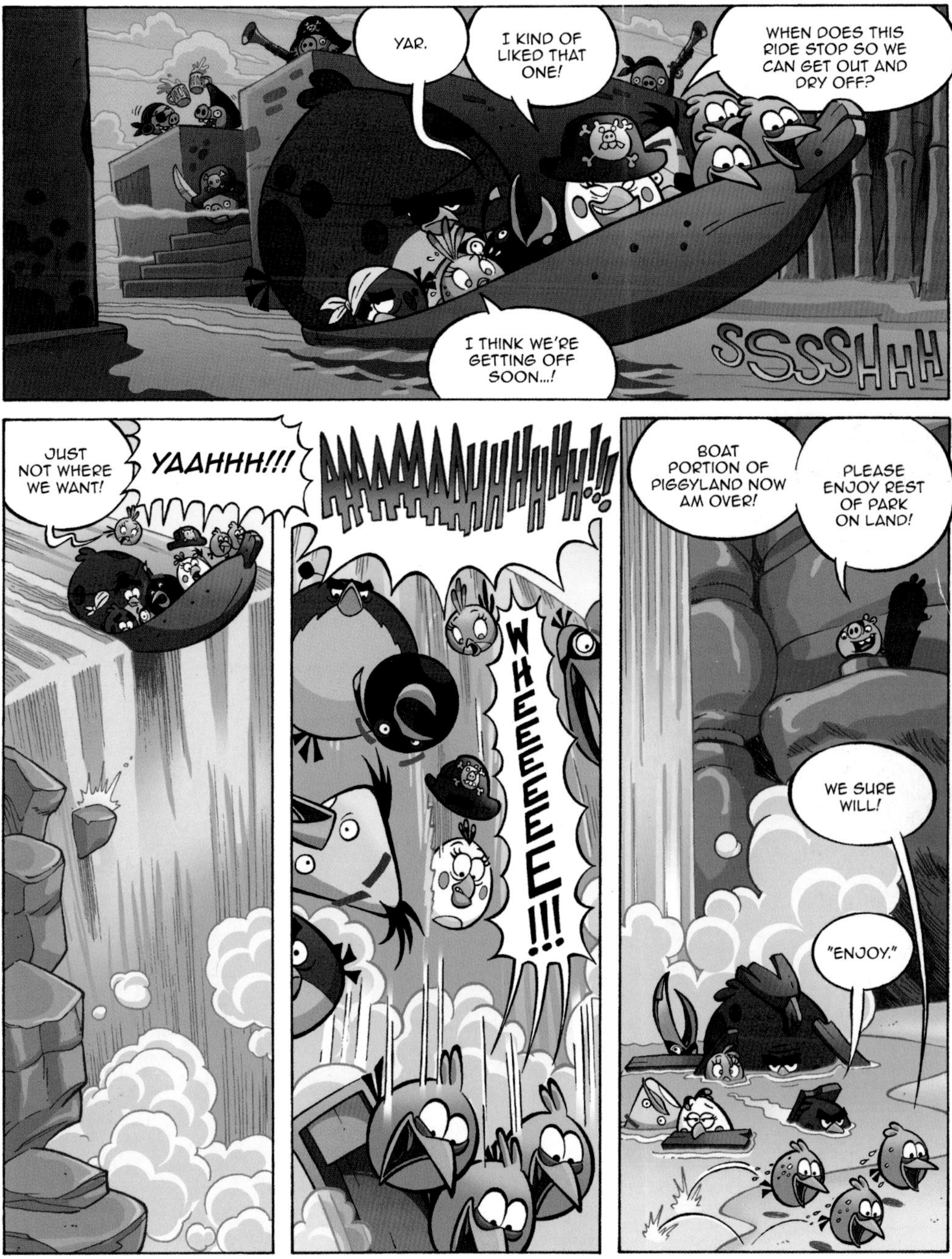
YAR.
I KIND OF LIKED THAT ONE!
WHEN DOES THIS RIDE STOP SO WE CAN GET OUT AND DRY OFF?
I THINK WE'RE GETTING OFF SOON...!
SSSSHHH
JUST NOT WHERE WE WANT!
YAAHHH!!!
AAAAAAAAHHHHHH!!!
WHEEEEEEE!!!
BOAT PORTION OF PIGGYLAND NOW AM OVER!
PLEASE ENJOY REST OF PARK ON LAND!
WE SURE WILL!
"ENJOY."

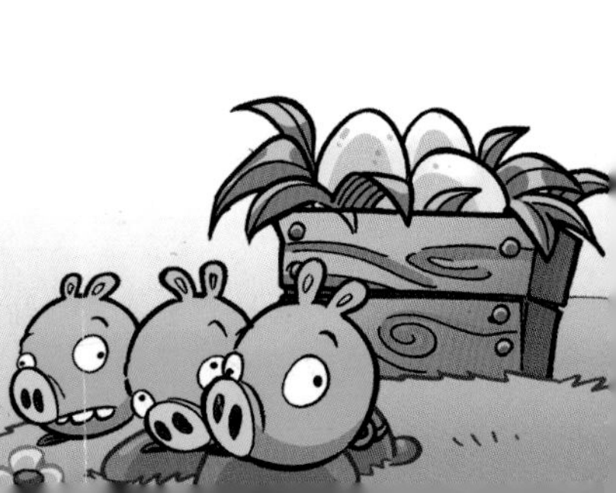

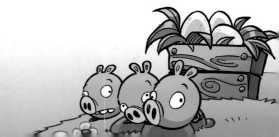

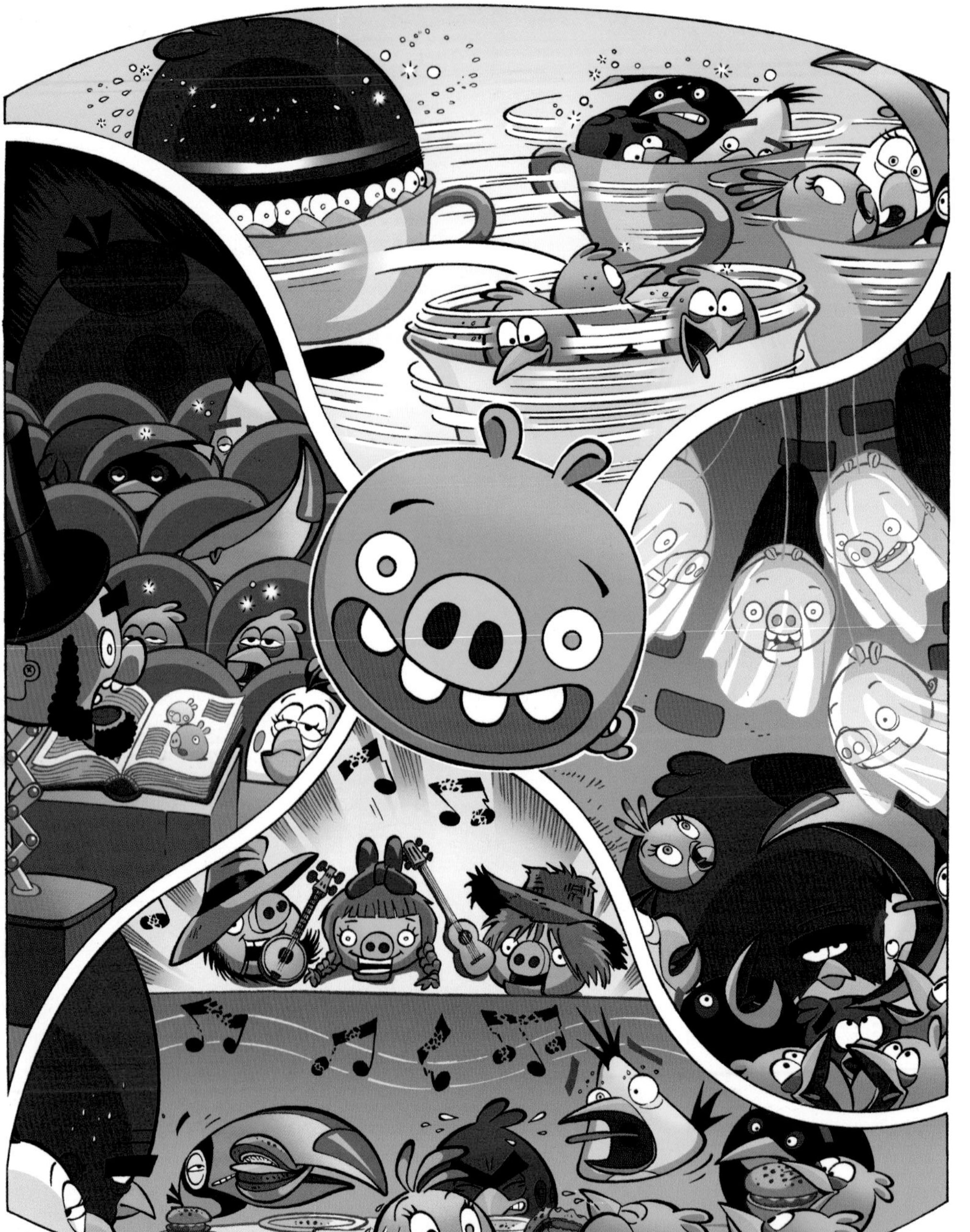

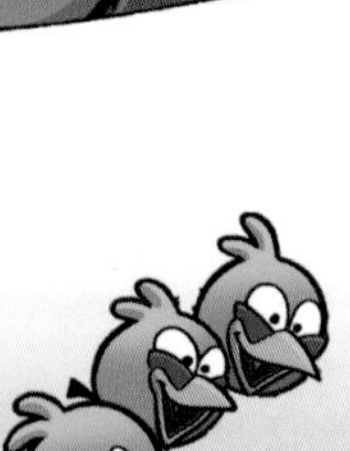

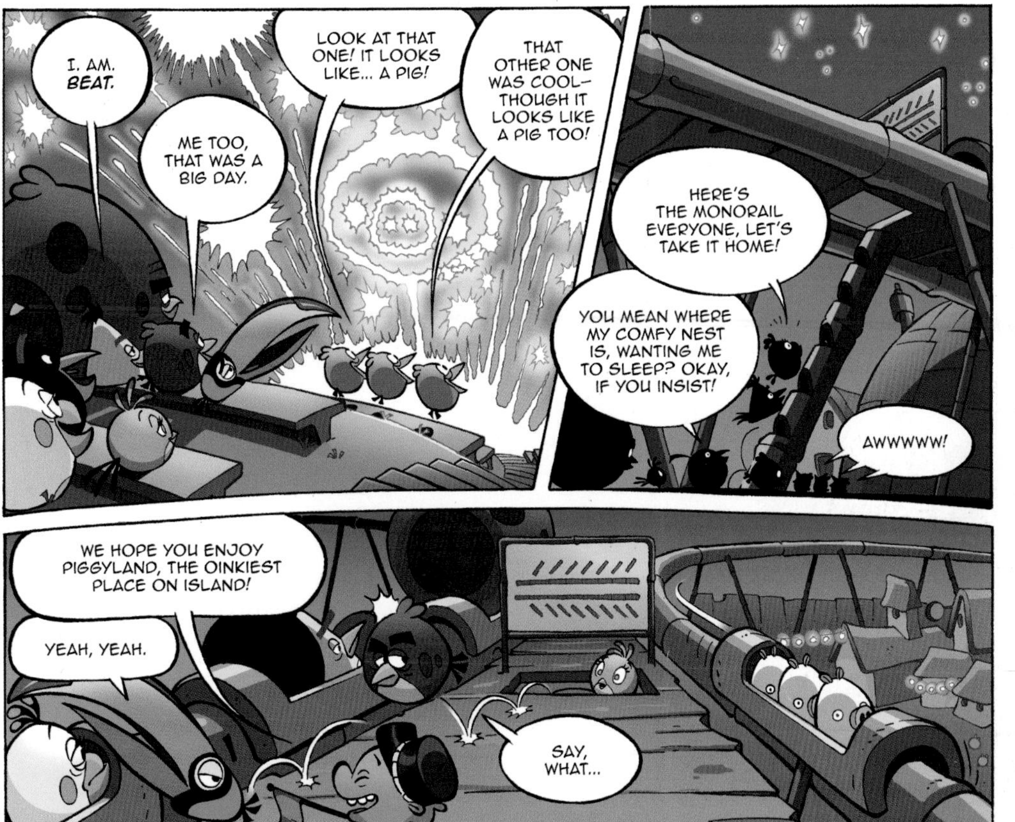
I. AM. **BEAT.**
ME TOO, THAT WAS A BIG DAY.
LOOK AT THAT ONE! IT LOOKS LIKE... A PIG!
THAT OTHER ONE WAS COOL— THOUGH IT LOOKS LIKE A PIG TOO!
HERE'S THE MONORAIL EVERYONE, LET'S TAKE IT HOME!
YOU MEAN WHERE MY COMFY NEST IS, WANTING ME TO SLEEP? OKAY, IF YOU INSIST!
AWWWWW!
WE HOPE YOU ENJOY PIGGYLAND, THE OINKIEST PLACE ON ISLAND!
YEAH, YEAH.
SAY, WHAT...
NOW I SEE THE PLAN!
MAKING US LOOK AT MECHANICAL CREA- TURES ALL DAY UNTIL IT SEEMS NORMAL TO US!
UH... HUH?
ARE YOU OKAY, RED? I MEAN, WE'RE ALL TIRED...
AND KEEPING US HERE ALL DAY SO THEY COULD SEARCH EVERY HIDING SPACE IN OUR HOME!
RED, WHAT ARE YOU TRYING TO SAY?

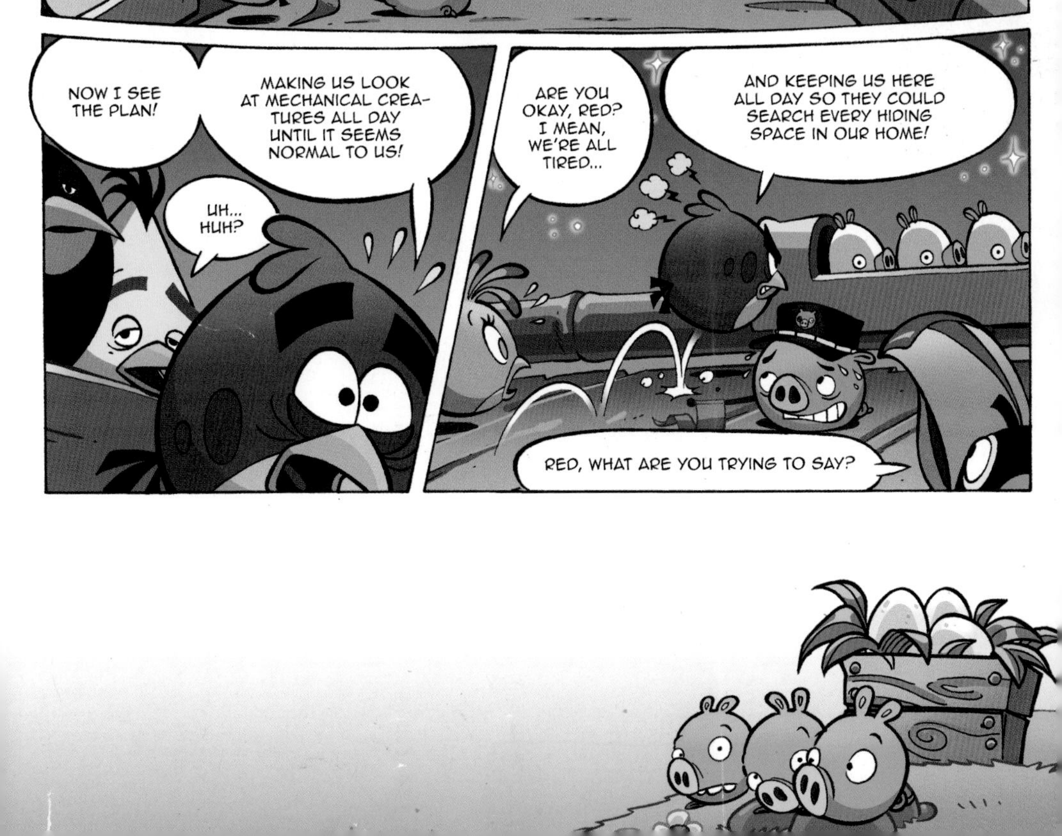

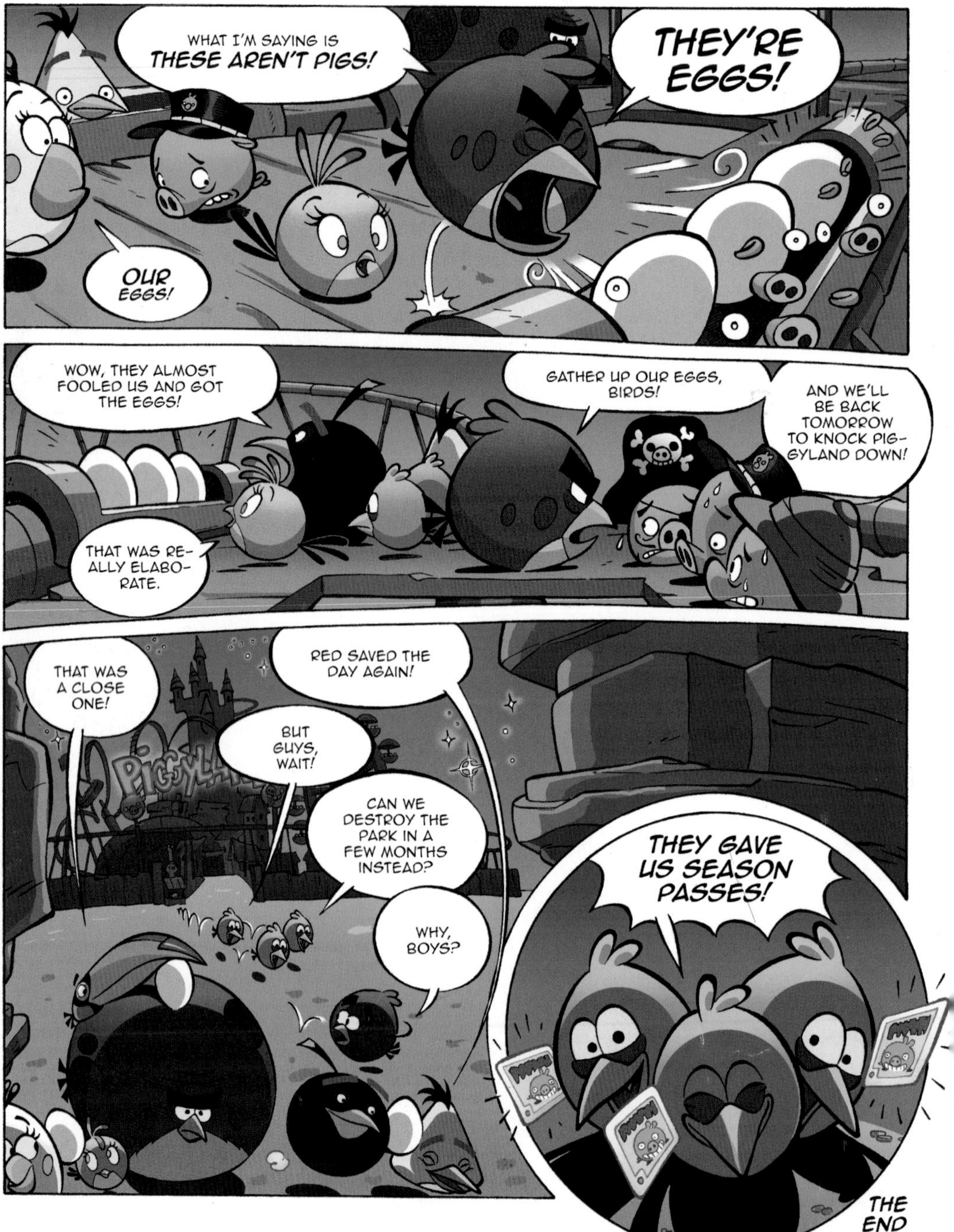
WHAT I'M SAYING IS THESE AREN'T PIGS!
THEY'RE EGGS!
OUR EGGS!
WOW, THEY ALMOST FOOLED US AND GOT THE EGGS!
THAT WAS REALLY ELABORATE.
GATHER UP OUR EGGS, BIRDS!
AND WE'LL BE BACK TOMORROW TO KNOCK PIGGYLAND DOWN!
THAT WAS A CLOSE ONE!
RED SAVED THE DAY AGAIN!
BUT GUYS, WAIT!
CAN WE DESTROY THE PARK IN A FEW MONTHS INSTEAD?
WHY, BOYS?
THEY GAVE US SEASON PASSES!
THE END

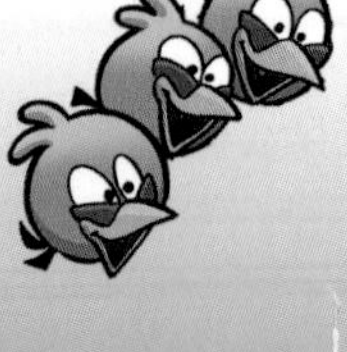

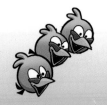

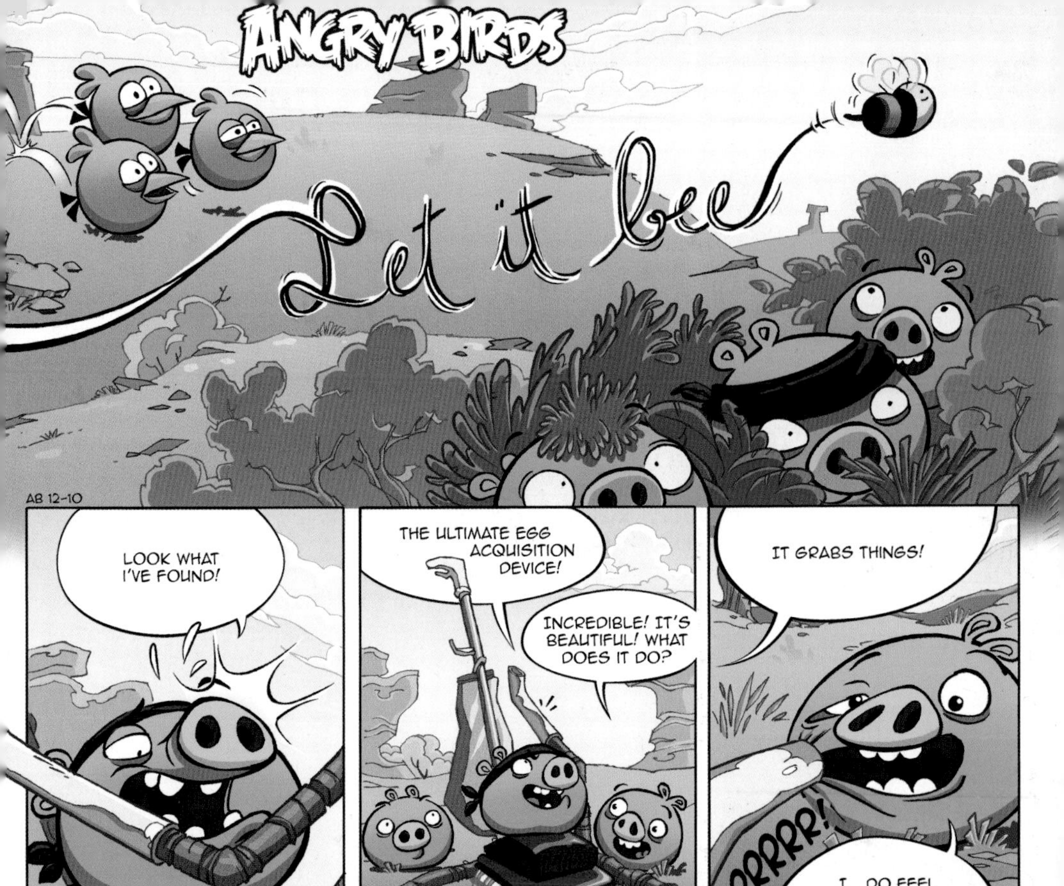
ANGRY BIRDS
Let it bee
AB 12-10
LOOK WHAT I'VE FOUND!
THE ULTIMATE EGG ACQUISITION DEVICE!
INCREDIBLE! IT'S BEAUTIFUL! WHAT DOES IT DO?
IT GRABS THINGS!
VRRRRR!
I... DO FEEL GRABBED!
I KNOW! ISN'T IT GREAT!
THE ULTIMATE EGG ACQUISITION DEVICE IS THE SOLUTION TO OUR PROBLEMS. JUST LISTEN TO THIS WONDERFUL PLAN!
WE USE THIS EXTENSION ATTACHMENT...

WRITTEN BY: PAUL TOBIN • ART BY: AUDREY BUSSI & ISA PYTHON • COLORS BY: DIGIKORE STUDIOS • LETTERS BY: ROVIO COMICS

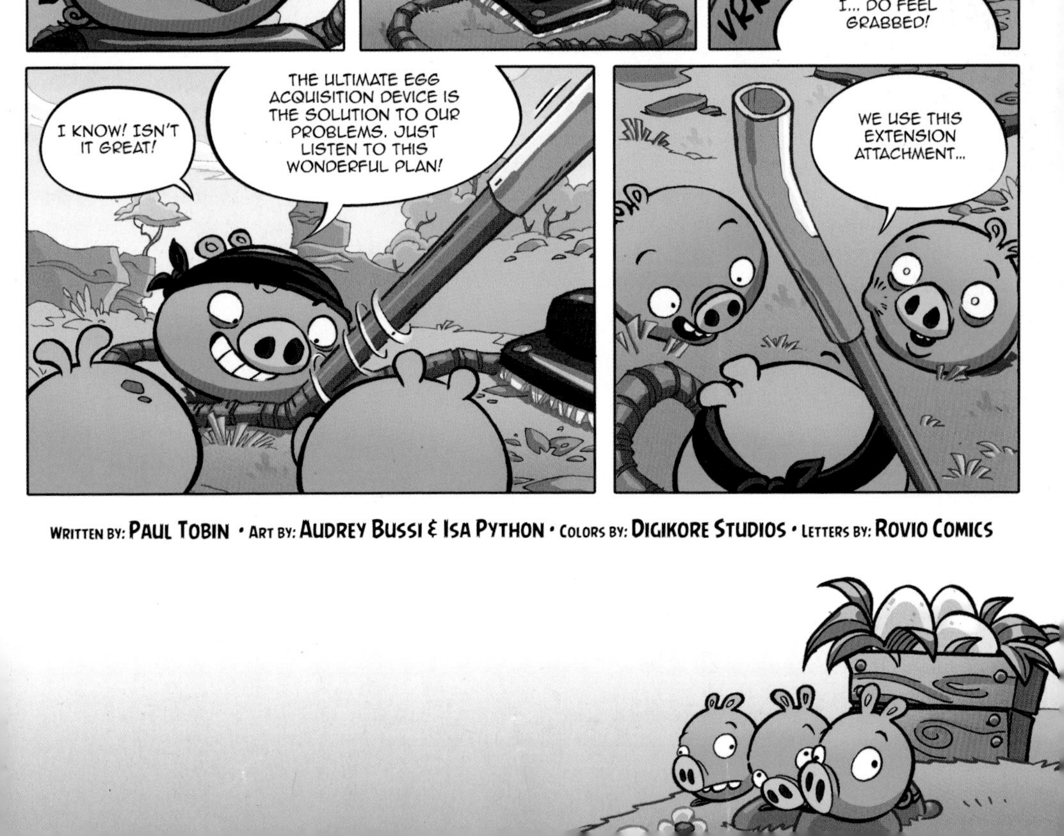

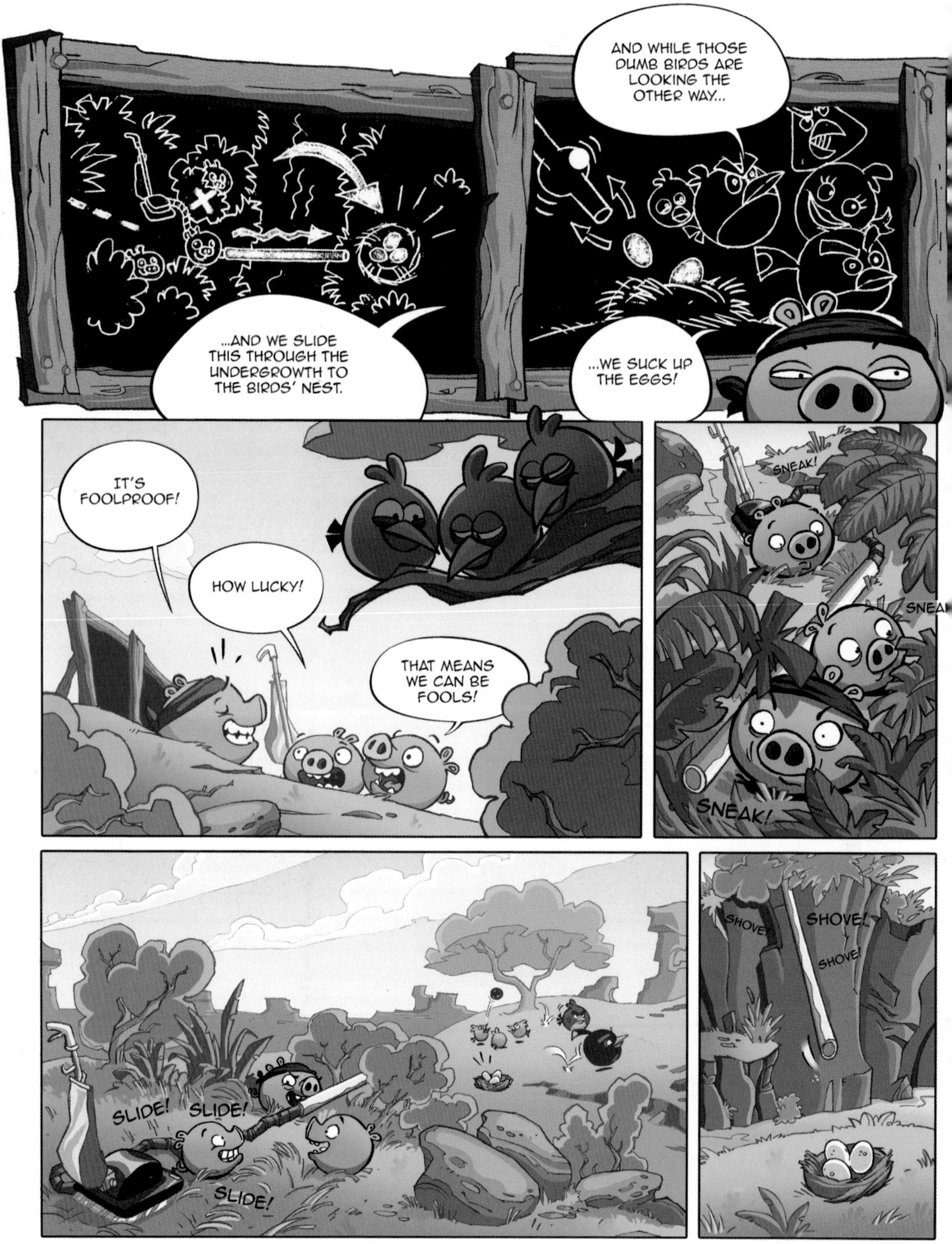
...AND WE SLIDE THIS THROUGH THE UNDERGROWTH TO THE BIRDS' NEST.
AND WHILE THOSE DUMB BIRDS ARE LOOKING THE OTHER WAY...
...WE SUCK UP THE EGGS!
IT'S FOOLPROOF!
HOW LUCKY!
THAT MEANS WE CAN BE FOOLS!
SNEAK!
SNEAK!
SLIDE!
SLIDE!
SLIDE!
SHOVE!
SHOVE!
SHOVE!

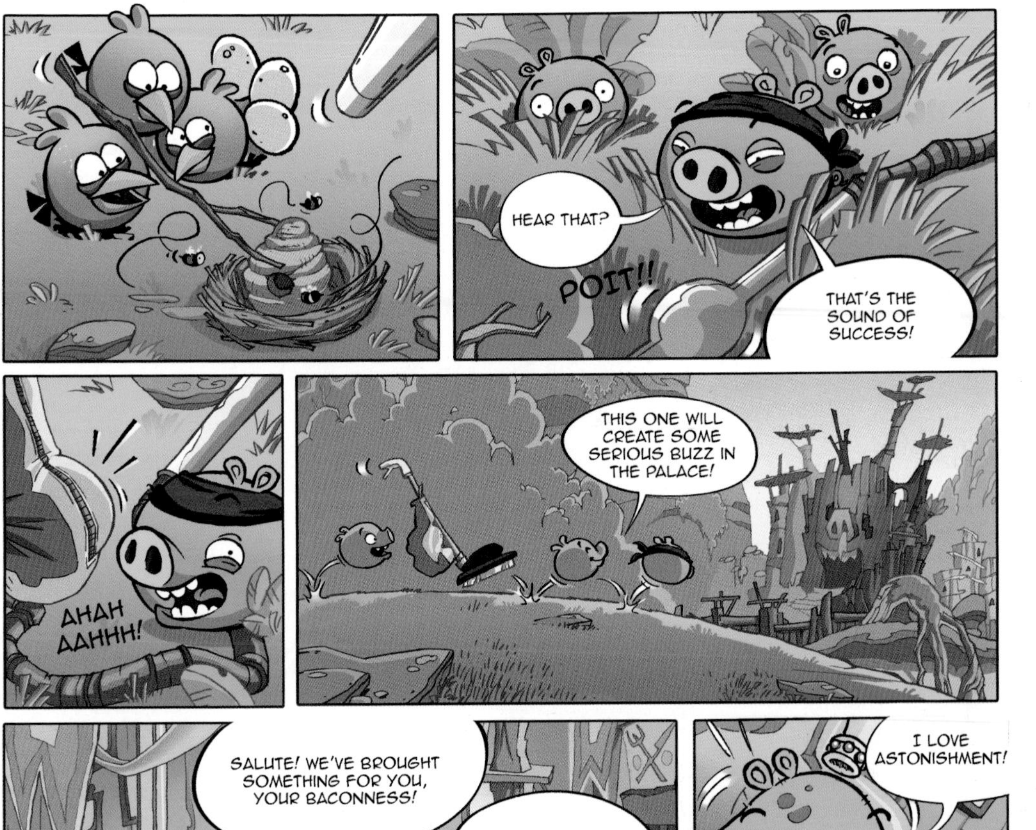
HEAR THAT?
POIT!!
THAT'S THE SOUND OF SUCCESS!
AHAH AAHHH!
THIS ONE WILL CREATE SOME SERIOUS BUZZ IN THE PALACE!
SALUTE! WE'VE BROUGHT SOMETHING FOR YOU, YOUR BACONNESS!
PREPARE TO HAVE ASTONISHMENT, SIRE!
I LOVE ASTONISHMENT!
UNZIP

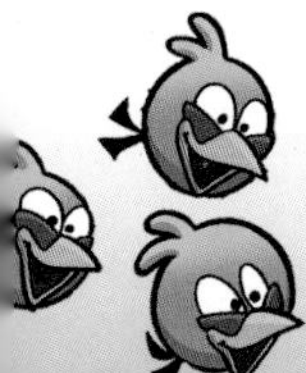

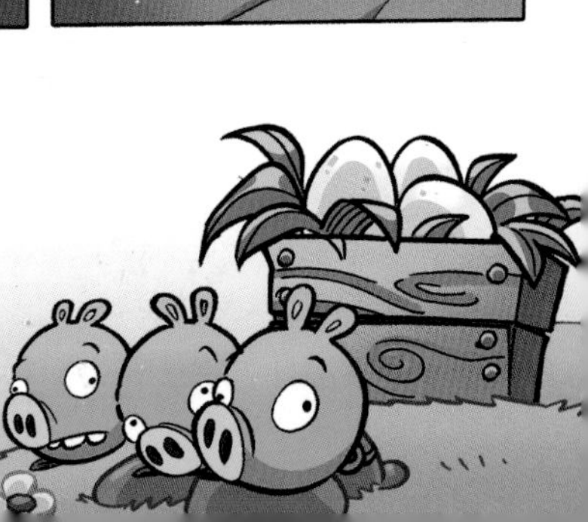

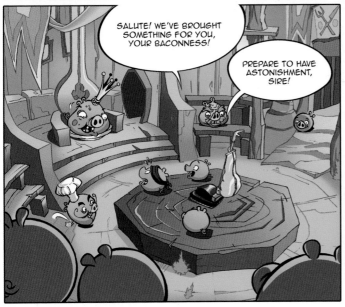

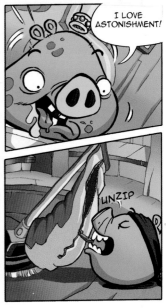

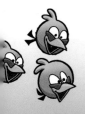

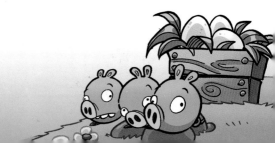

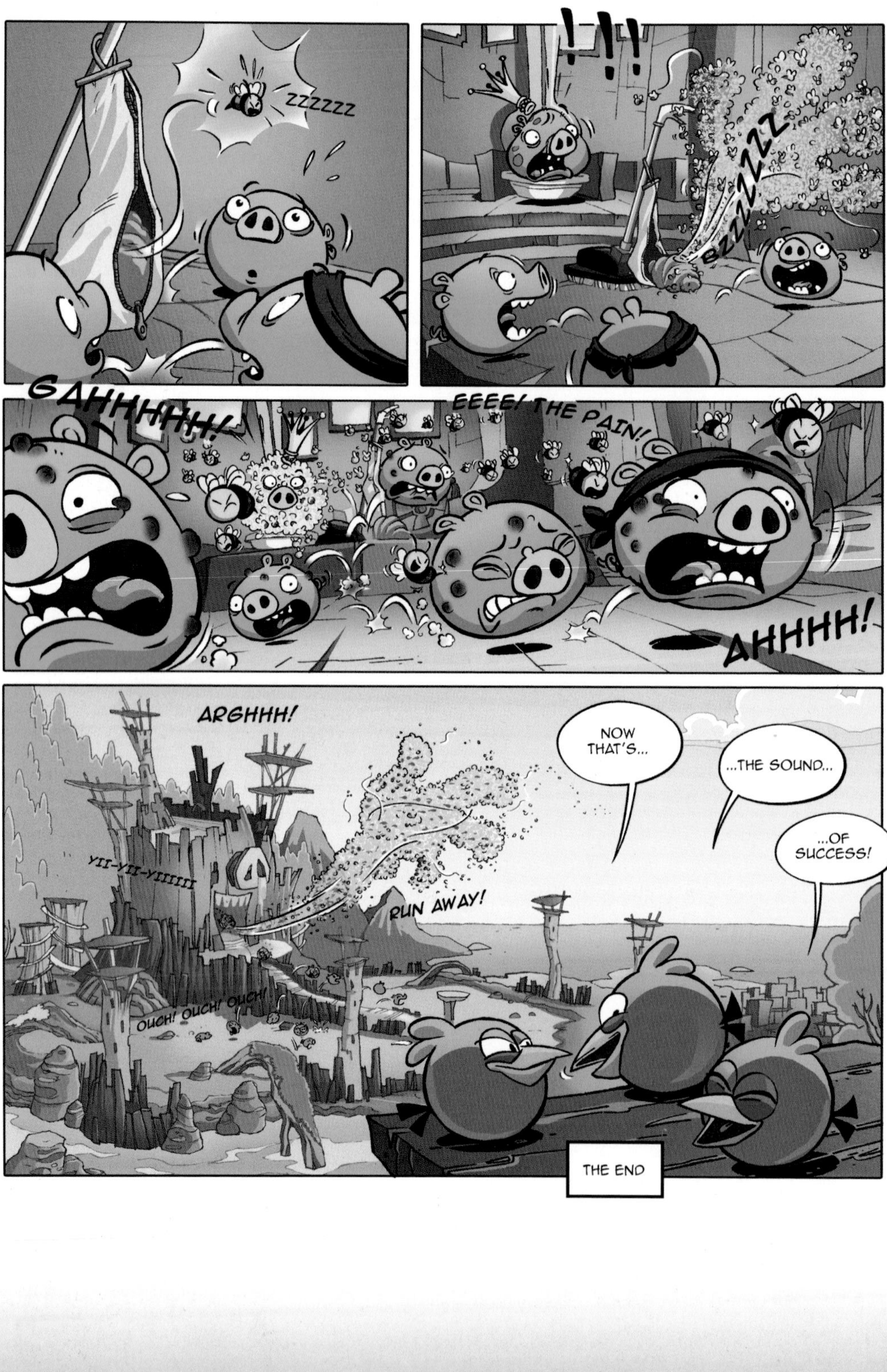
ZZZZZZ
!!!
BZZZZZZZZ
GAHHHHHH!
EEEE! THE PAIN!
AHHHH!
ARGHHH!
YII-YII-YIIIIII
RUN AWAY!
OUCH! OUCH! OUCH!
NOW THAT'S...
...THE SOUND...
...OF SUCCESS!
THE END

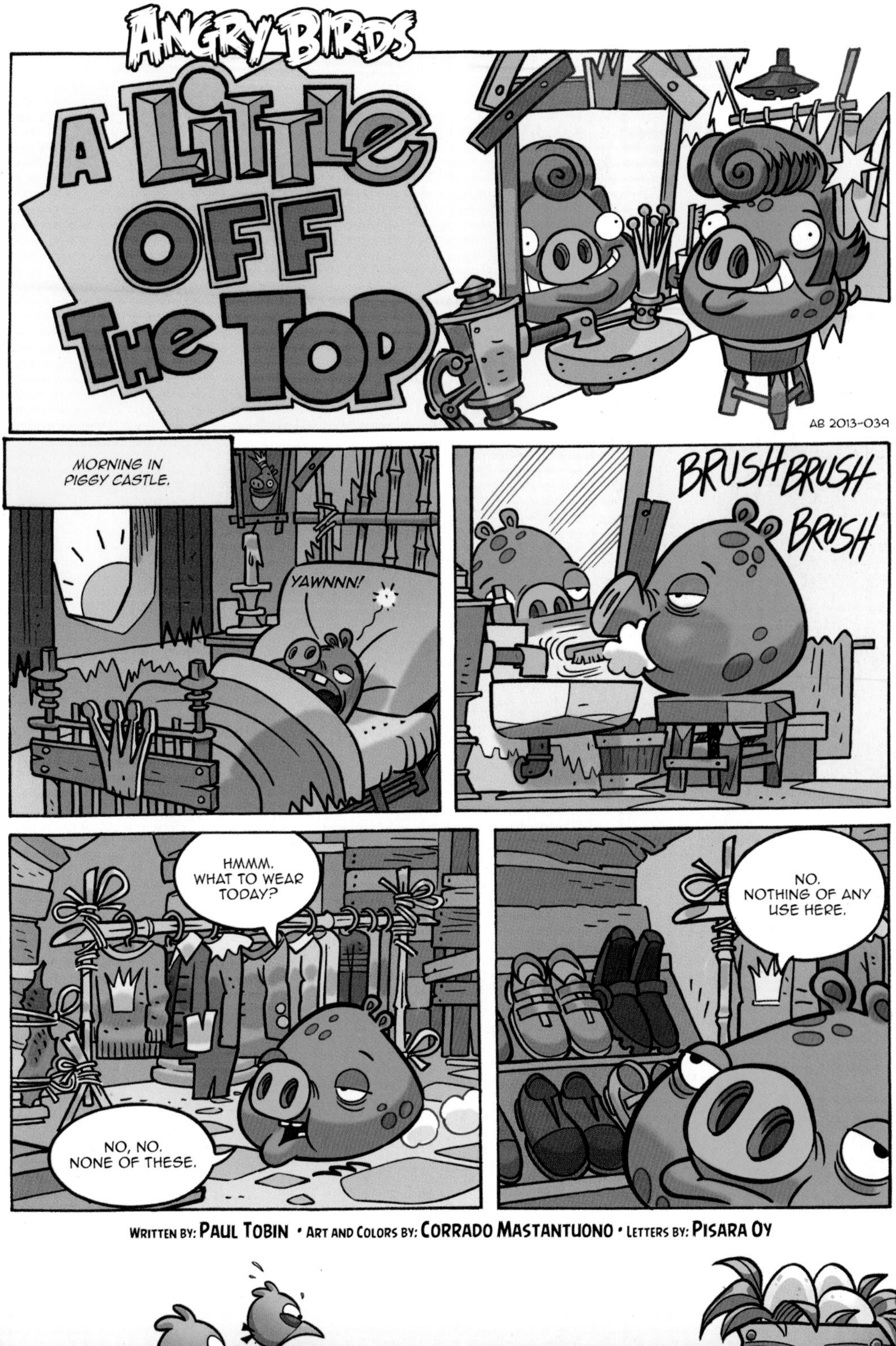
ANGRY BIRDS
A LITTLE OFF THE TOP
AB 2013-039
MORNING IN PIGGY CASTLE.
YAWNNN!
BRUSH BRUSH BRUSH
HMMM. WHAT TO WEAR TODAY?
NO, NO. NONE OF THESE.
NO. NOTHING OF ANY USE HERE.

WRITTEN BY: PAUL TOBIN • ART AND COLORS BY: CORRADO MASTANTUONO • LETTERS BY: PISARA OY

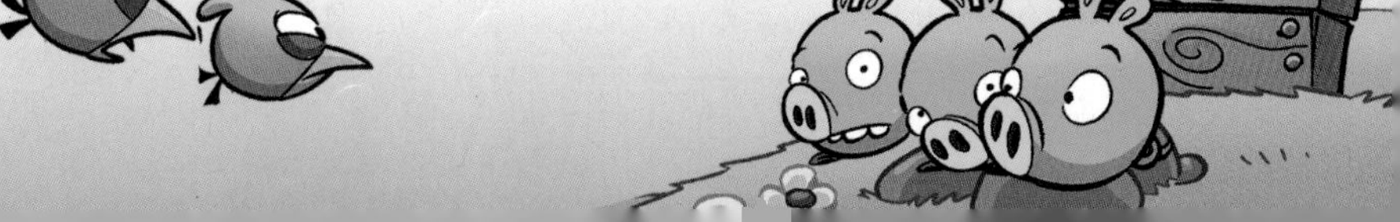

AHHH, YES!
THAT WOULD LOOK GOOD!
NOW FOR TODAY'S AGENDA. I WOULD THINK SOME BOISTEROUS YELLING. SOME EGG-STEALING.
HOPEFULLY SOME WAFFLES AND DONUTS AND CAKES AND I WOULD LIKE SOME BALLOONS AND MORE WAFFLES AND NAPS AND...
KING!
WOOOOOOSHHHH
OOOOMPFERS!
THWAKK
SLAAAPP
GRRRRRR!
UH-OH!

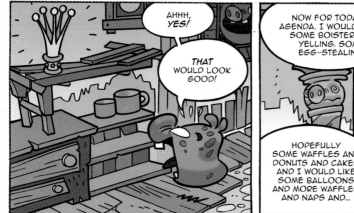

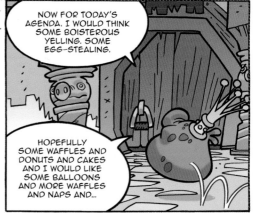

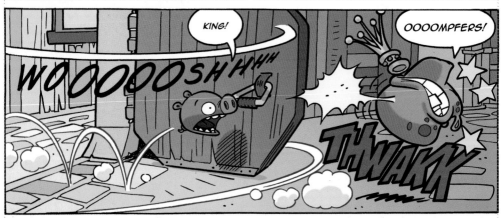

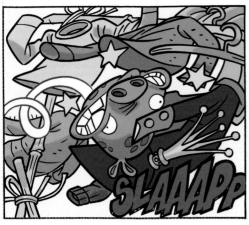

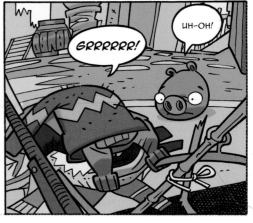

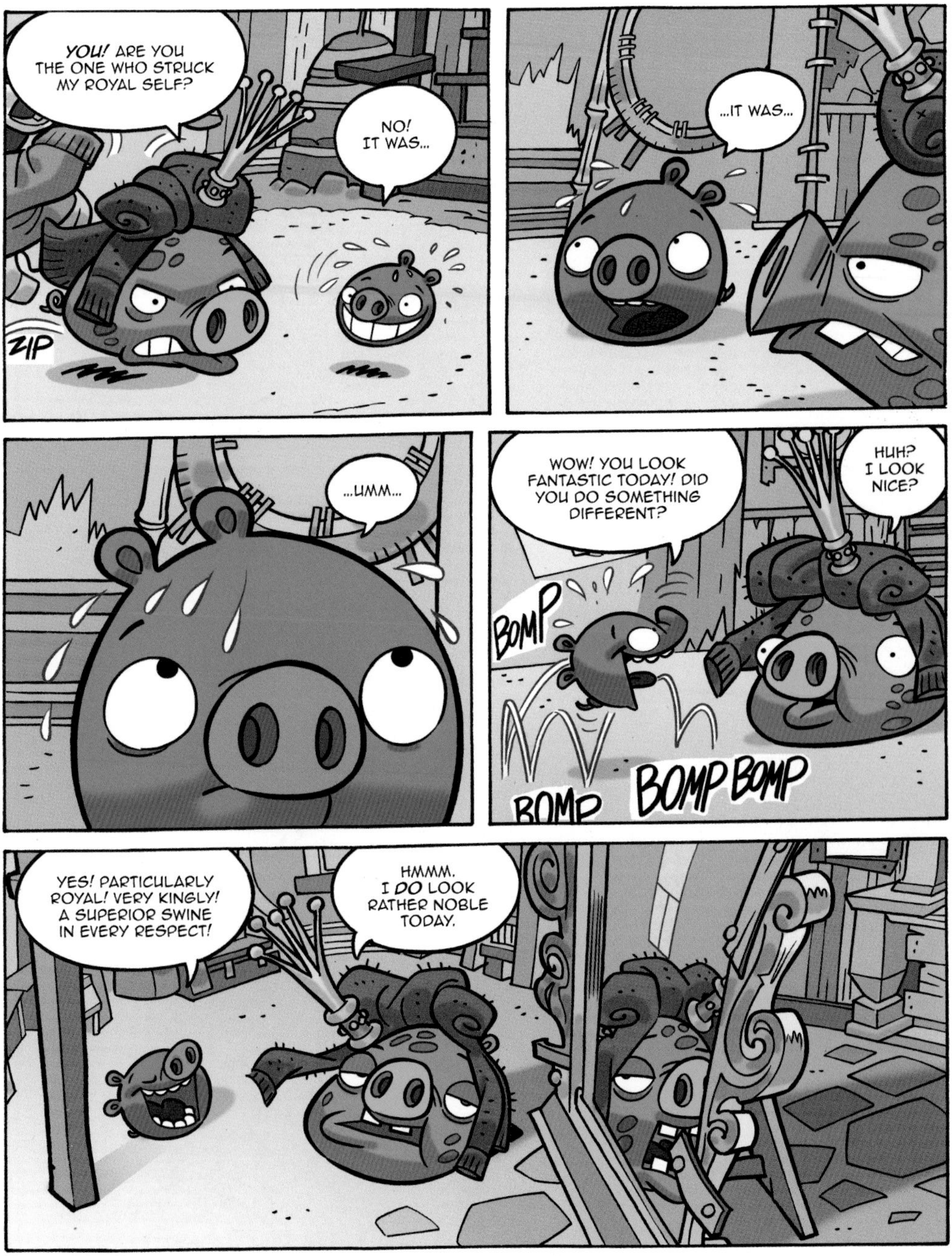
YOU! ARE YOU THE ONE WHO STRUCK MY ROYAL SELF?
ZIP
NO! IT WAS...
...IT WAS...
...UMM...
WOW! YOU LOOK FANTASTIC TODAY! DID YOU DO SOMETHING DIFFERENT?
HUH? I LOOK NICE?
BOMP
BOMP
BOMP BOMP
YES! PARTICULARLY ROYAL! VERY KINGLY! A SUPERIOR SWINE IN EVERY RESPECT!
HMMM. I DO LOOK RATHER NOBLE TODAY.

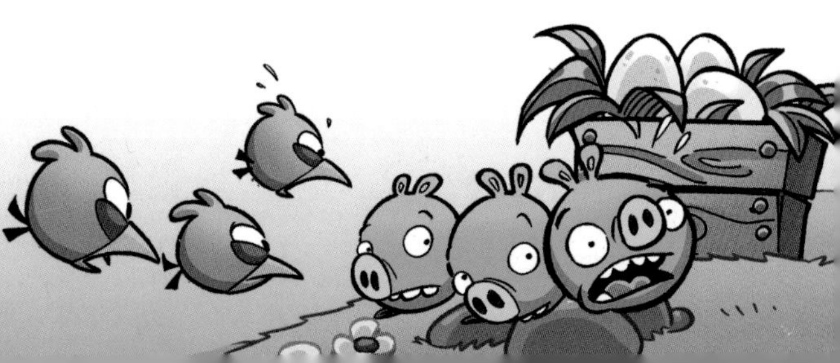

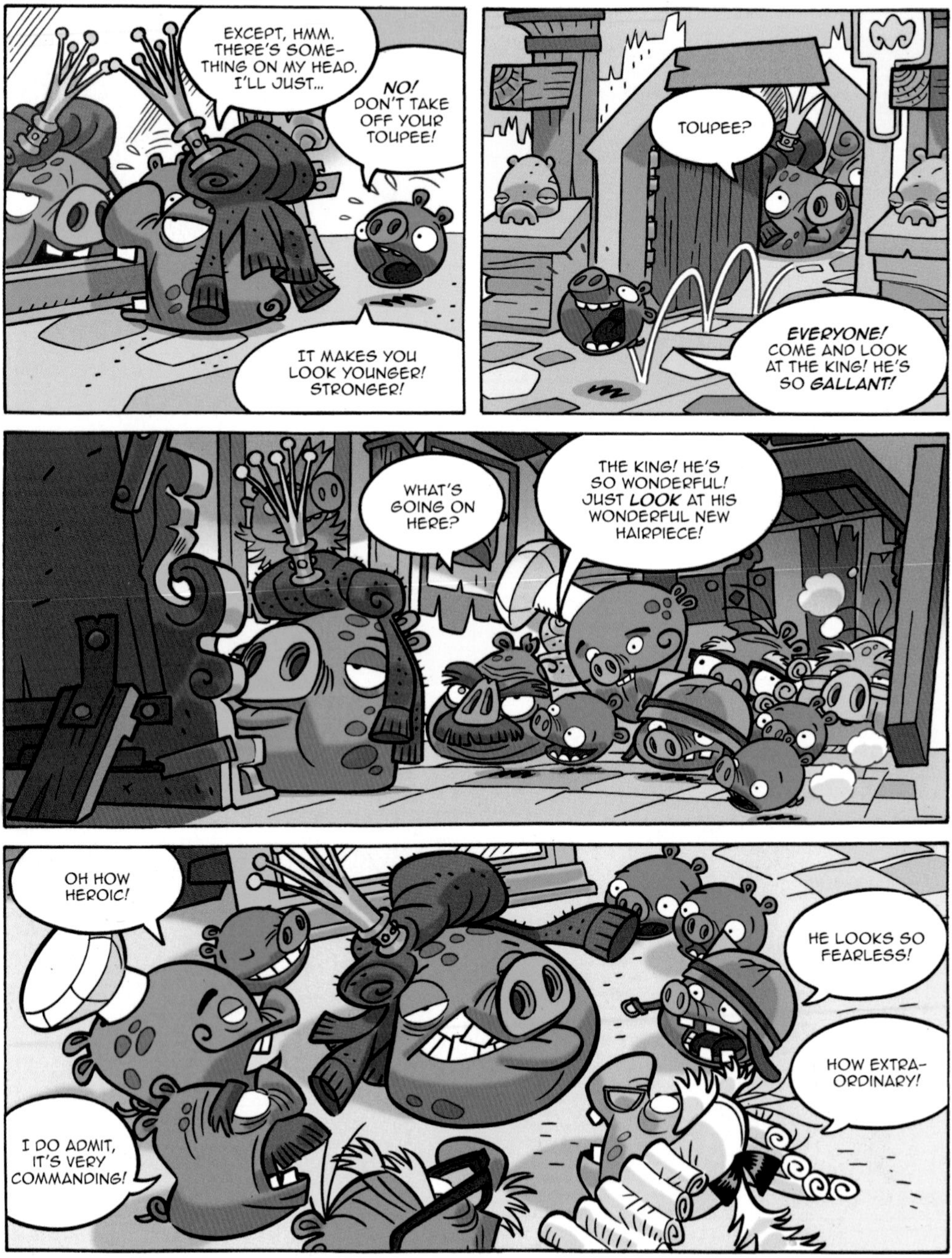
EXCEPT, HMM. THERE'S SOME-THING ON MY HEAD. I'LL JUST...
*NO!* DON'T TAKE OFF YOUR TOUPEE!
IT MAKES YOU LOOK YOUNGER! STRONGER!
TOUPEE?
*EVERYONE!* COME AND LOOK AT THE KING! HE'S SO *GALLANT!*
WHAT'S GOING ON HERE?
THE KING! HE'S SO WONDERFUL! JUST *LOOK* AT HIS WONDERFUL NEW HAIRPIECE!
OH HOW HEROIC!
HE LOOKS SO FEARLESS!
HOW EXTRA-ORDINARY!
I DO ADMIT, IT'S VERY COMMANDING!

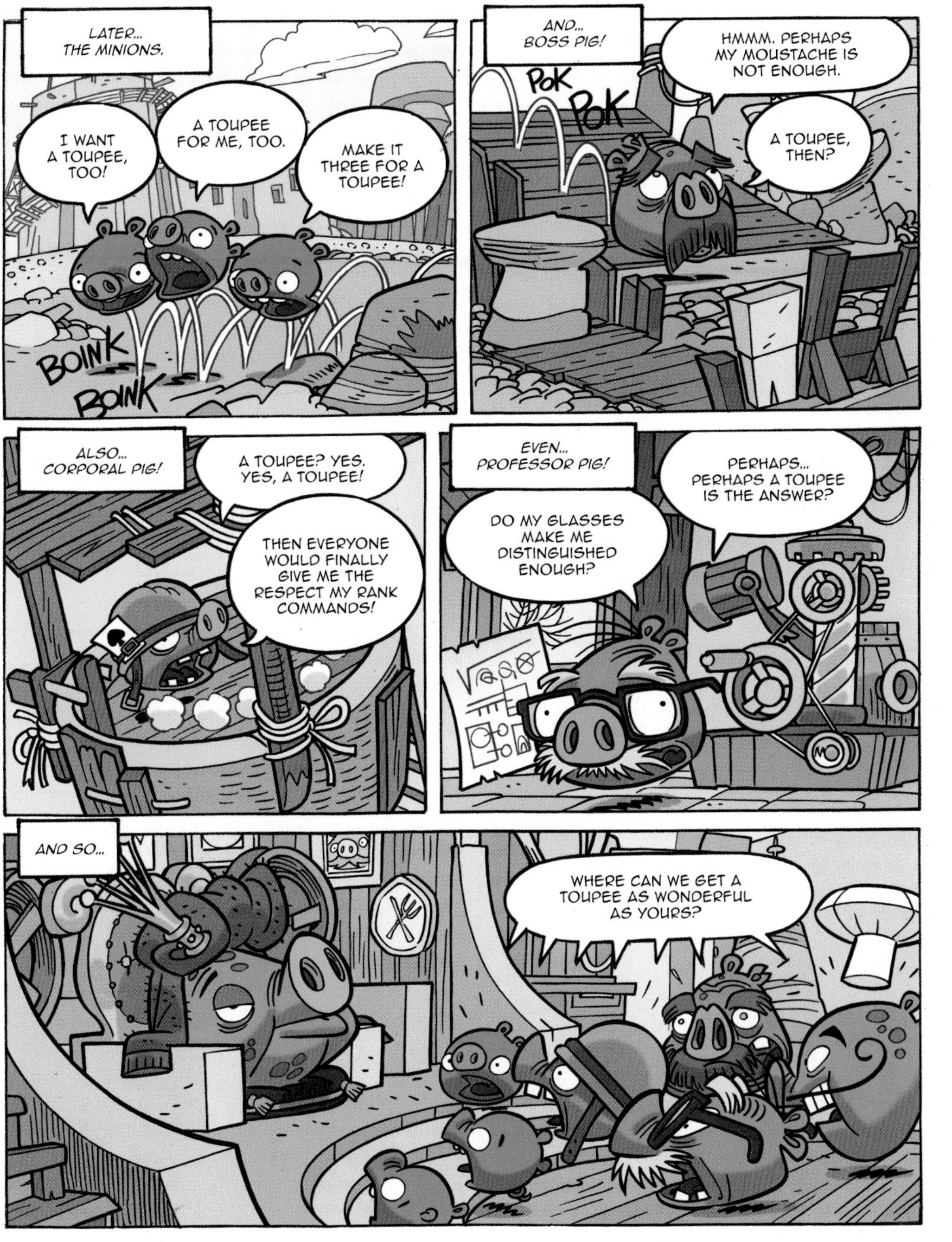
LATER... THE MINIONS.
I WANT A TOUPEE, TOO!
A TOUPEE FOR ME, TOO.
MAKE IT THREE FOR A TOUPEE!
BOINK
BOINK
AND... BOSS PIG!
POK
POK
HMMM. PERHAPS MY MOUSTACHE IS NOT ENOUGH.
A TOUPEE, THEN?
ALSO... CORPORAL PIG!
A TOUPEE? YES. YES, A TOUPEE!
THEN EVERYONE WOULD FINALLY GIVE ME THE RESPECT MY RANK COMMANDS!
EVEN... PROFESSOR PIG!
DO MY GLASSES MAKE ME DISTINGUISHED ENOUGH?
PERHAPS... PERHAPS A TOUPEE IS THE ANSWER?
AND SO...
WHERE CAN WE GET A TOUPEE AS WONDERFUL AS YOURS?

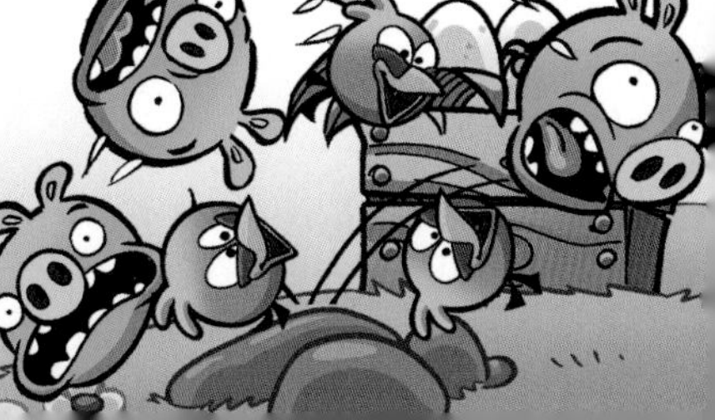

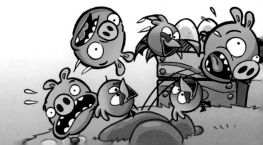

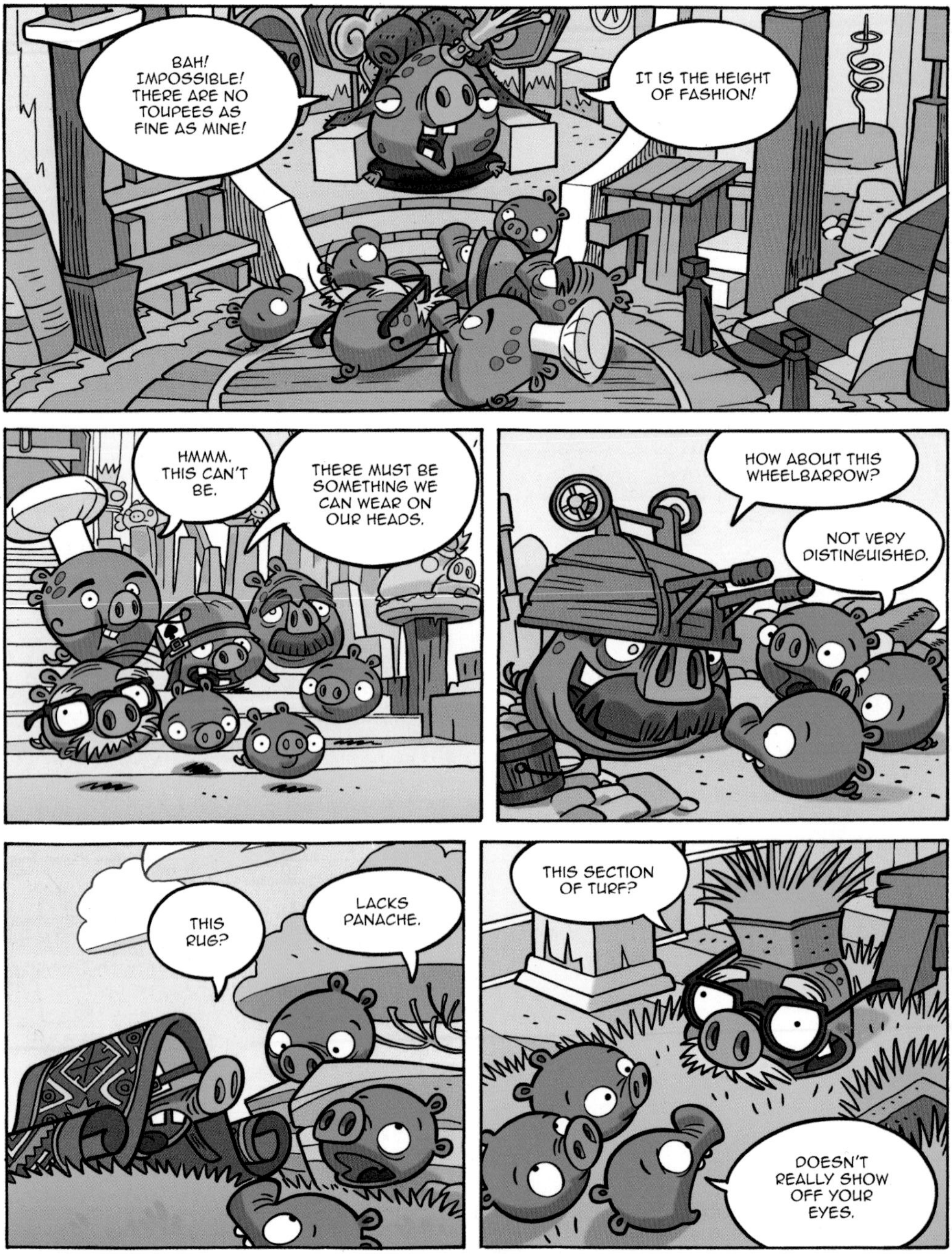
BAH! IMPOSSIBLE! THERE ARE NO TOUPEES AS FINE AS MINE!
IT IS THE HEIGHT OF FASHION!
HMMM. THIS CAN'T BE.
THERE MUST BE SOMETHING WE CAN WEAR ON OUR HEADS.
HOW ABOUT THIS WHEELBARROW?
NOT VERY DISTINGUISHED.
THIS RUG?
LACKS PANACHE.
THIS SECTION OF TURF?
DOESN'T REALLY SHOW OFF YOUR EYES.

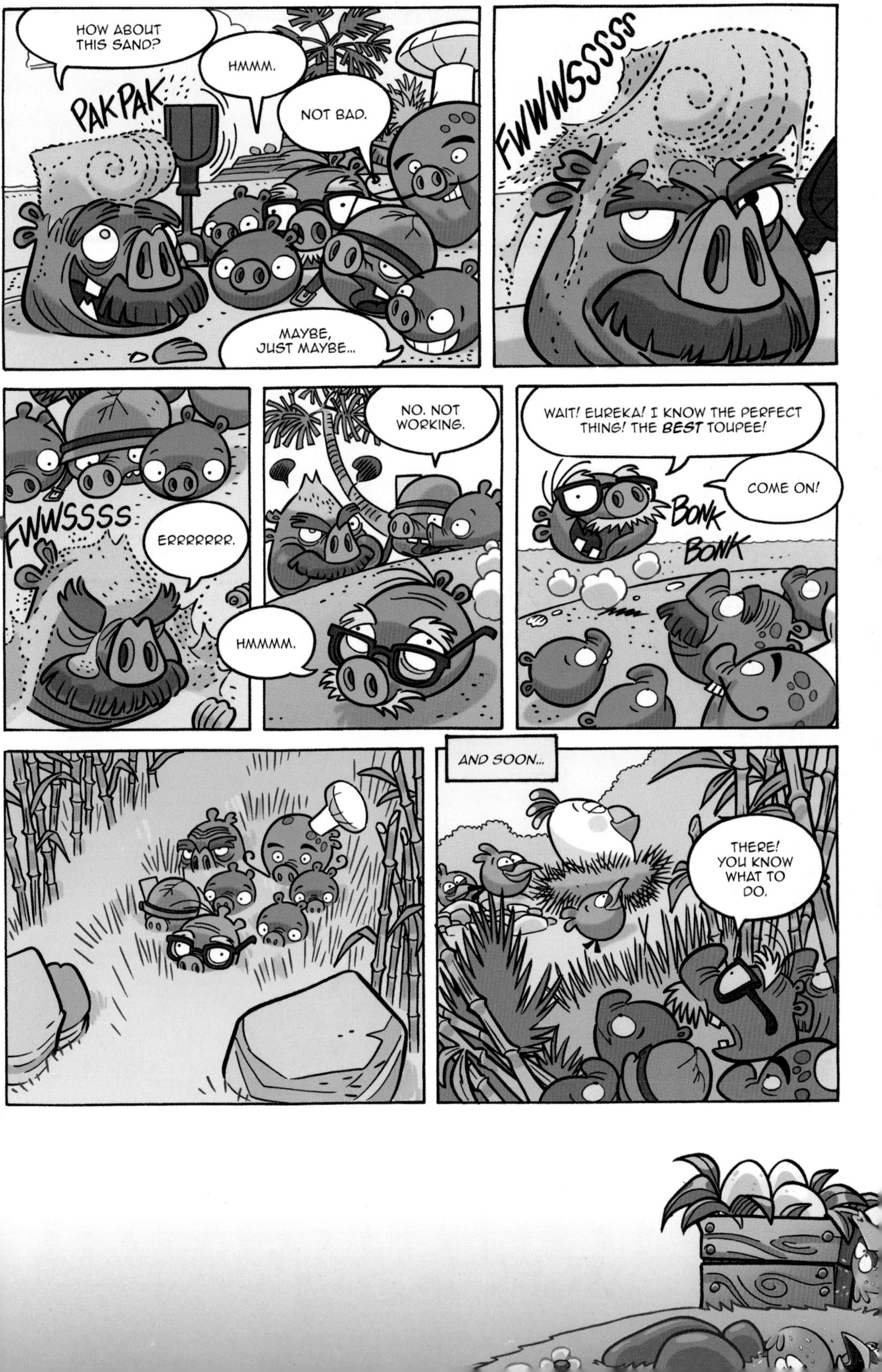
HOW ABOUT THIS SAND?
HMMM.
PAKPAK
NOT BAD.
MAYBE, JUST MAYBE...
FWWWSSSSS
FWWSSSS
ERRRRRRR.
NO. NOT WORKING.
HMMMM.
WAIT! EUREKA! I KNOW THE PERFECT THING! THE **BEST** TOUPEE!
COME ON!
BONK
BONK
AND SOON...
THERE! YOU KNOW WHAT TO DO.

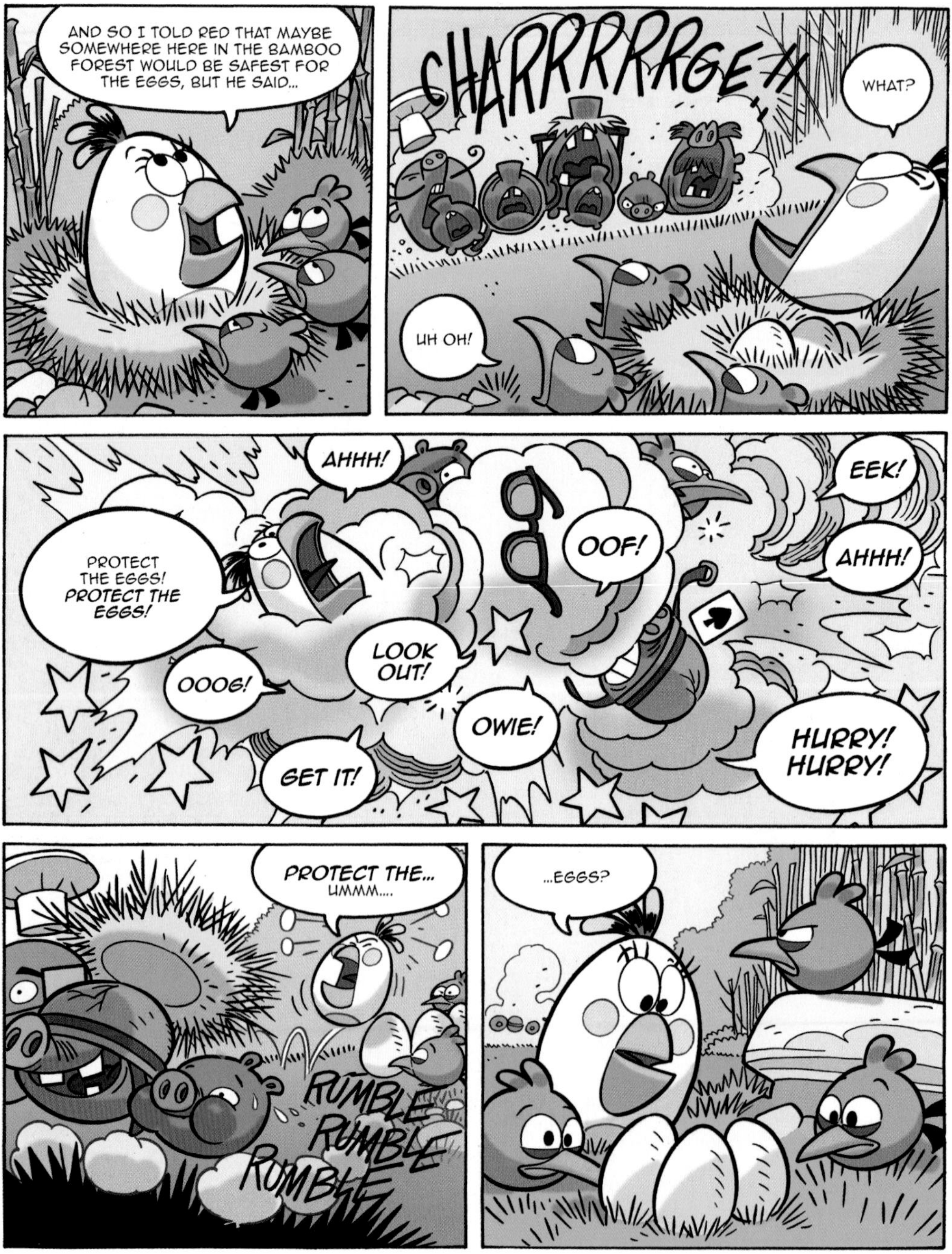
AND SO I TOLD RED THAT MAYBE SOMEWHERE HERE IN THE BAMBOO FOREST WOULD BE SAFEST FOR THE EGGS, BUT HE SAID...
CHARRRRRRGE!!
WHAT?
UH OH!
AHHH!
EEK!
PROTECT THE EGGS! PROTECT THE EGGS!
OOF!
AHHH!
LOOK OUT!
OOOG!
OWIE!
HURRY! HURRY!
GET IT!
PROTECT THE... UMMM....
RUMBLE RUMBLE RUMBLE
...EGGS?

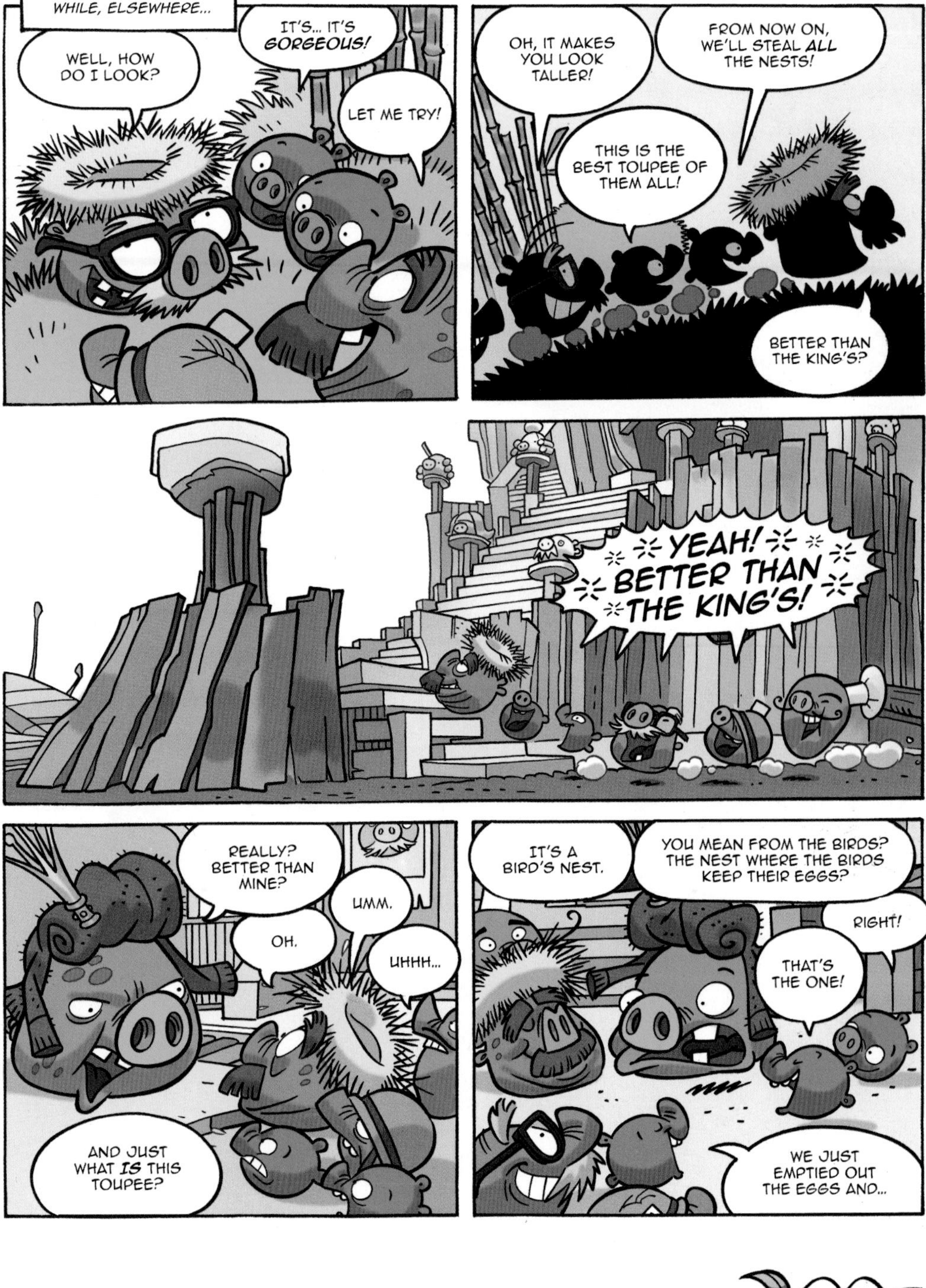
WHILE, ELSEWHERE...
WELL, HOW DO I LOOK?
IT'S... IT'S GORGEOUS!
LET ME TRY!
OH, IT MAKES YOU LOOK TALLER!
FROM NOW ON, WE'LL STEAL ALL THE NESTS!
THIS IS THE BEST TOUPEE OF THEM ALL!
BETTER THAN THE KING'S?
YEAH! BETTER THAN THE KING'S!
REALLY? BETTER THAN MINE?
UMM.
OH.
UHHH...
AND JUST WHAT IS THIS TOUPEE?
IT'S A BIRD'S NEST.
YOU MEAN FROM THE BIRDS? THE NEST WHERE THE BIRDS KEEP THEIR EGGS?
RIGHT!
THAT'S THE ONE!
WE JUST EMPTIED OUT THE EGGS AND...

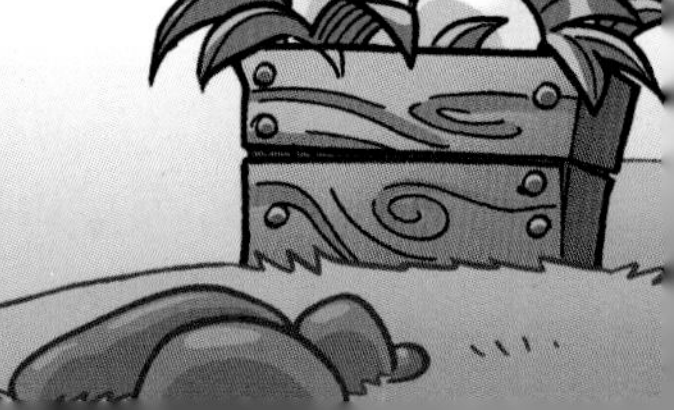

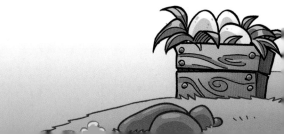

YOU **HAD** THE EGGS?!
SURE, BUT WE... ***OH!***
ZIP
SAY, WE... DID.
WE DID HAVE THE EGGS.
OH, NOW I SEE WHAT THE KING IS SAYING.
YES. WE'VE LOST SIGHT OF WHAT'S IMPORTANT.
WE'VE BEEN CAUGHT UP IN NOTHING BUT FASHION, BUT IT'S NOT FASHION WHAT'S IMPORTANT... IT'S WHAT'S INSIDE A PERSON.
RIGHT.
AND EGGS.
RIGHT. EGGS ARE ***VERY*** IMPORTANT.
I SUPPOSE... AHEM...
...THERE'S NOTHING WRONG WITH LOVING EGGS ***AND*** BEING FASHIONABLE.
ZIP
THE END

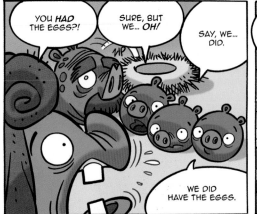

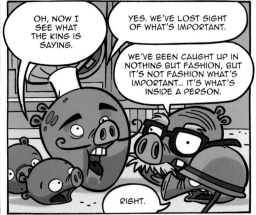

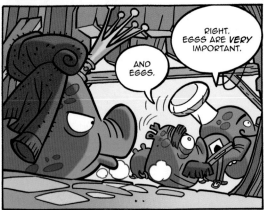

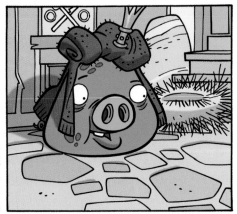

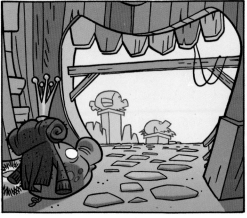

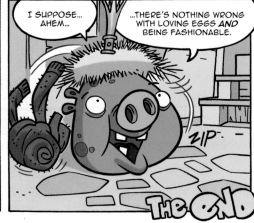

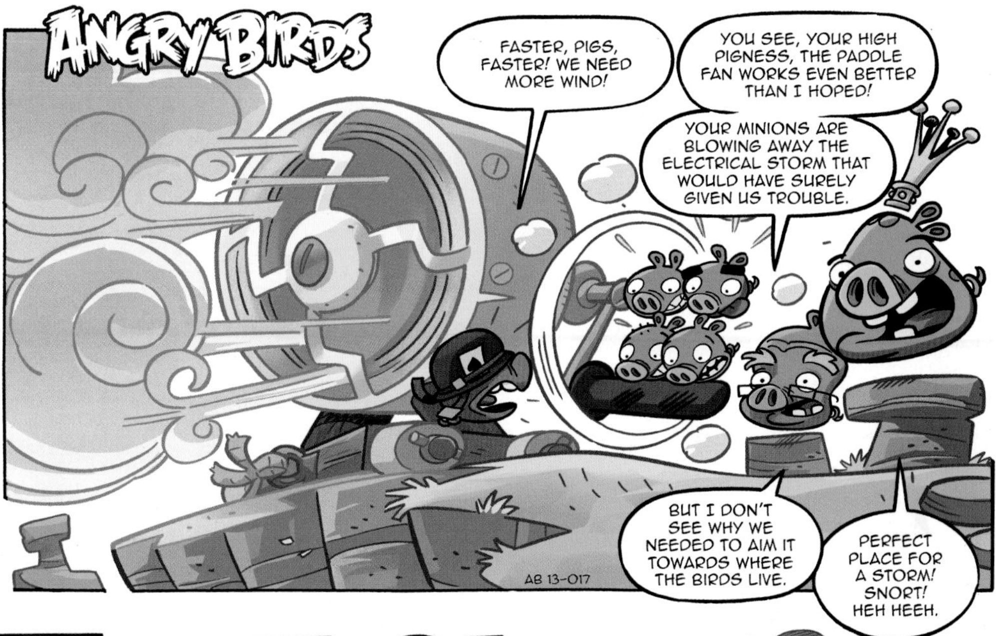
ANGRY BIRDS
FASTER, PIGS, FASTER! WE NEED MORE WIND!
YOU SEE, YOUR HIGH PIGNESS, THE PADDLE FAN WORKS EVEN BETTER THAN I HOPED!
YOUR MINIONS ARE BLOWING AWAY THE ELECTRICAL STORM THAT WOULD HAVE SURELY GIVEN US TROUBLE.
BUT I DON'T SEE WHY WE NEEDED TO AIM IT TOWARDS WHERE THE BIRDS LIVE.
PERFECT PLACE FOR A STORM! SNORT! HEH HEEH.
AB 13-017

# Static Cling

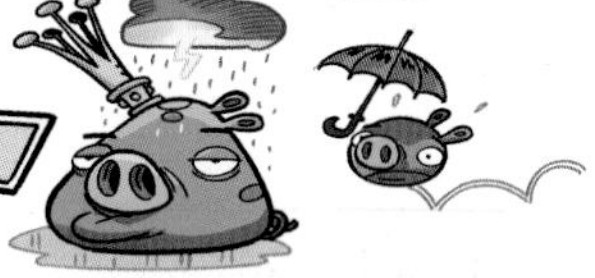

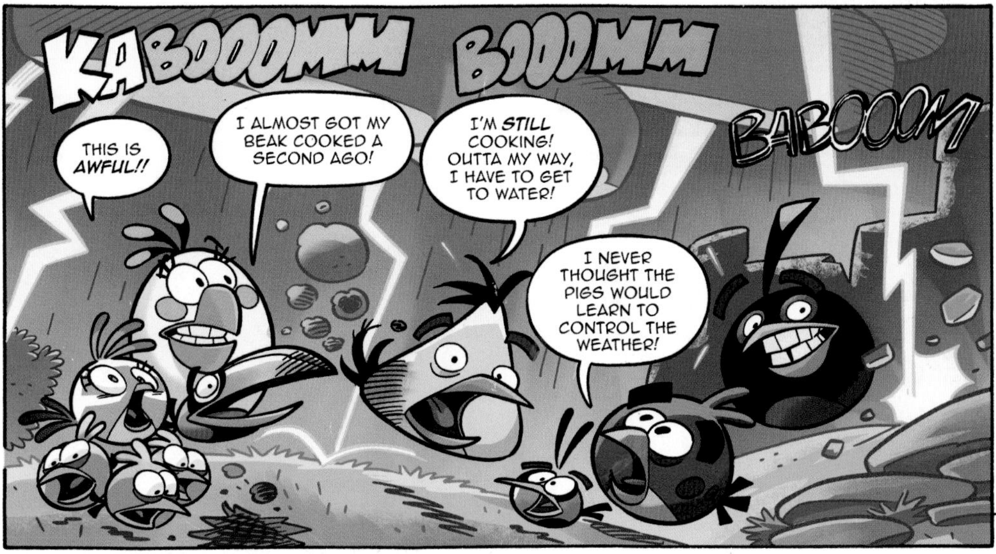
KABOOOMM
BOOOMM
BABOOOM
THIS IS AWFUL!!
I ALMOST GOT MY BEAK COOKED A SECOND AGO!
I'M STILL COOKING! OUTTA MY WAY, I HAVE TO GET TO WATER!
I NEVER THOUGHT THE PIGS WOULD LEARN TO CONTROL THE WEATHER!

WRITTEN BY: JEFF PARKER • ART BY: STEFANO INTINI • COLORS BY: NICOLA PASQUETTO • LETTERS BY: PISARA OY

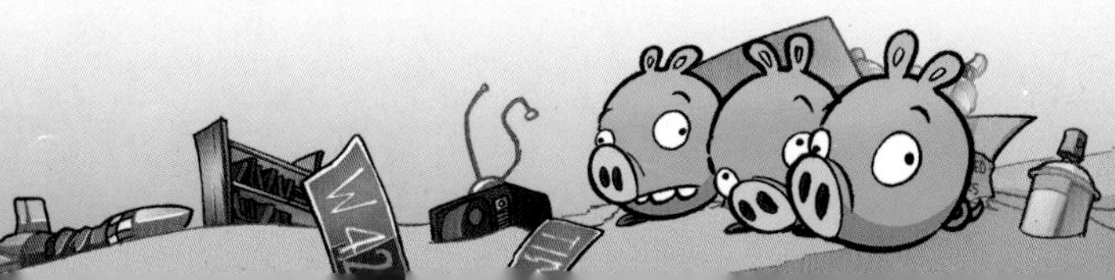

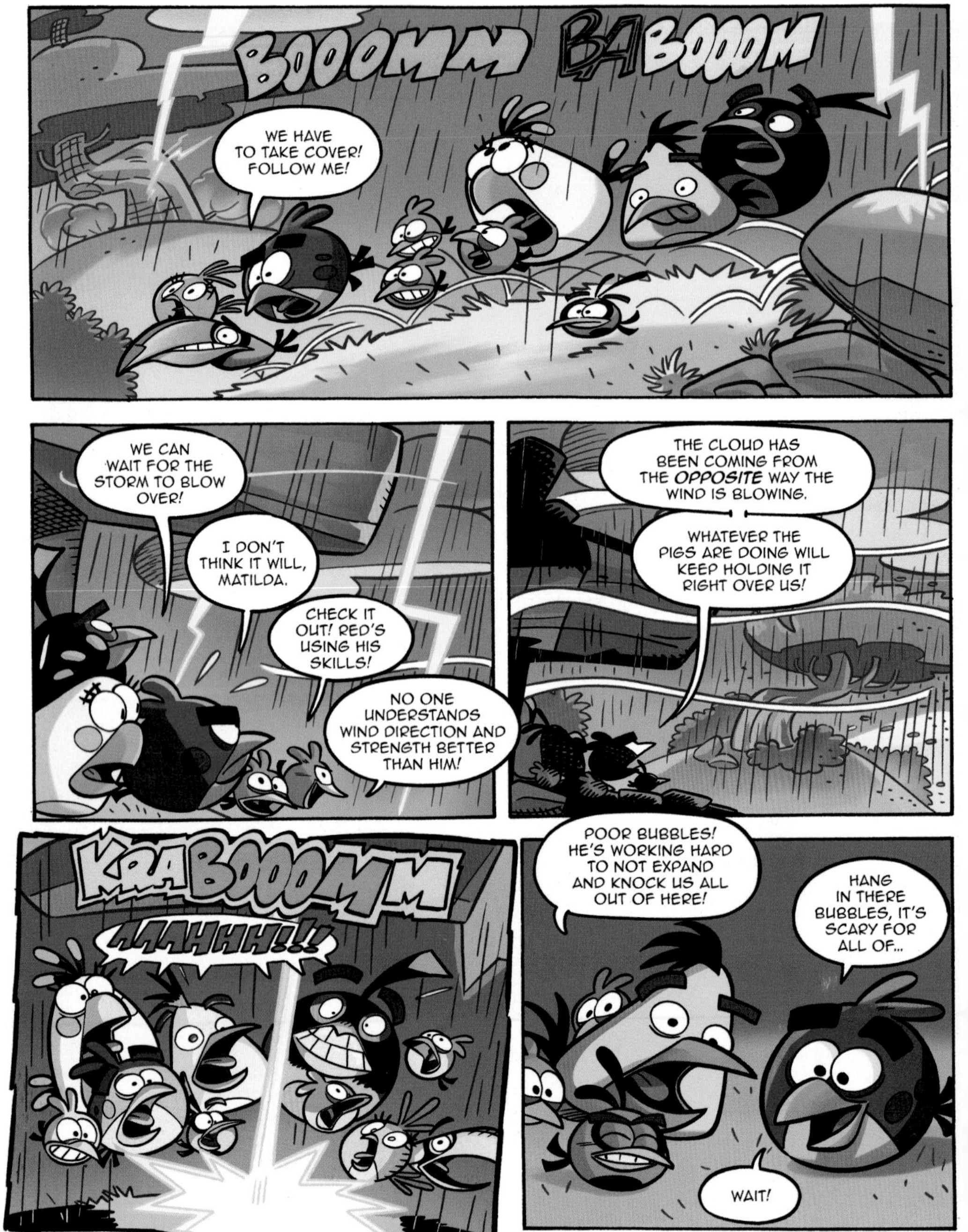
BOOOMM BABOOOM
WE HAVE TO TAKE COVER! FOLLOW ME!
WE CAN WAIT FOR THE STORM TO BLOW OVER!
I DON'T THINK IT WILL, MATILDA.
CHECK IT OUT! RED'S USING HIS SKILLS!
NO ONE UNDERSTANDS WIND DIRECTION AND STRENGTH BETTER THAN HIM!
THE CLOUD HAS BEEN COMING FROM THE *OPPOSITE* WAY THE WIND IS BLOWING.
WHATEVER THE PIGS ARE DOING WILL KEEP HOLDING IT RIGHT OVER US!
KRABOOOMM
AAAHHH!!!
POOR BUBBLES! HE'S WORKING HARD TO NOT EXPAND AND KNOCK US ALL OUT OF HERE!
HANG IN THERE BUBBLES, IT'S SCARY FOR ALL OF...
WAIT!

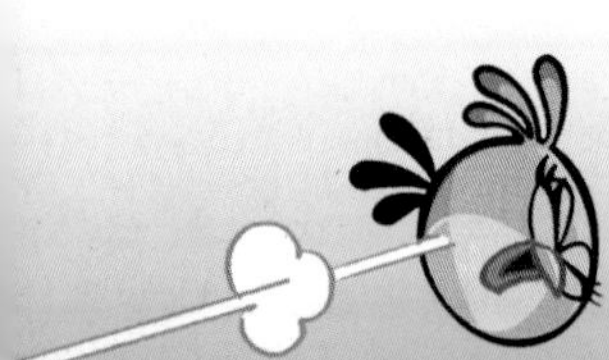

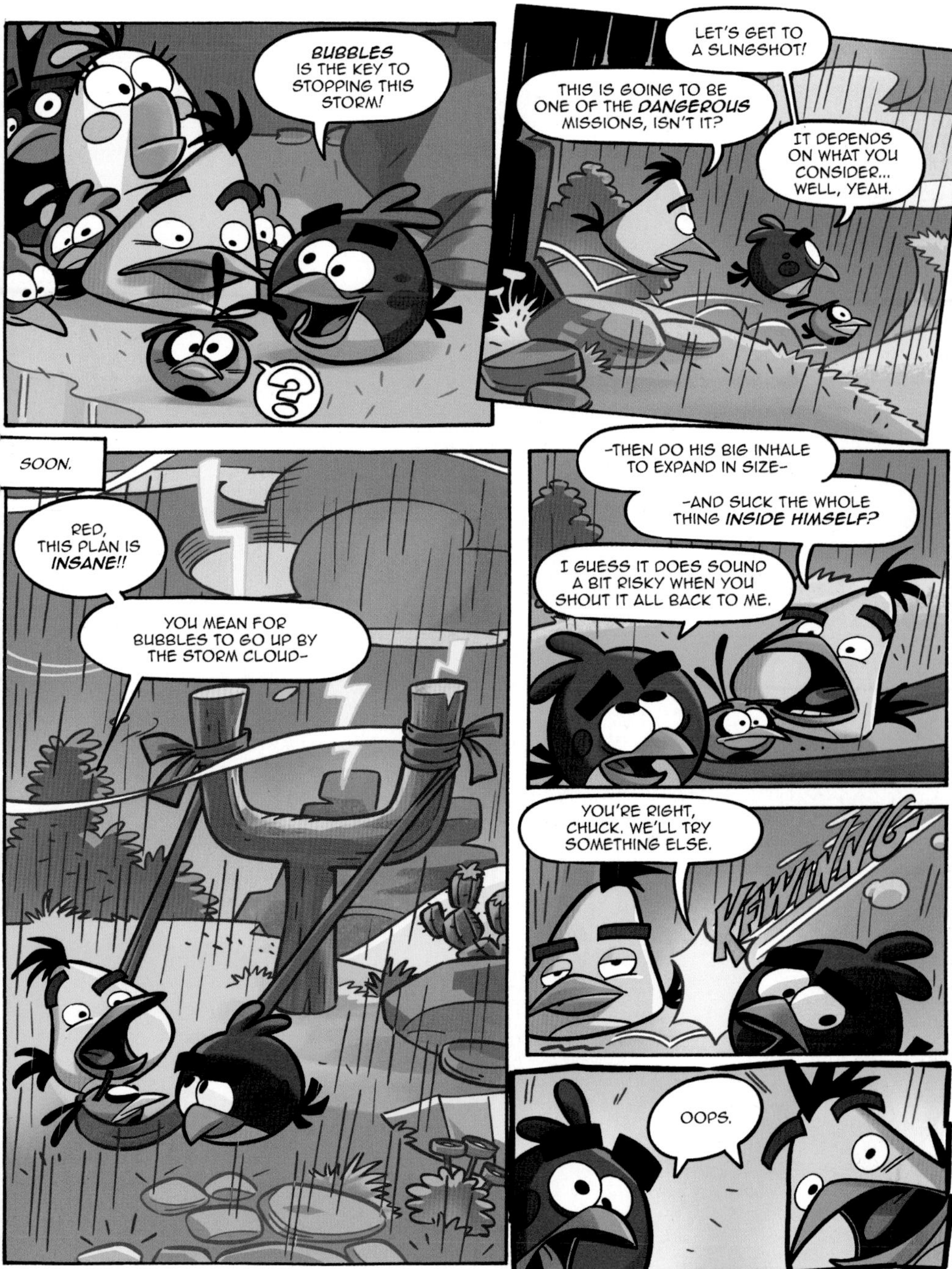
BUBBLES IS THE KEY TO STOPPING THIS STORM!
?
LET'S GET TO A SLINGSHOT!
THIS IS GOING TO BE ONE OF THE DANGEROUS MISSIONS, ISN'T IT?
IT DEPENDS ON WHAT YOU CONSIDER... WELL, YEAH.
SOON.
RED, THIS PLAN IS INSANE!!
YOU MEAN FOR BUBBLES TO GO UP BY THE STORM CLOUD-
-THEN DO HIS BIG INHALE TO EXPAND IN SIZE-
-AND SUCK THE WHOLE THING INSIDE HIMSELF?
I GUESS IT DOES SOUND A BIT RISKY WHEN YOU SHOUT IT ALL BACK TO ME.
YOU'RE RIGHT, CHUCK. WE'LL TRY SOMETHING ELSE.
OOPS.

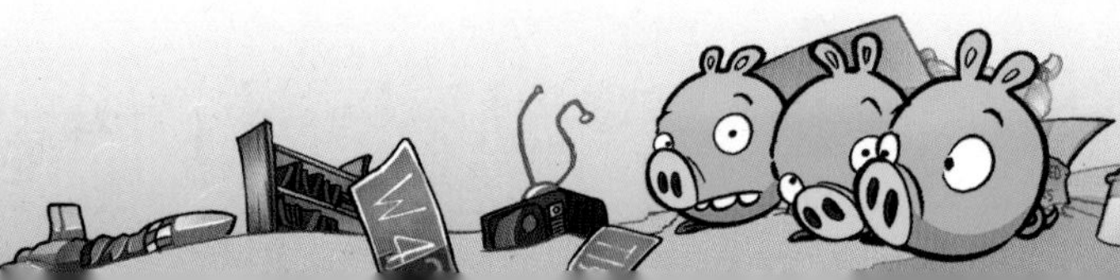

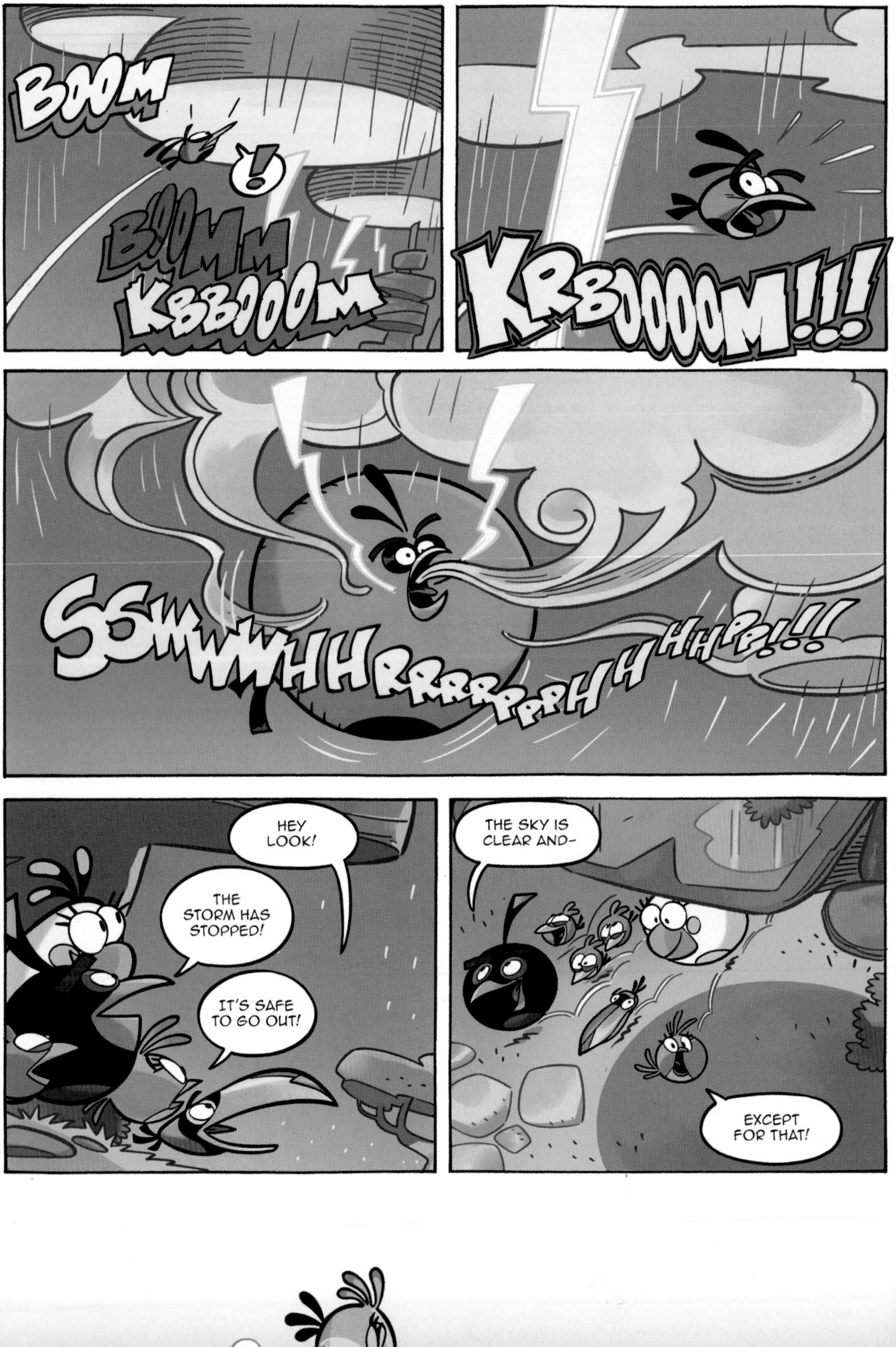
BOOM
!
BOOMM
KBBOOOM
KRBOOOOM!!!
SSHWWHHRRRRRPPPHHHHPP!!!
HEY LOOK!
THE STORM HAS STOPPED!
IT'S SAFE TO GO OUT!
THE SKY IS CLEAR AND-
EXCEPT FOR THAT!

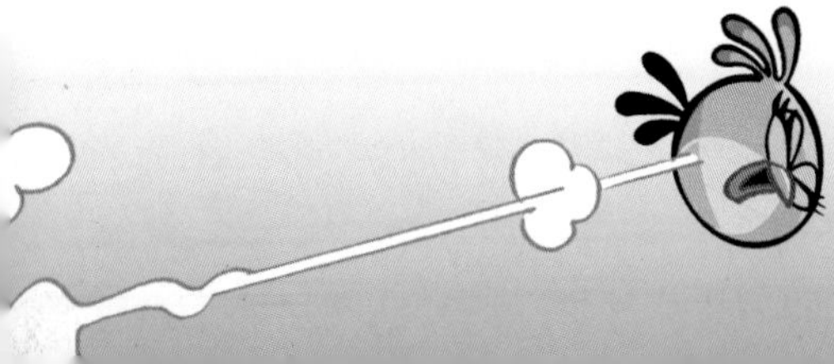

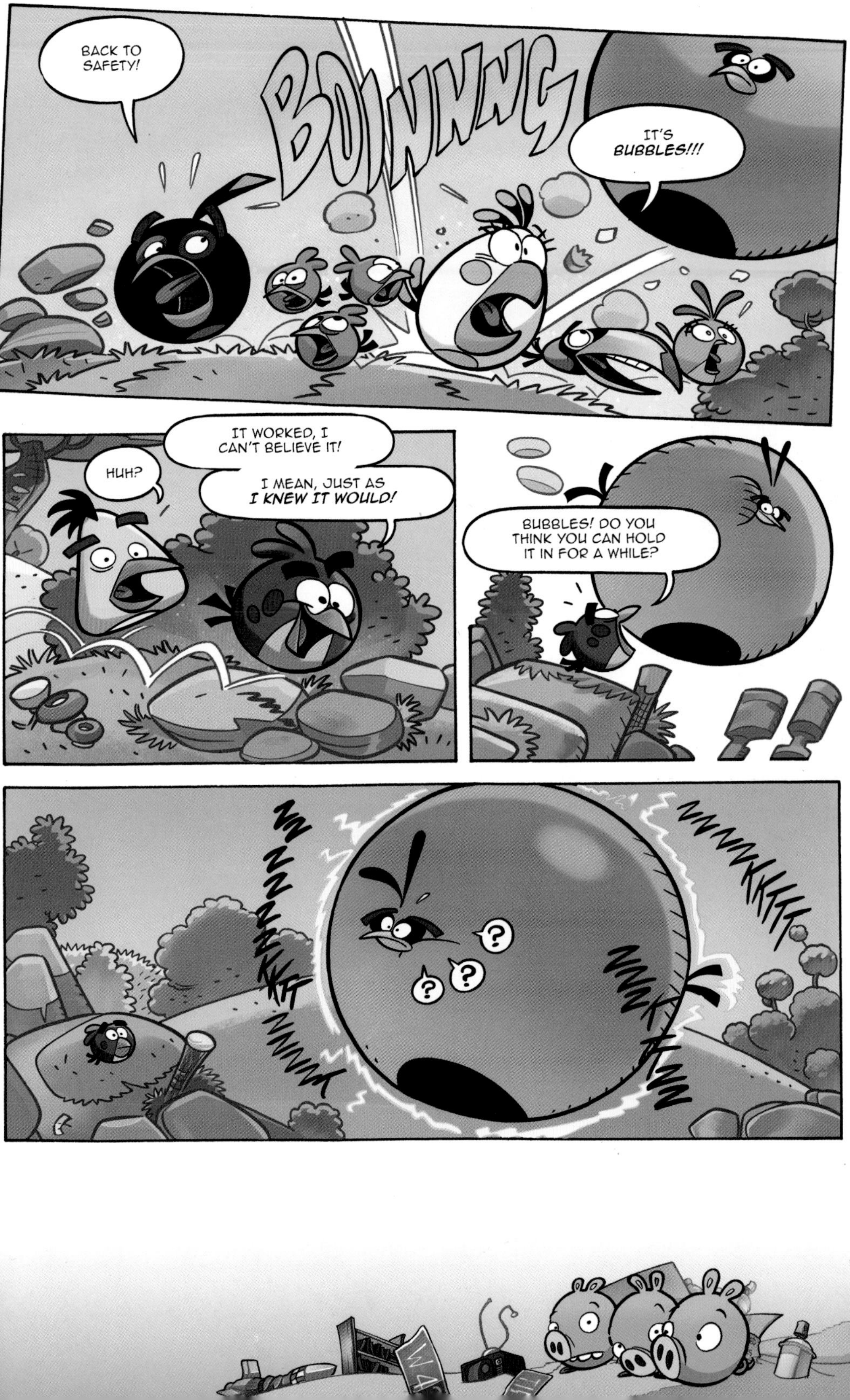
BACK TO SAFETY!
BOINNNG
IT'S *BUBBLES!!!*
HUH?
IT WORKED, I CAN'T BELIEVE IT!
I MEAN, JUST AS *I KNEW IT WOULD!*
BUBBLES! DO YOU THINK YOU CAN HOLD IT IN FOR A WHILE?
?
?
?
ZZZZZZZZKKK
ZZZZZZZZKKKK
ZZZZZZZZKKKK
ZZZZZZZ
W4

I FEEL... WEIRD...
SOMETHING IS HAPPENING TO ME!
TO ALL OF US, LOOK!
EEP!
MATILDA CAN FLY?
DON'T TAKE THIS THE WRONG WAY BUBBLES...
...BUT I'M STUCK ON YOU.
UH-OH.
MIGHT WANT TO LOOK OUT BELOW, GANG.
THIS IS WORSE THAN THE STORM!
IT'S A STORM-**BALL**.
THAT CAN FLATTEN US ALL!

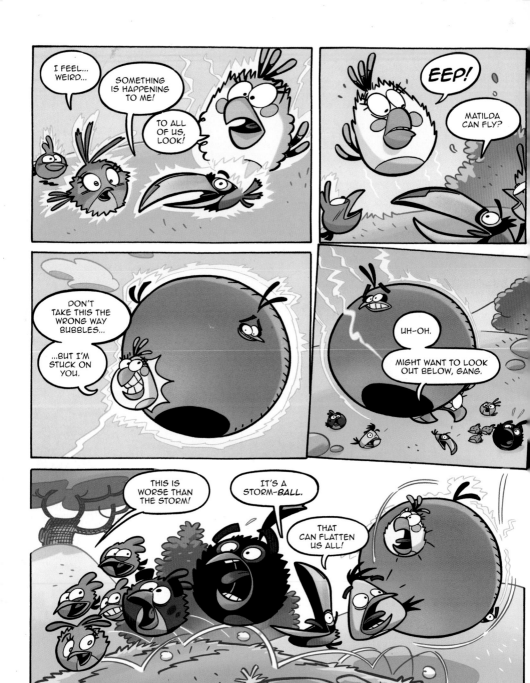

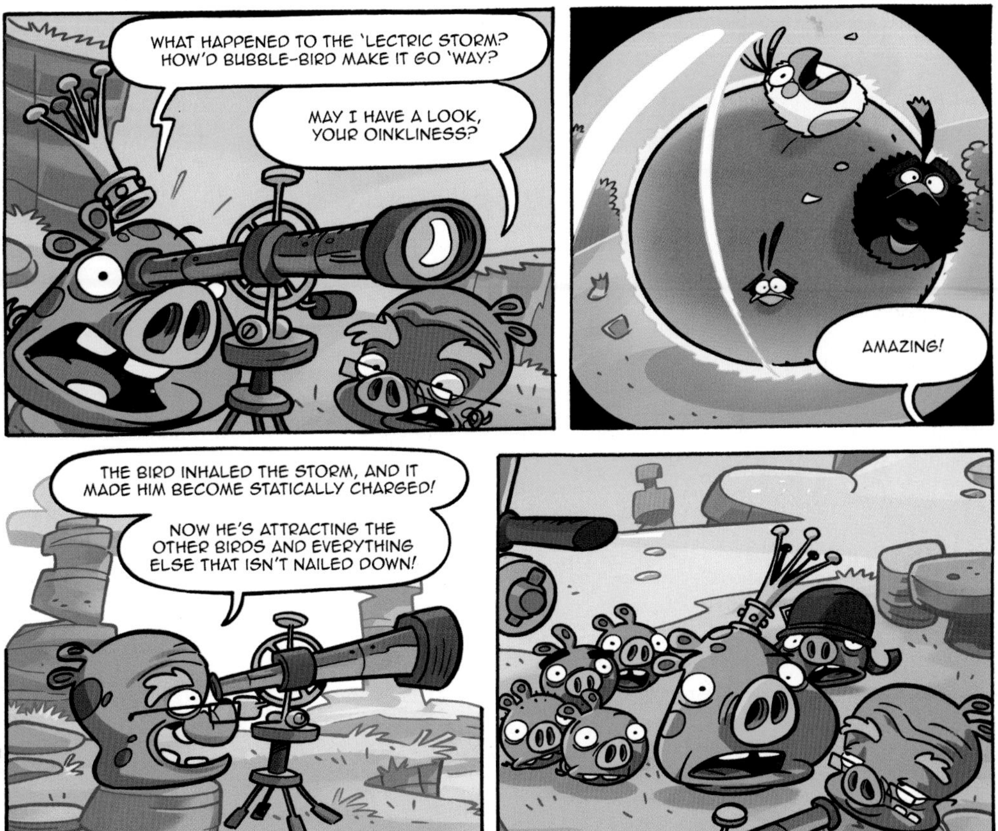
WHAT HAPPENED TO THE 'LECTRIC STORM? HOW'D BUBBLE-BIRD MAKE IT GO 'WAY?
MAY I HAVE A LOOK, YOUR OINKLINESS?
AMAZING!
THE BIRD INHALED THE STORM, AND IT MADE HIM BECOME STATICALLY CHARGED!
NOW HE'S ATTRACTING THE OTHER BIRDS AND EVERYTHING ELSE THAT ISN'T NAILED DOWN!
THE SKY-GHOSTS MADE BUBBLES STICKY SO NOW EVERYTHING IS STICKING TO HIM.
AH!! OF COURSE.
SKY-GHOSTS! I KNEW IT!
MY HEROES!

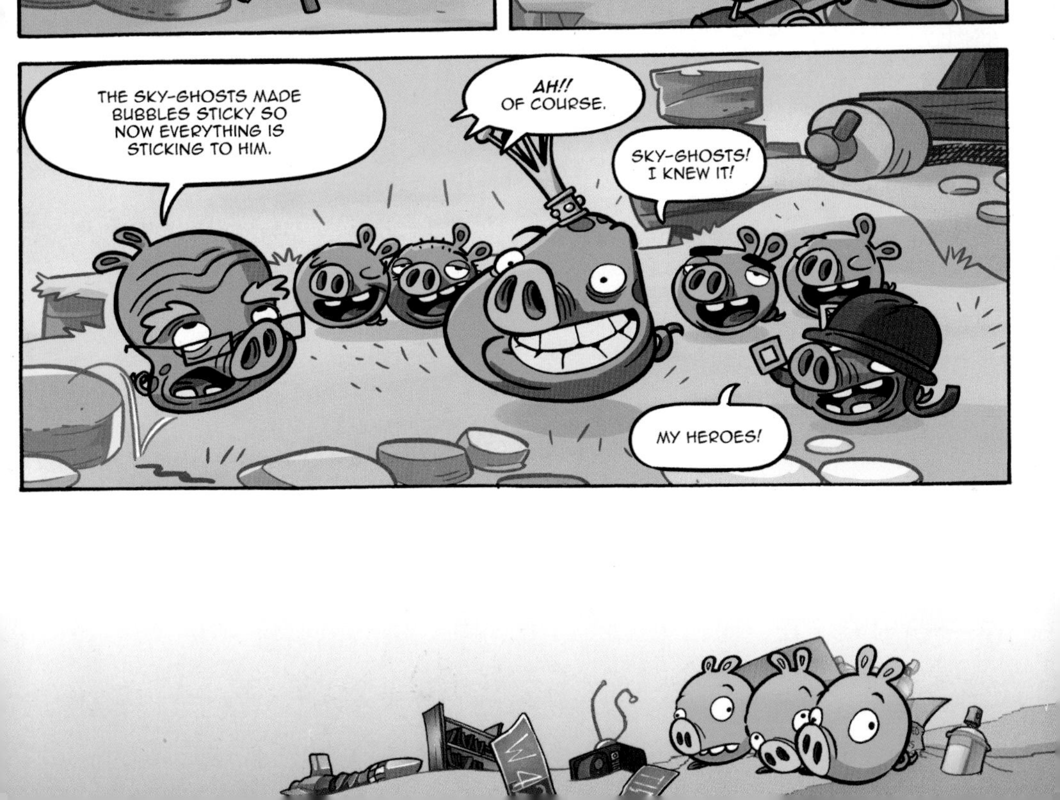

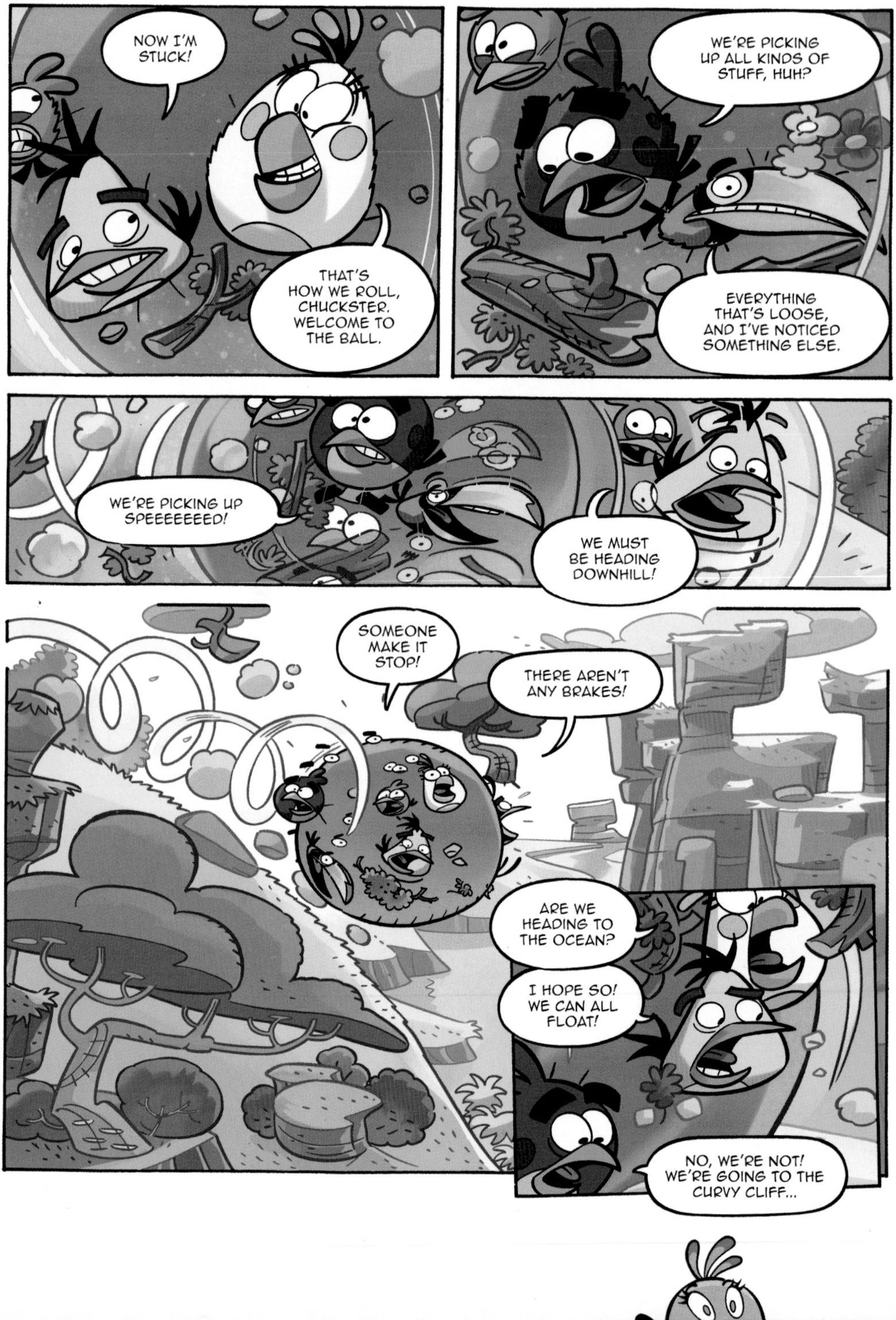
NOW I'M STUCK!
THAT'S HOW WE ROLL, CHUCKSTER. WELCOME TO THE BALL.
WE'RE PICKING UP ALL KINDS OF STUFF, HUH?
EVERYTHING THAT'S LOOSE, AND I'VE NOTICED SOMETHING ELSE.
WE'RE PICKING UP SPEEEEEEED!
WE MUST BE HEADING DOWNHILL!
SOMEONE MAKE IT STOP!
THERE AREN'T ANY BRAKES!
ARE WE HEADING TO THE OCEAN?
I HOPE SO! WE CAN ALL FLOAT!
NO, WE'RE NOT! WE'RE GOING TO THE CURVY CLIFF...

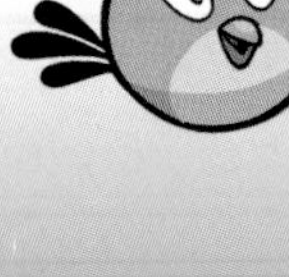

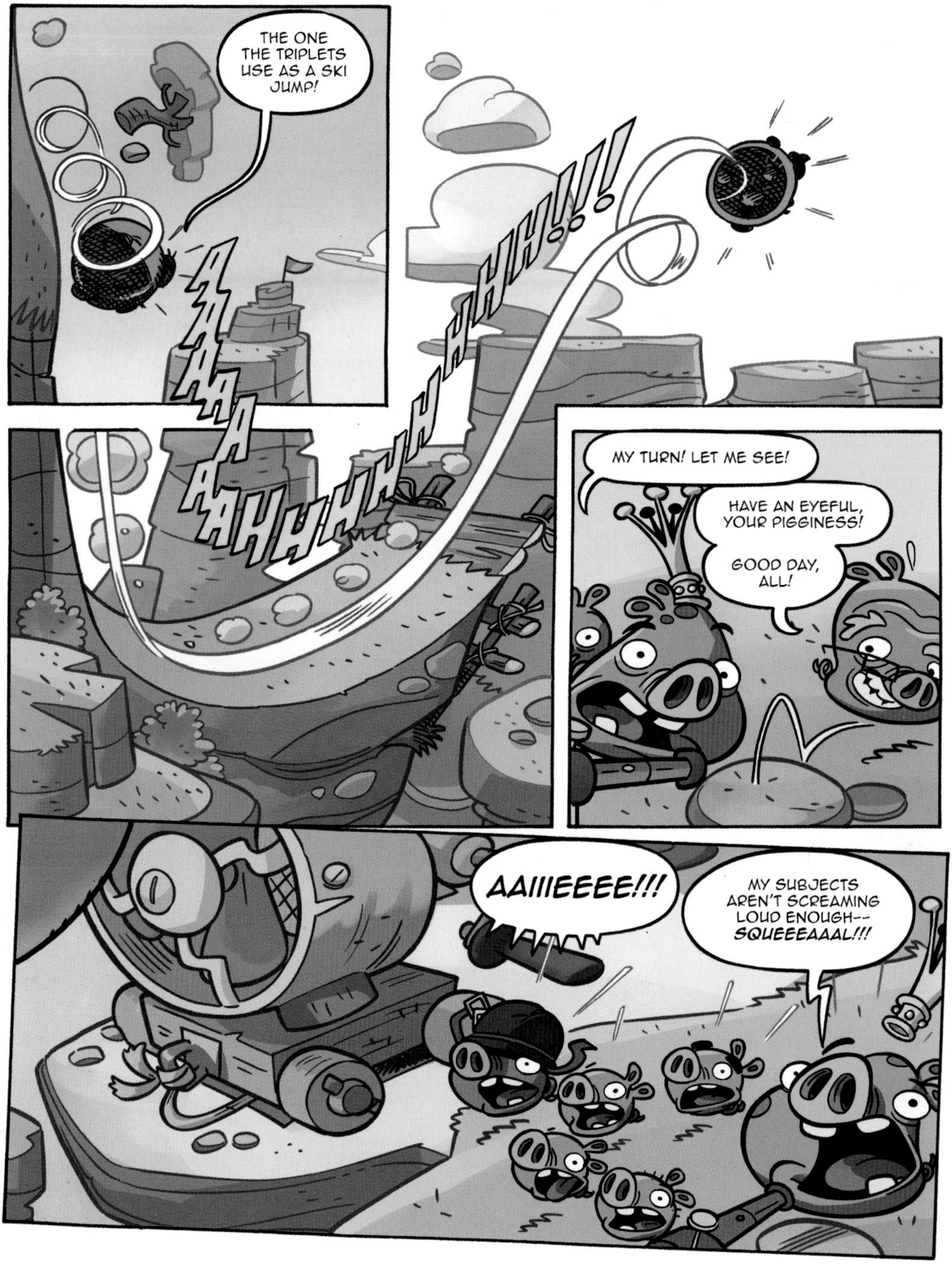
THE ONE THE TRIPLETS USE AS A SKI JUMP!
AAAAAAAHHHHHHHHHHHHHH!!!
MY TURN! LET ME SEE!
HAVE AN EYEFUL, YOUR PIGGINESS!
GOOD DAY, ALL!
AAIIIEEEE!!!
MY SUBJECTS AREN'T SCREAMING LOUD ENOUGH-- SQUEEEAAAL!!!

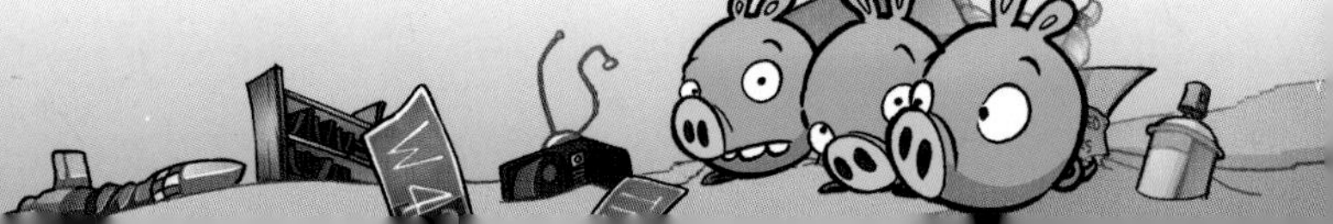

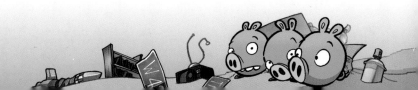

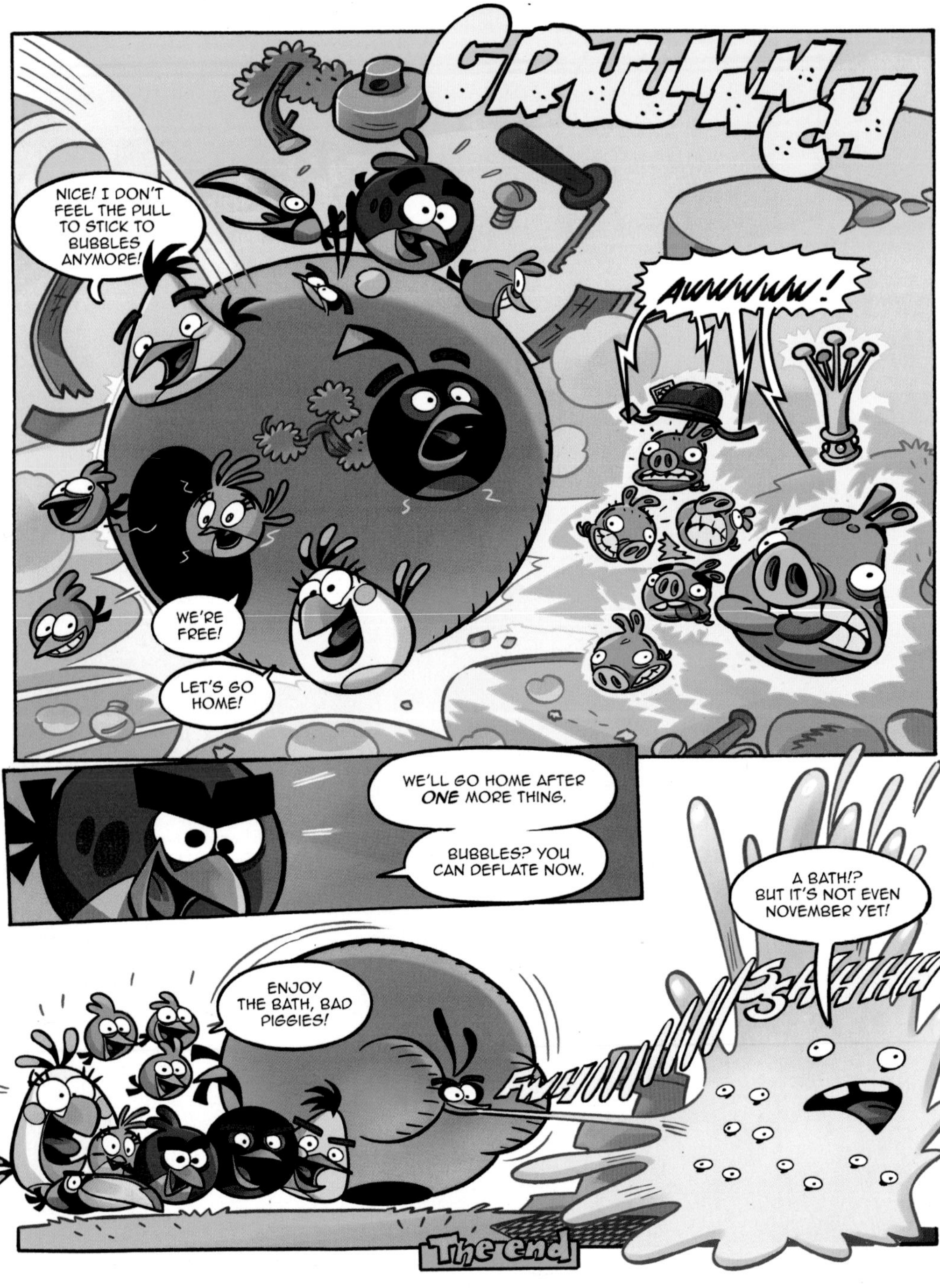
CRUNNNCH
NICE! I DON'T FEEL THE PULL TO STICK TO BUBBLES ANYMORE!
AWWWWW!
WE'RE FREE!
LET'S GO HOME!
WE'LL GO HOME AFTER ONE MORE THING.
BUBBLES? YOU CAN DEFLATE NOW.
A BATH!? BUT IT'S NOT EVEN NOVEMBER YET!
ENJOY THE BATH, BAD PIGGIES!
SPLASHHH
FWHHH
The end

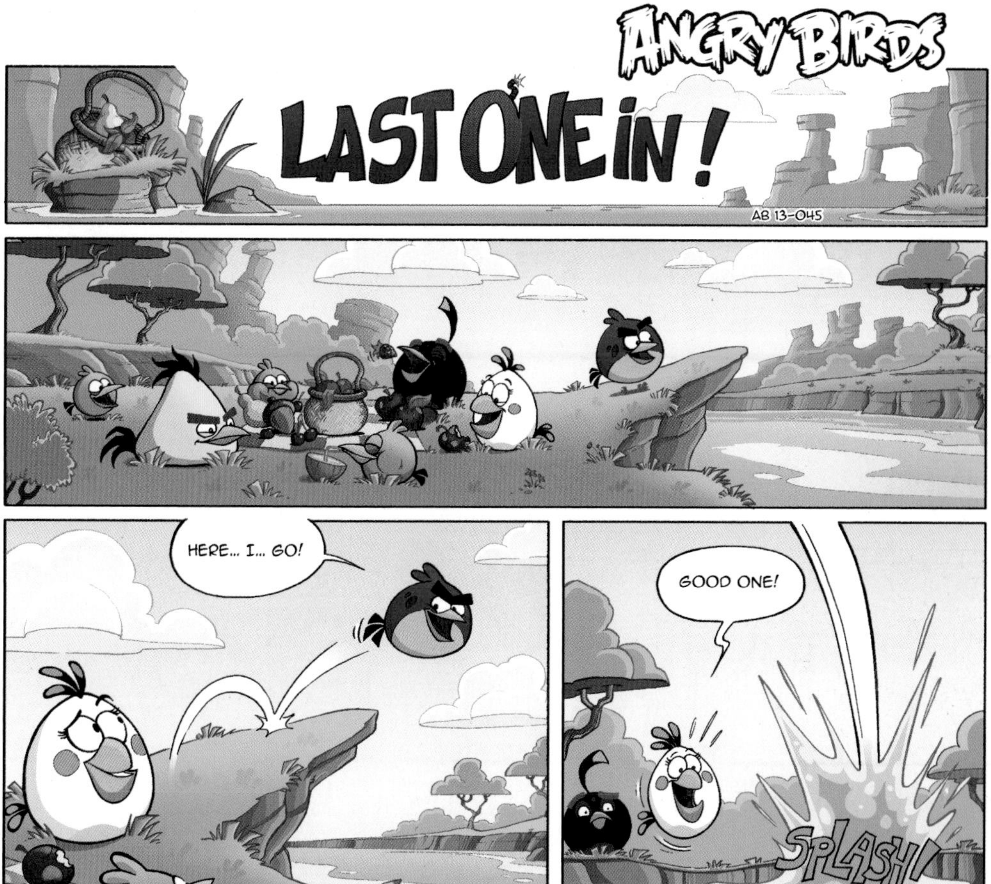
ANGRY BIRDS
LAST ONE IN!
AB 13-045
HERE... I... GO!
GOOD ONE!
SPLASH!
MY TURN!
SPLASH!
AMAZING!
CHECK THIS OUT!

WRITTEN BY: PAUL TOBIN • ART BY: DIANE FAYOLLE • COLORS BY: DIGIKORE STUDIOS • LETTERS BY: ROVIO COMICS

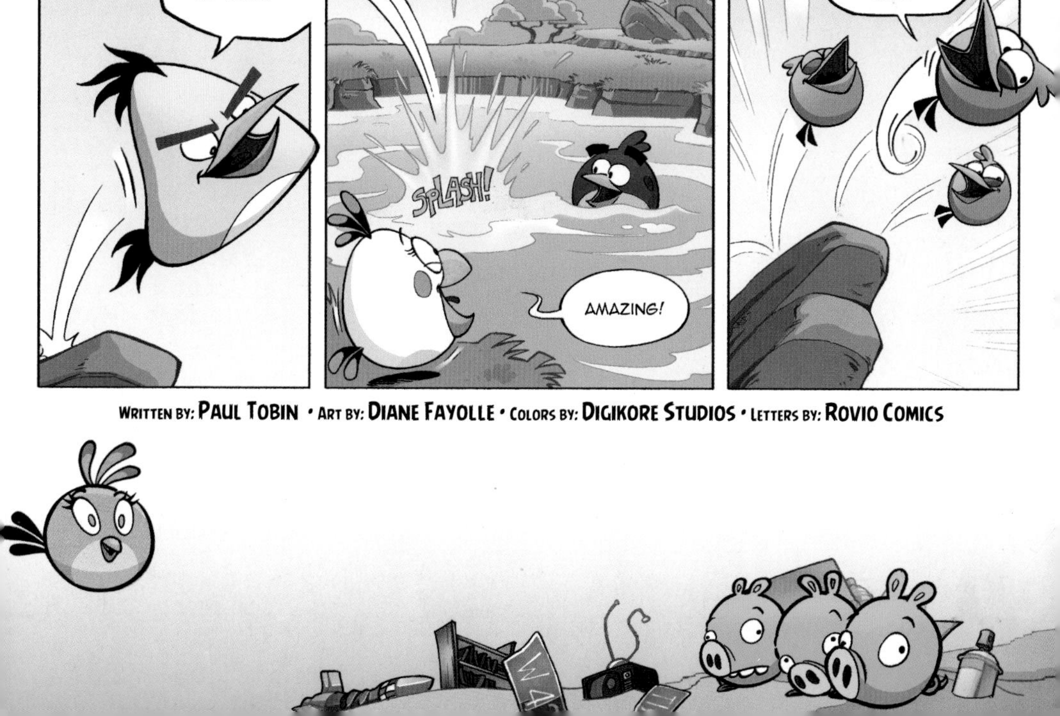

SPLISH!
SPLASH!
SPLOSH!
CANNON-BALL!
BOMB, NO!
KABOOOM!!!!
GRRRRRRRR...
THE END!

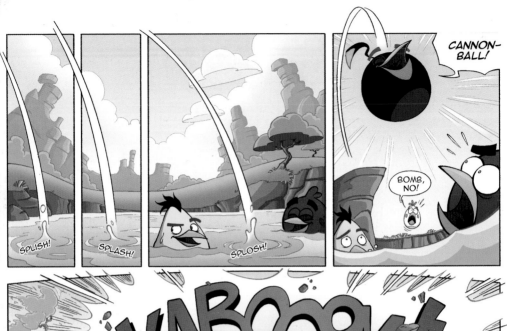

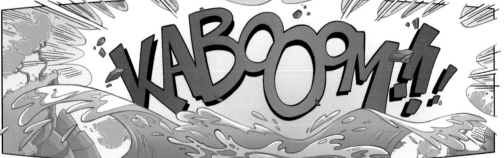

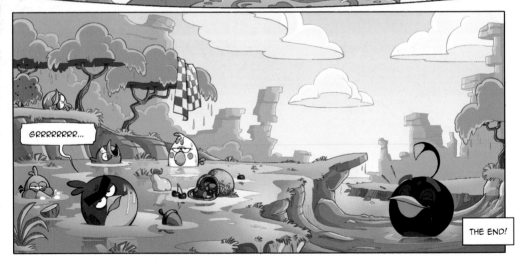

# THE GREEN ROOKIE

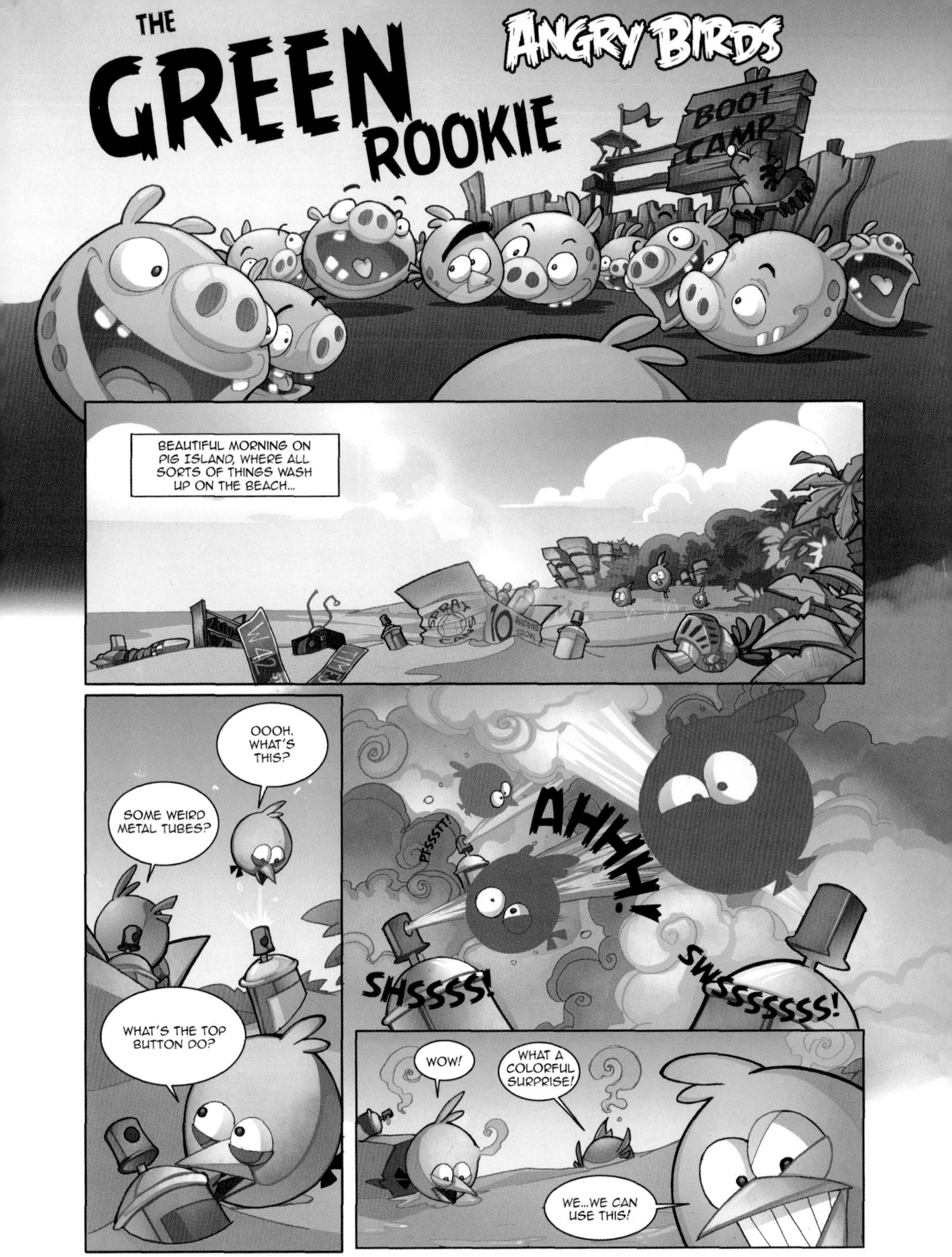

ANGRY BIRDS
BOOT CAMP
BEAUTIFUL MORNING ON PIG ISLAND, WHERE ALL SORTS OF THINGS WASH UP ON THE BEACH...
OOOH. WHAT'S THIS?
SOME WEIRD METAL TUBES?
WHAT'S THE TOP BUTTON DO?
PSSSTT!
AHHH!
SHSSSS!
SWSSSSSSS!
WOW!
WHAT A COLORFUL SURPRISE!
WE...WE CAN USE THIS!


WRITTEN BY: PAUL TOBIN • ART BY: DAVID BALDEÓN • COLORS BY: DAVID GARCIA • LETTERS BY: CLAYTON COWLES

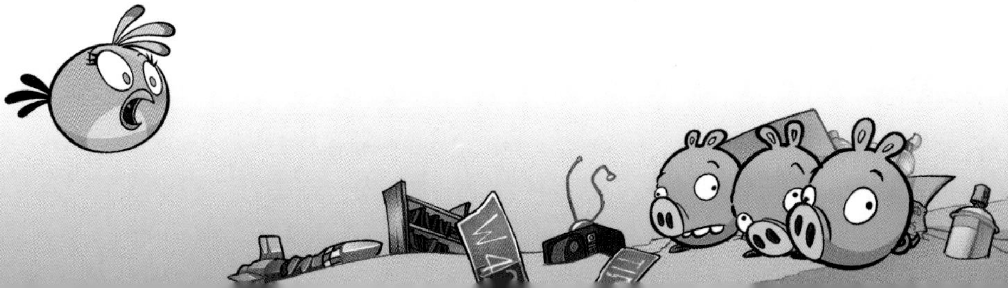

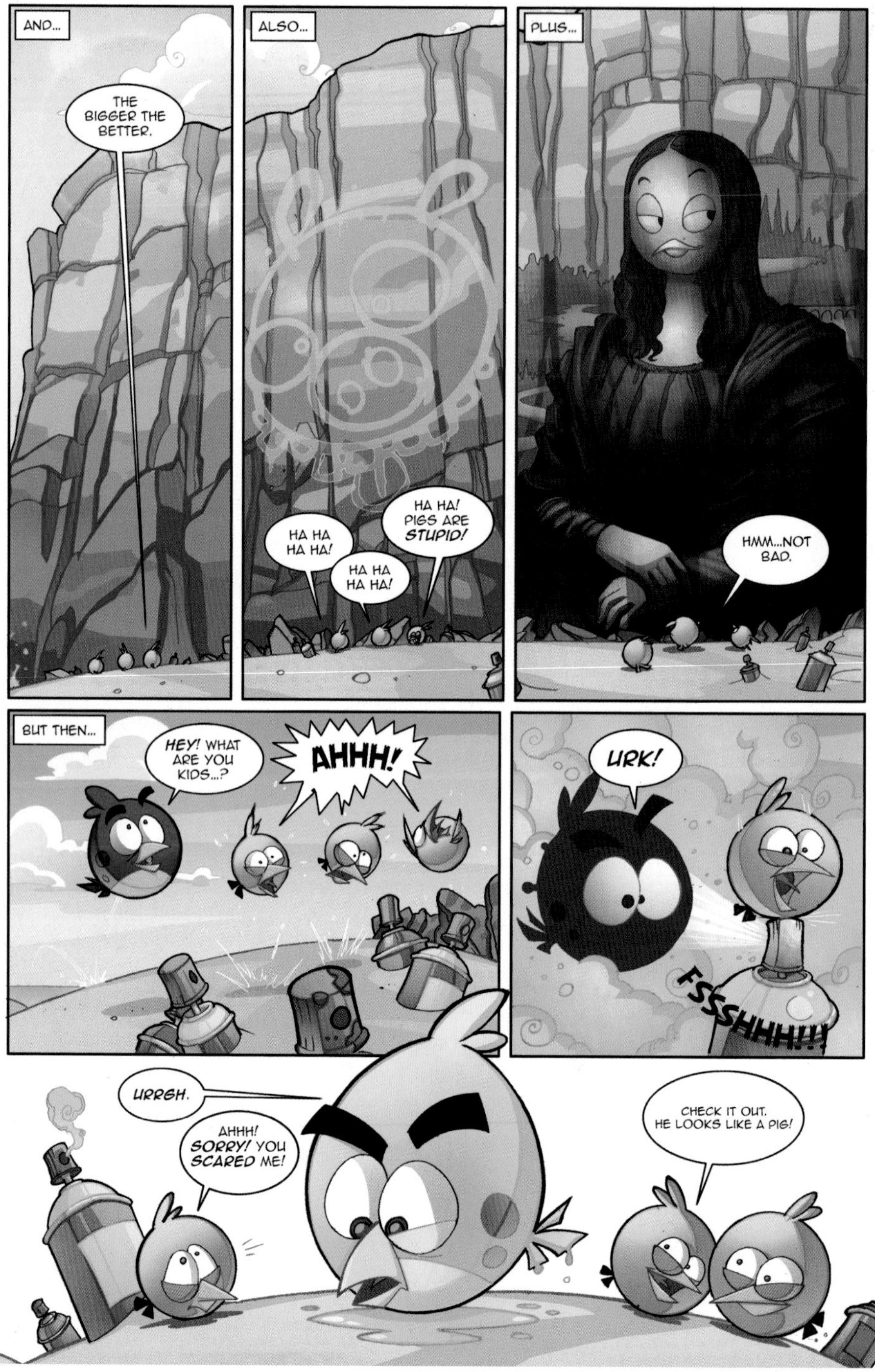
AND...
THE BIGGER THE BETTER.
ALSO...
HA HA HA HA!
HA HA HA HA!
HA HA! PIGS ARE STUPID!
PLUS...
HMM...NOT BAD.
BUT THEN...
HEY! WHAT ARE YOU KIDS...?
AHHH!
URK!
FSSSHHH!!!
URRGH.
AHHH! SORRY! YOU SCARED ME!
CHECK IT OUT. HE LOOKS LIKE A PIG!

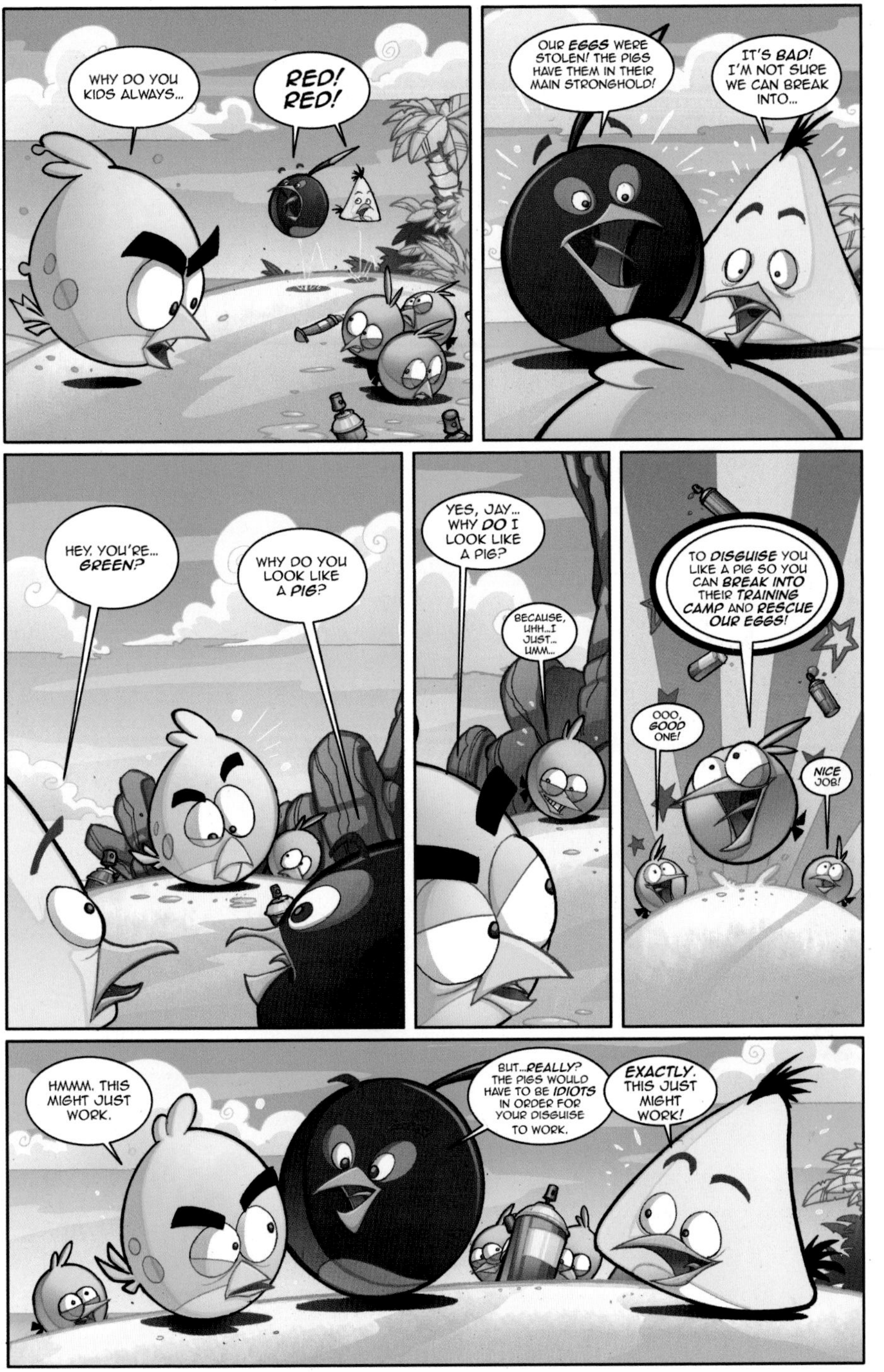
WHY DO YOU KIDS ALWAYS...
RED! RED!
OUR EGGS WERE STOLEN! THE PIGS HAVE THEM IN THEIR MAIN STRONGHOLD!
IT'S BAD! I'M NOT SURE WE CAN BREAK INTO...
HEY, YOU'RE... GREEN?
WHY DO YOU LOOK LIKE A PIG?
YES, JAY... WHY DO I LOOK LIKE A PIG?
BECAUSE, UHH...I JUST... UMM...
TO DISGUISE YOU LIKE A PIG SO YOU CAN BREAK INTO THEIR TRAINING CAMP AND RESCUE OUR EGGS!
OOO, GOOD ONE!
NICE JOB!
HMMM. THIS MIGHT JUST WORK.
BUT...REALLY? THE PIGS WOULD HAVE TO BE IDIOTS IN ORDER FOR YOUR DISGUISE TO WORK.
EXACTLY. THIS JUST MIGHT WORK!

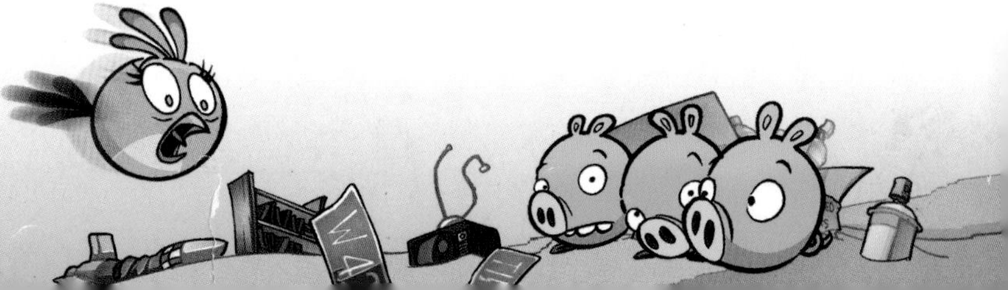

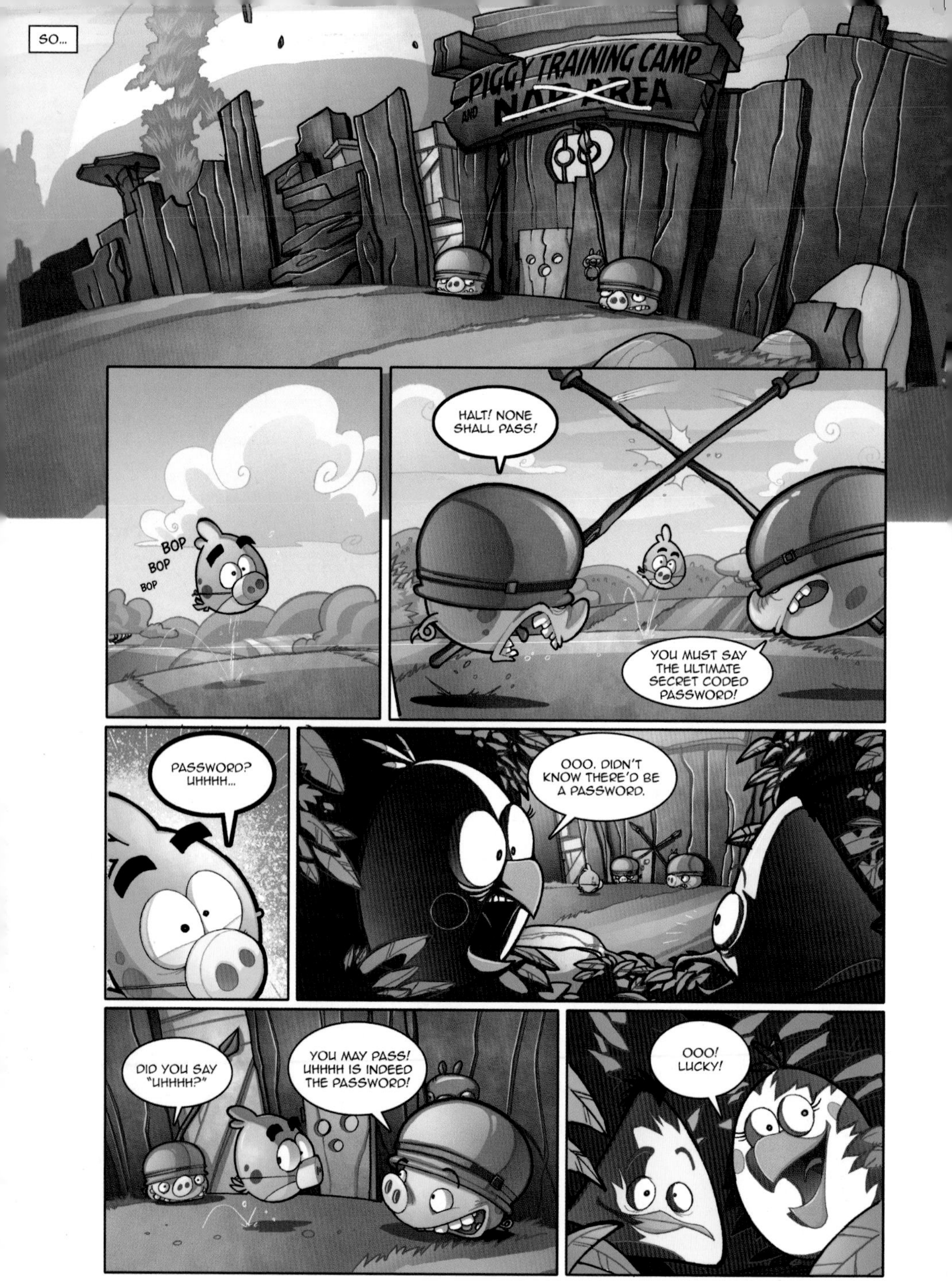
SO...
PIGGY TRAINING CAMP
AND NAP AREA
BOP
BOP
BOP
HALT! NONE SHALL PASS!
YOU MUST SAY THE ULTIMATE SECRET CODED PASSWORD!
PASSWORD? UHHHH...
OOO. DIDN'T KNOW THERE'D BE A PASSWORD.
DID YOU SAY "UHHHH?"
YOU MAY PASS! UHHHH IS INDEED THE PASSWORD!
OOO! LUCKY!

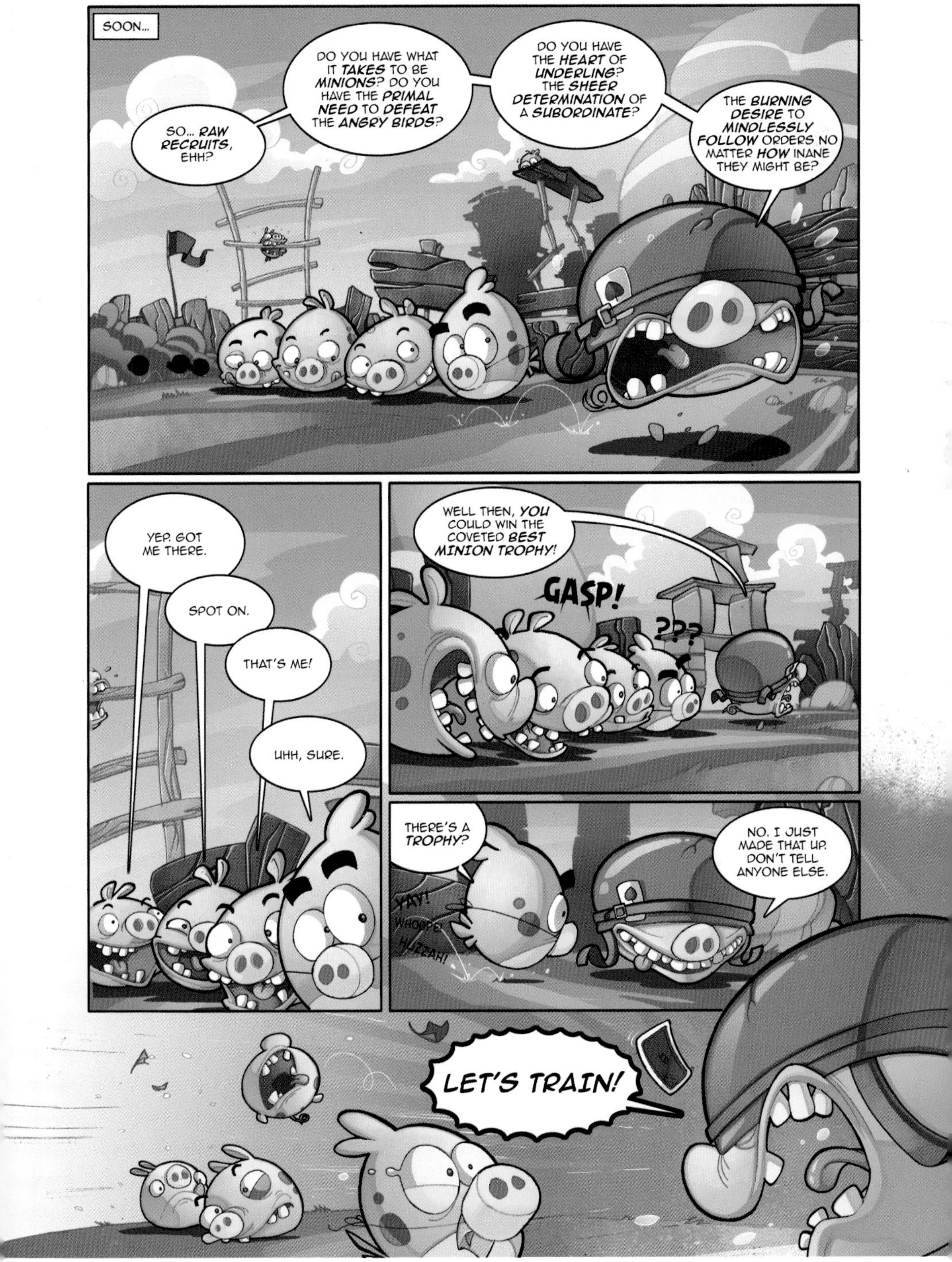
SOON...
SO... RAW RECRUITS, EHH?
DO YOU HAVE WHAT IT TAKES TO BE MINIONS? DO YOU HAVE THE PRIMAL NEED TO DEFEAT THE ANGRY BIRDS?
DO YOU HAVE THE HEART OF UNDERLING? THE SHEER DETERMINATION OF A SUBORDINATE?
THE BURNING DESIRE TO MINDLESSLY FOLLOW ORDERS NO MATTER HOW INANE THEY MIGHT BE?
YEP. GOT ME THERE.
SPOT ON.
THAT'S ME!
UHH, SURE.
WELL THEN, YOU COULD WIN THE COVETED BEST MINION TROPHY!
GASP!
???
THERE'S A TROPHY?
NO. I JUST MADE THAT UP. DON'T TELL ANYONE ELSE.
YAY!
WHOOPE!
HUZZAH!
LET'S TRAIN!

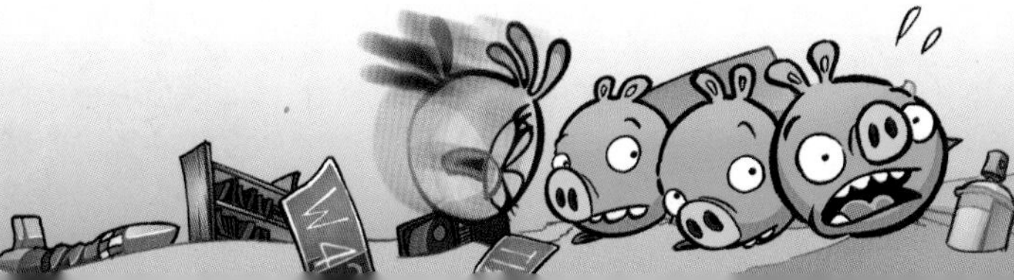

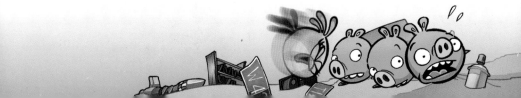

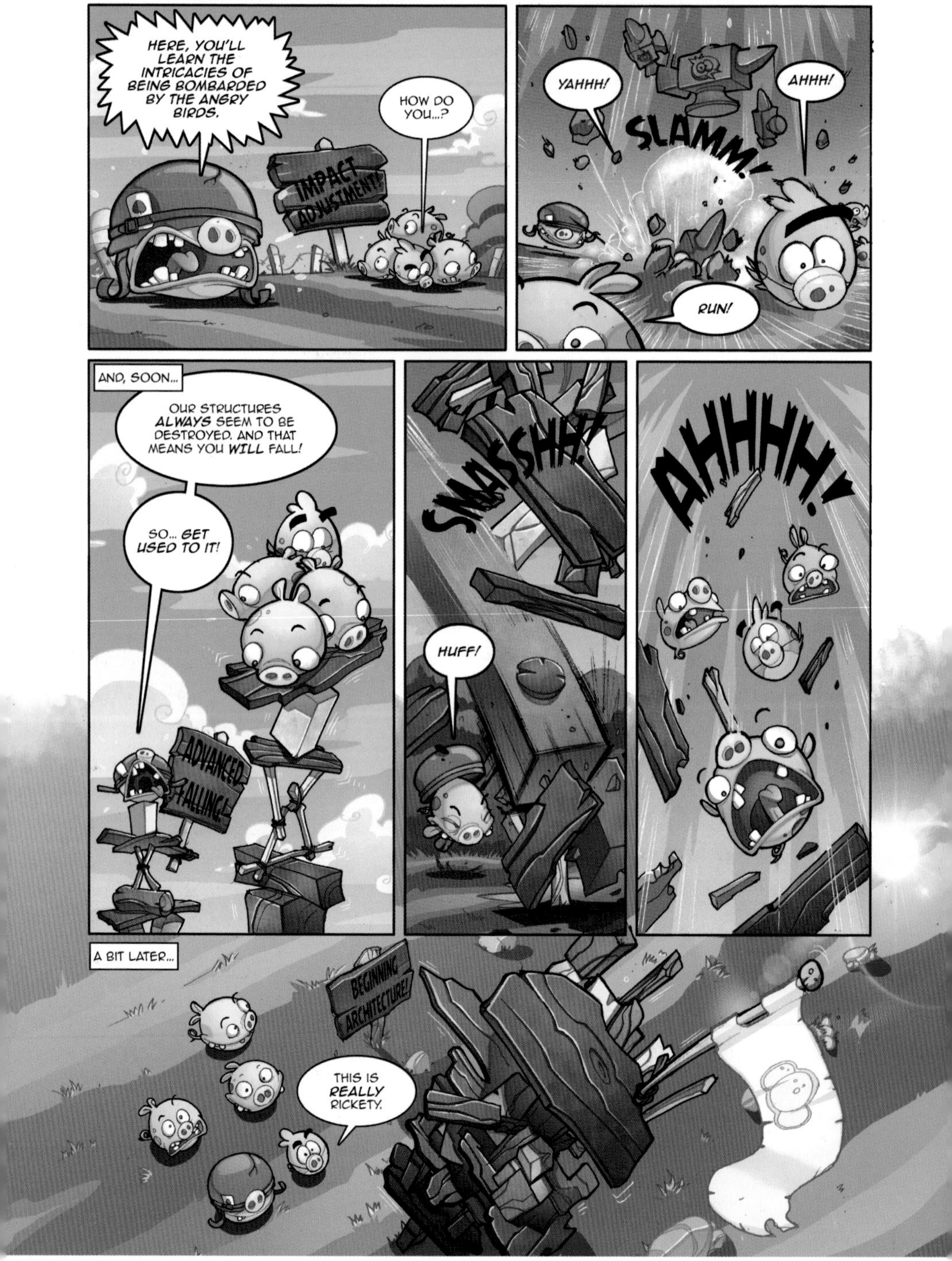
HERE, YOU'LL LEARN THE INTRICACIES OF BEING BOMBARDED BY THE ANGRY BIRDS.
IMPACT ADJUSTMENT!
HOW DO YOU...?
YAHHH!
AHHH!
SLAMM!
RUN!
AND, SOON...
OUR STRUCTURES ALWAYS SEEM TO BE DESTROYED. AND THAT MEANS YOU WILL FALL!
SO... GET USED TO IT!
ADVANCED FALLING!
SMASSHH!
HUFF!
AHHHH!
A BIT LATER...
BEGINNING ARCHITECTURE!
THIS IS REALLY RICKETY.

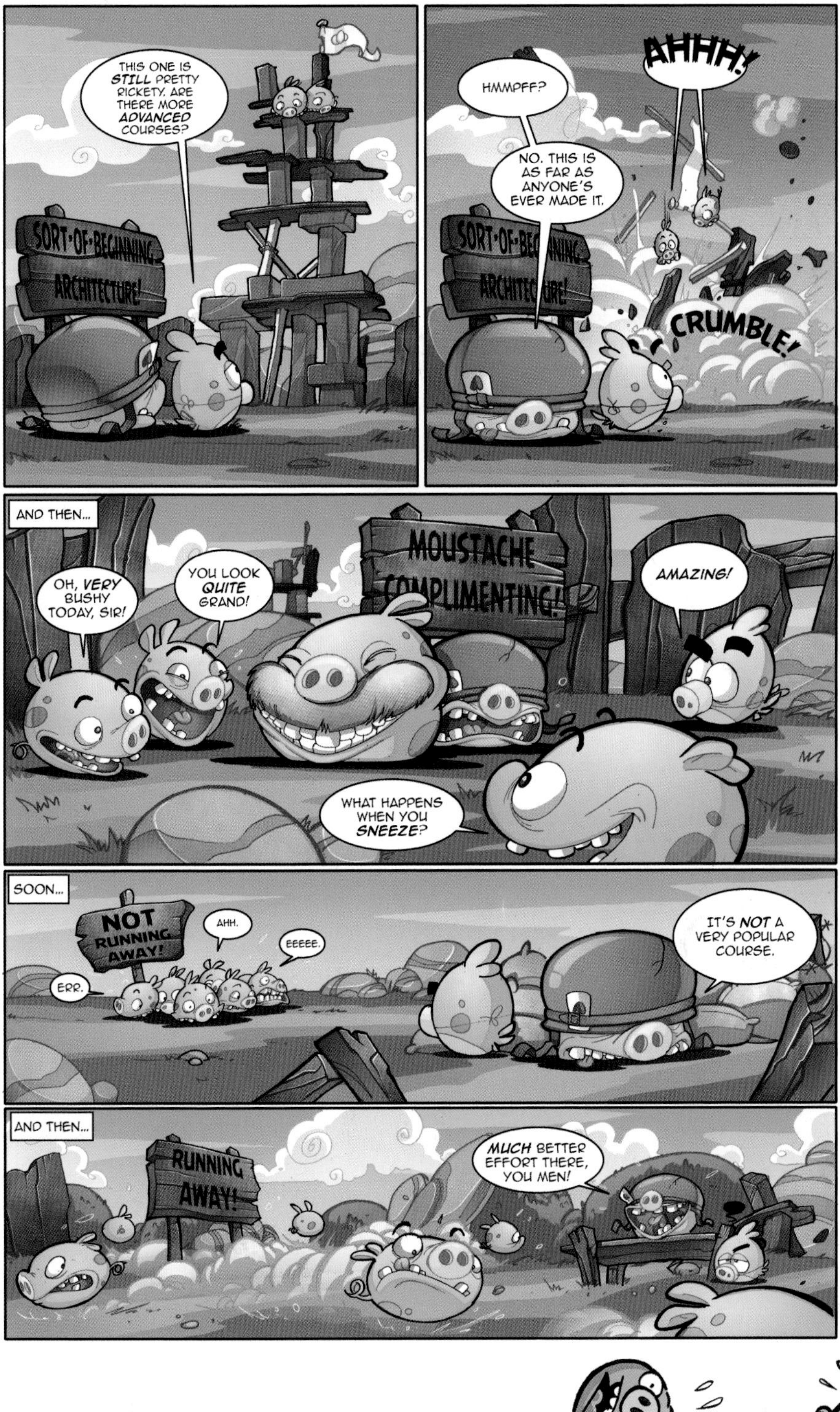
THIS ONE IS *STILL* PRETTY RICKETY. ARE THERE MORE *ADVANCED* COURSES?
SORT-OF-BEGINNING ARCHITECTURE!
HMMPFF?
NO. THIS IS AS FAR AS ANYONE'S EVER MADE IT.
AHHH!
CRUMBLE!
AND THEN...
MOUSTACHE COMPLIMENTING!
OH, *VERY* BUSHY TODAY, SIR!
YOU LOOK *QUITE* GRAND!
*AMAZING!*
WHAT HAPPENS WHEN YOU *SNEEZE*?
SOON...
NOT RUNNING AWAY!
ERR.
AHH.
EEEEE.
IT'S *NOT* A VERY POPULAR COURSE.
AND THEN...
RUNNING AWAY!
*MUCH* BETTER EFFORT THERE, YOU MEN!

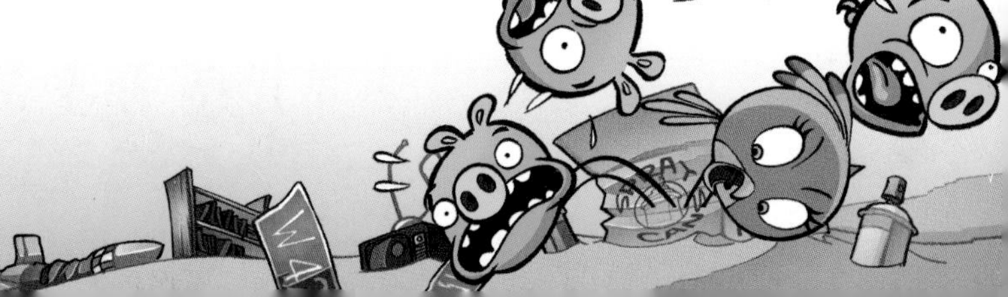

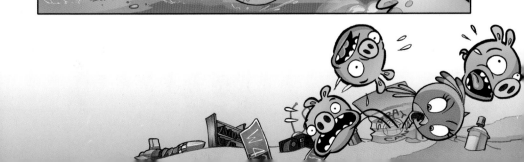

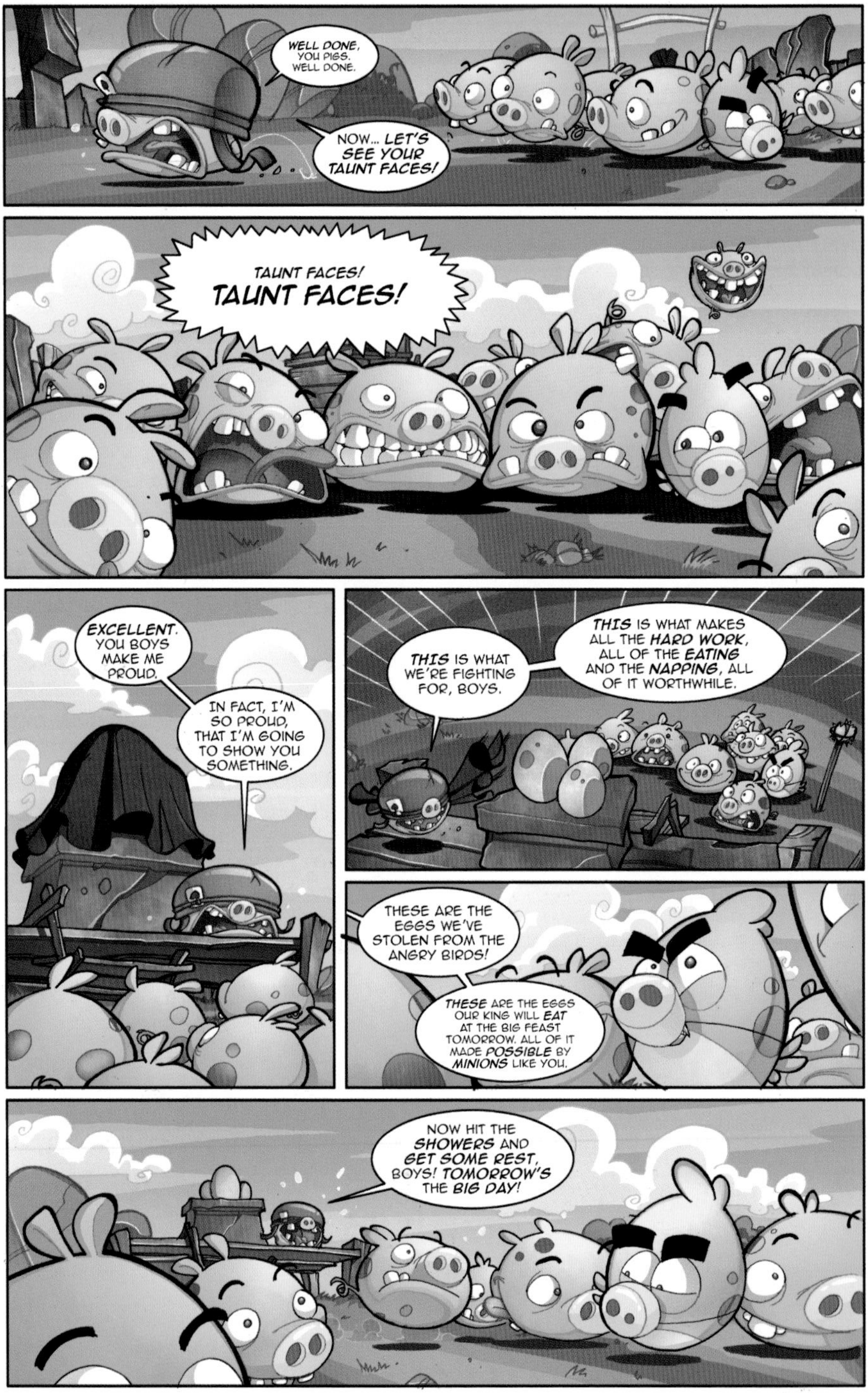
WELL DONE, YOU PIGS. WELL DONE.
NOW... LET'S SEE YOUR TAUNT FACES!
TAUNT FACES! TAUNT FACES!
EXCELLENT. YOU BOYS MAKE ME PROUD.
IN FACT, I'M SO PROUD, THAT I'M GOING TO SHOW YOU SOMETHING.
THIS IS WHAT WE'RE FIGHTING FOR, BOYS.
THIS IS WHAT MAKES ALL THE HARD WORK, ALL OF THE EATING AND THE NAPPING, ALL OF IT WORTHWHILE.
THESE ARE THE EGGS WE'VE STOLEN FROM THE ANGRY BIRDS!
THESE ARE THE EGGS OUR KING WILL EAT AT THE BIG FEAST TOMORROW. ALL OF IT MADE POSSIBLE BY MINIONS LIKE YOU.
NOW HIT THE SHOWERS AND GET SOME REST, BOYS! TOMORROW'S THE BIG DAY!

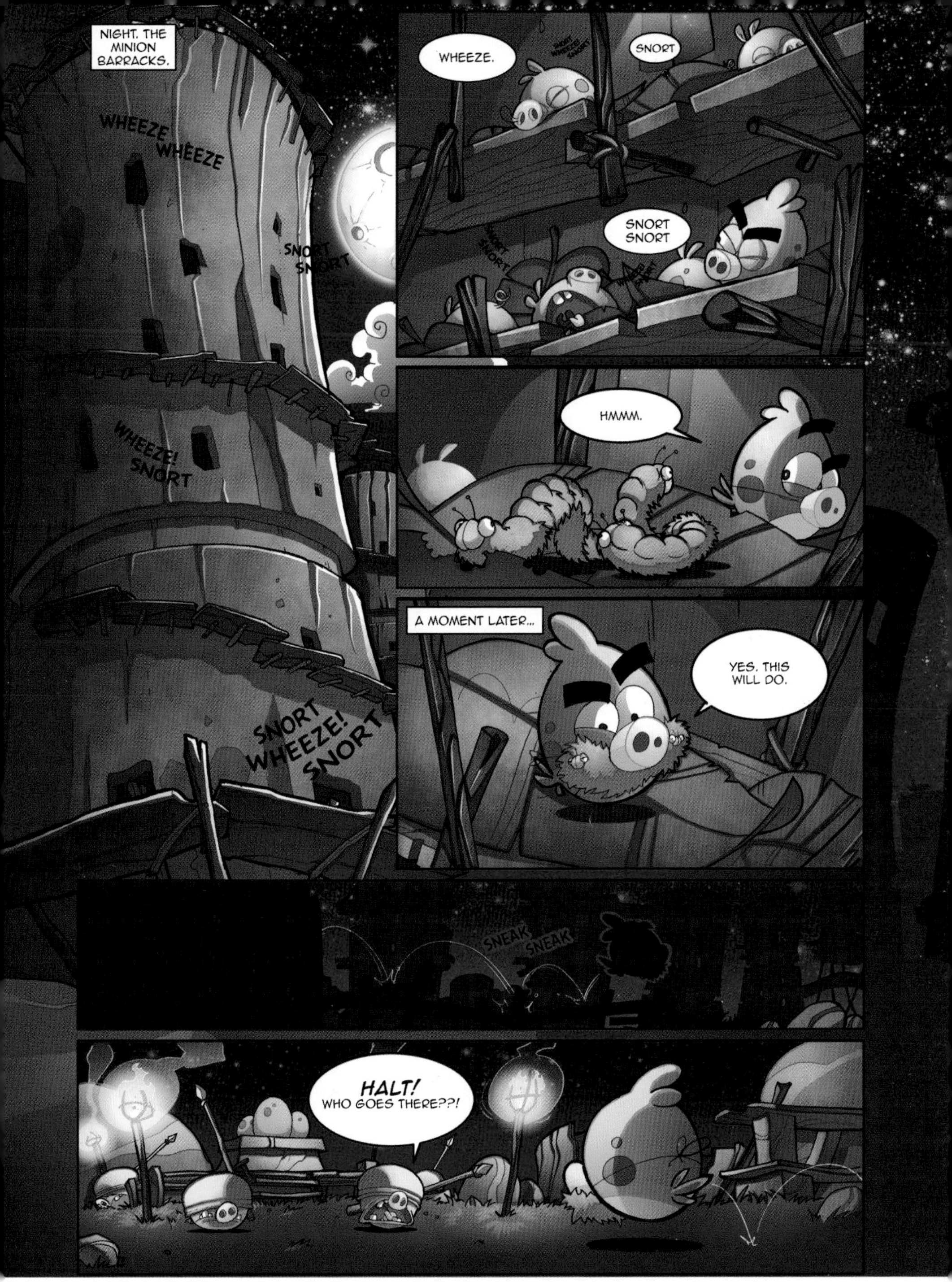

NIGHT. THE MINION BARRACKS.
WHEEZE WHEEZE
SNORT SNORT
WHEEZE! SNORT
SNORT WHEEZE! SNORT
WHEEZE.
SNORT
SNORT SNORT
HMMM.
A MOMENT LATER...
YES. THIS WILL DO.
SNEAK SNEAK
HALT! WHO GOES THERE??!


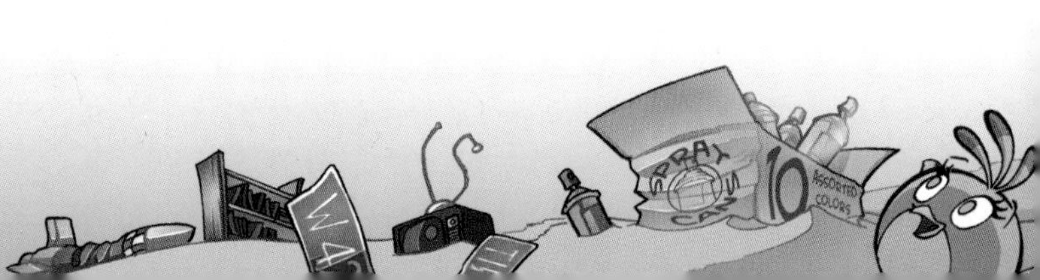

SPRAY CAN
10
ASSORTED COLORS

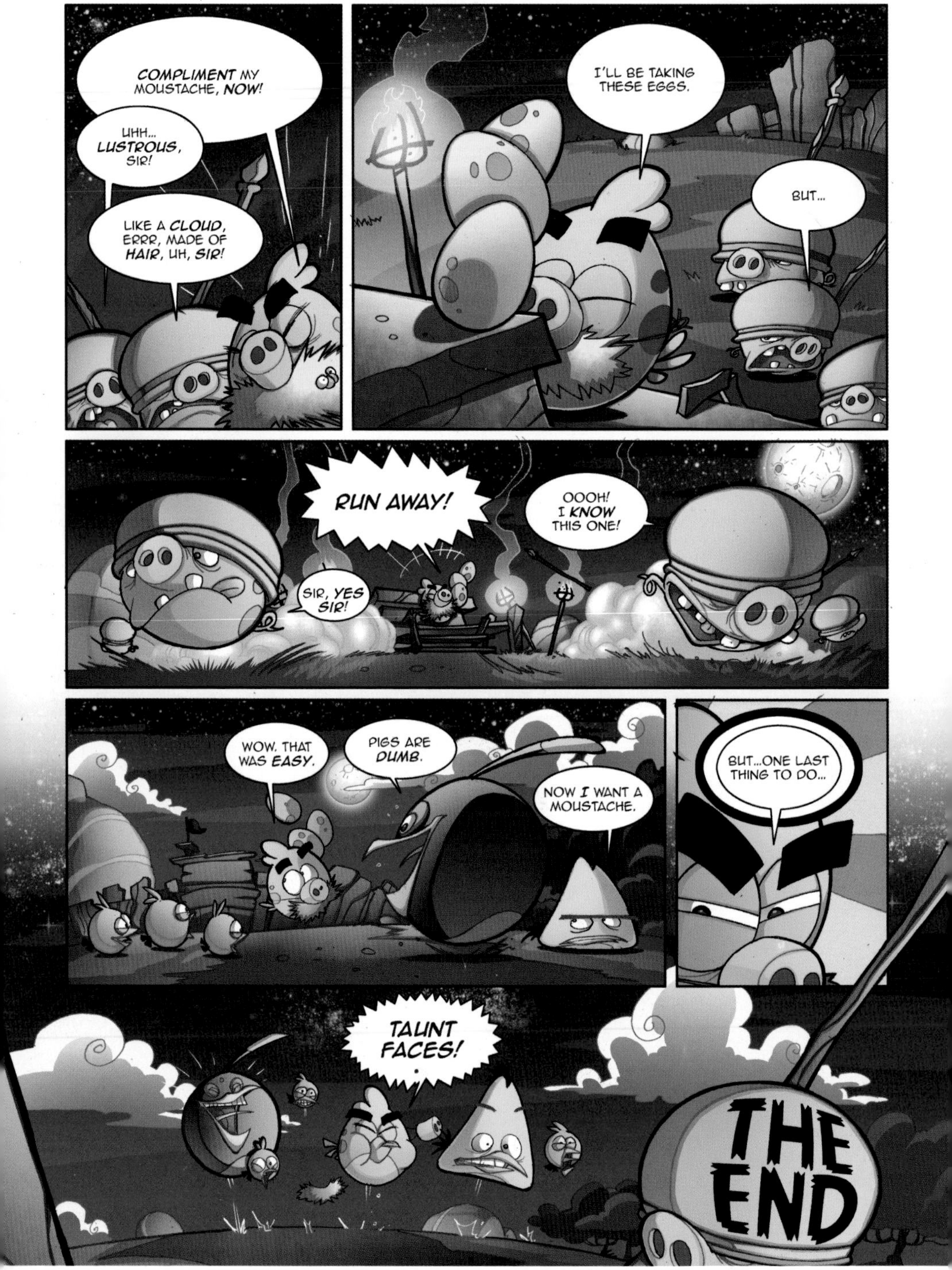
COMPLIMENT MY MOUSTACHE, NOW!
UHH... LUSTROUS, SIR!
LIKE A CLOUD, ERRR, MADE OF HAIR, UH, SIR!
I'LL BE TAKING THESE EGGS.
BUT...
RUN AWAY!
SIR, YES SIR!
OOOH! I KNOW THIS ONE!
WOW. THAT WAS EASY.
PIGS ARE DUMB.
NOW I WANT A MOUSTACHE.
BUT...ONE LAST THING TO DO...
TAUNT FACES!
THE END

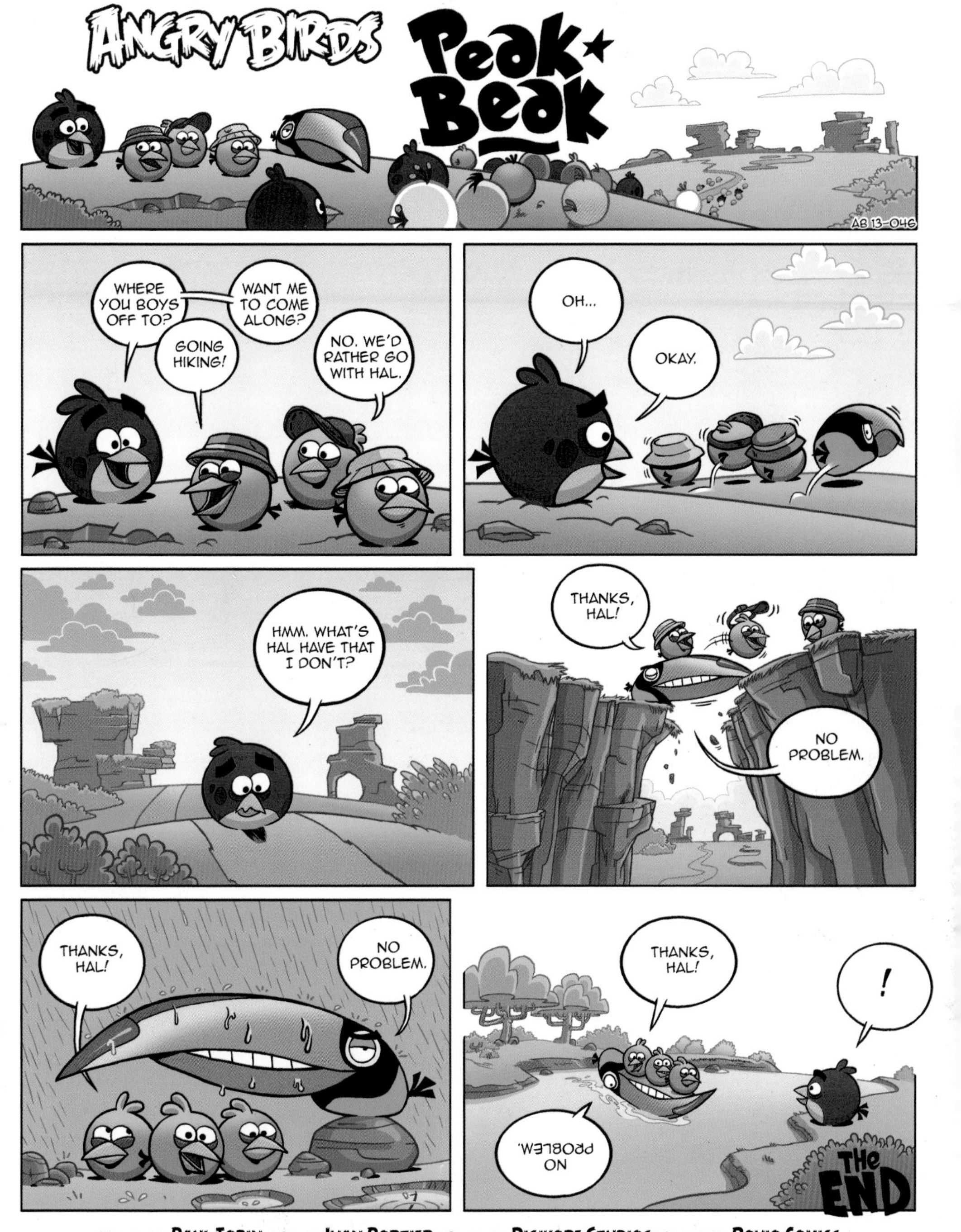
ANGRY BIRDS
Peak Beak
AB 13-046
WHERE YOU BOYS OFF TO?
GOING HIKING!
WANT ME TO COME ALONG?
NO. WE'D RATHER GO WITH HAL.
OH...
OKAY.
HMM. WHAT'S HAL HAVE THAT I DON'T?
THANKS, HAL!
NO PROBLEM.
THANKS, HAL!
NO PROBLEM.
THANKS, HAL!
NO PROBLEM.
!
THE END

WRITTEN BY: PAUL TOBIN • ART BY: IVAN PORTIER • COLORS BY: DIGIKORE STUDIOS • LETTERS BY: ROVIO COMICS

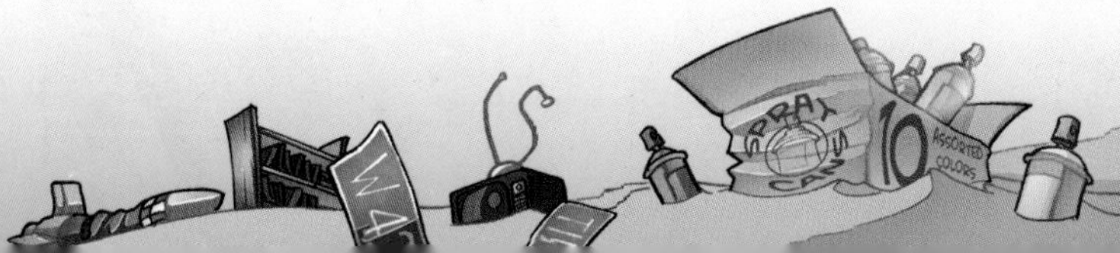

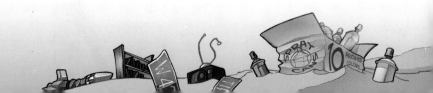

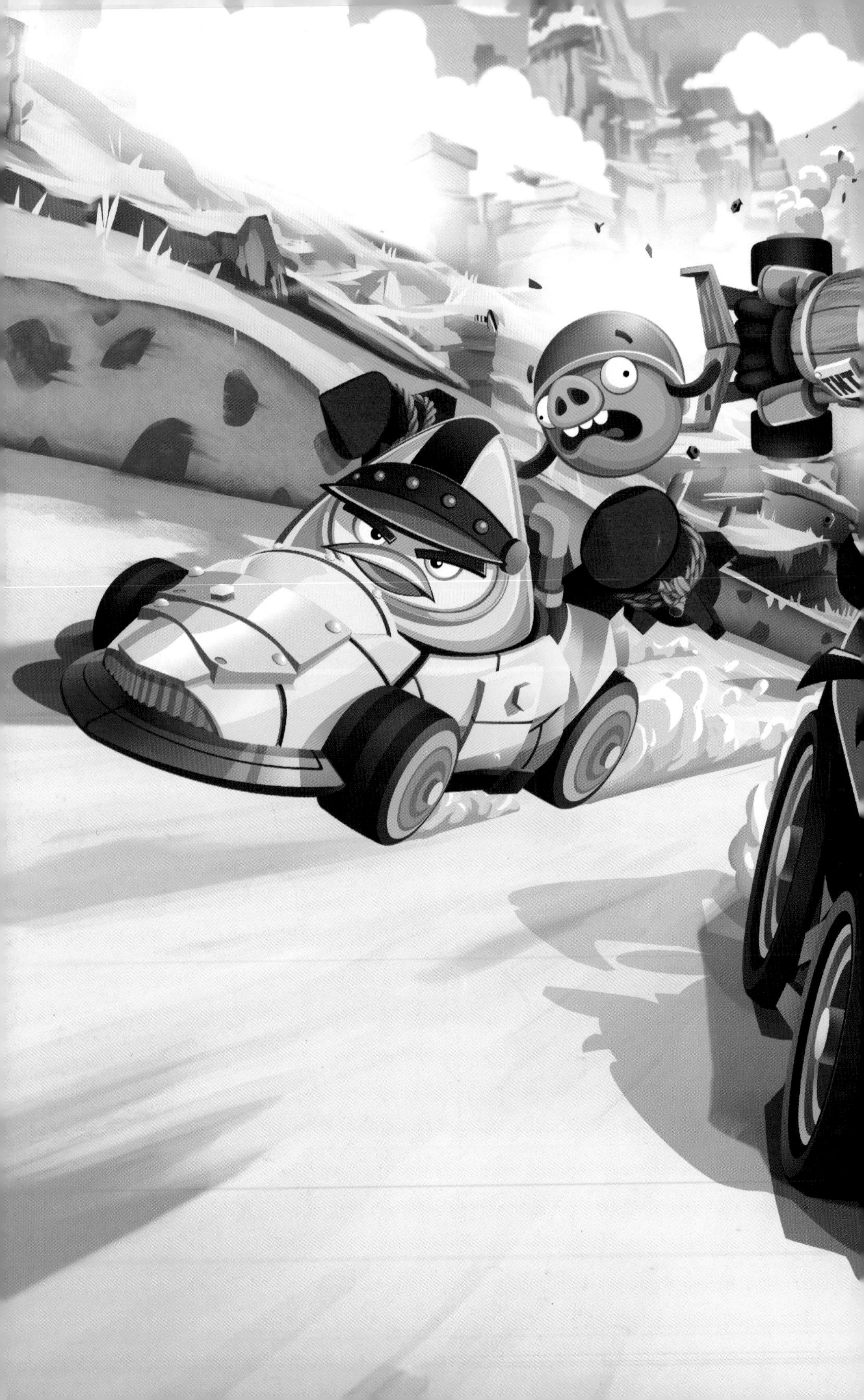
TNT

Artwork by Pilot Studios

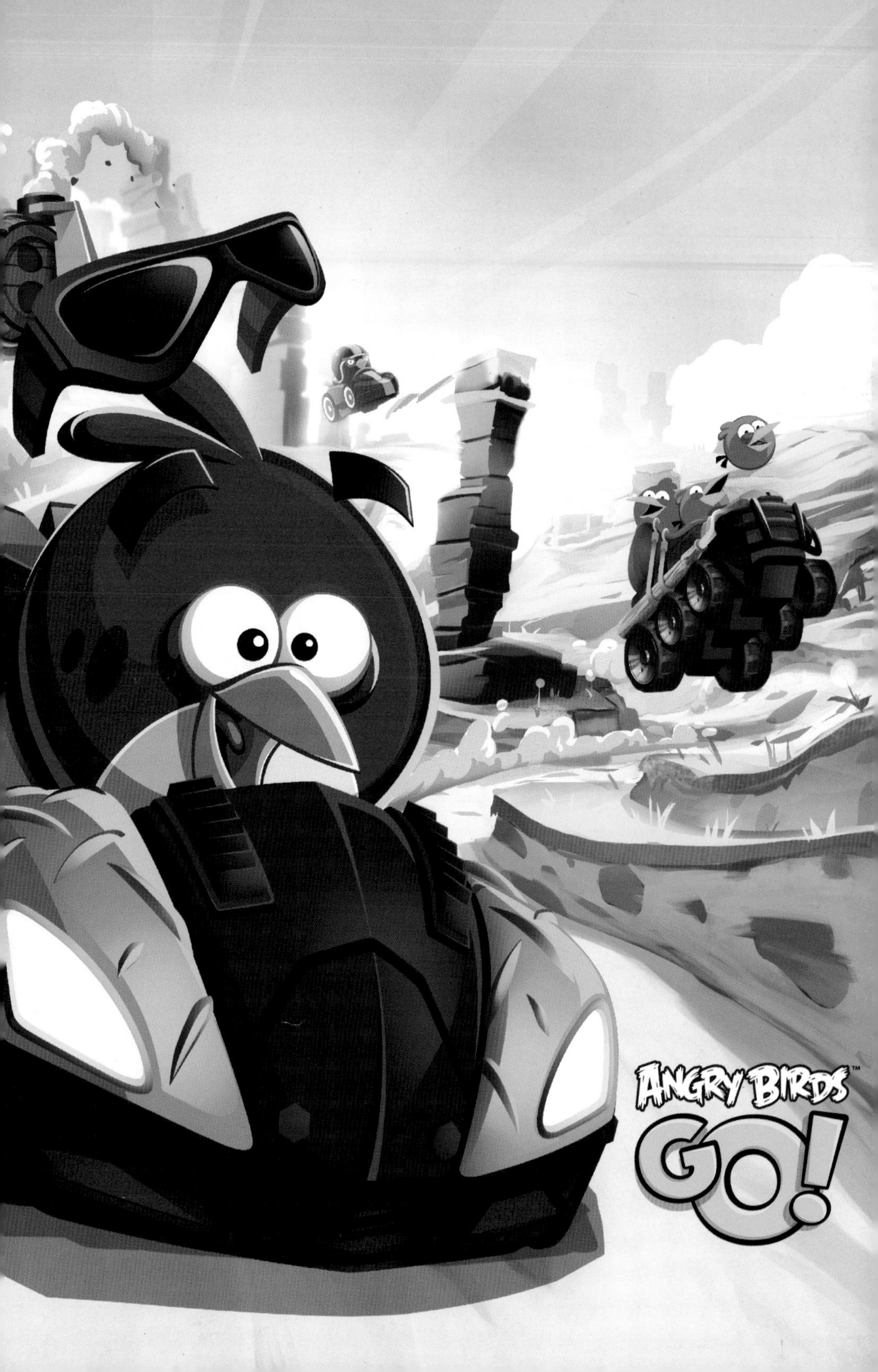
ANGRY BIRDS™
GO!

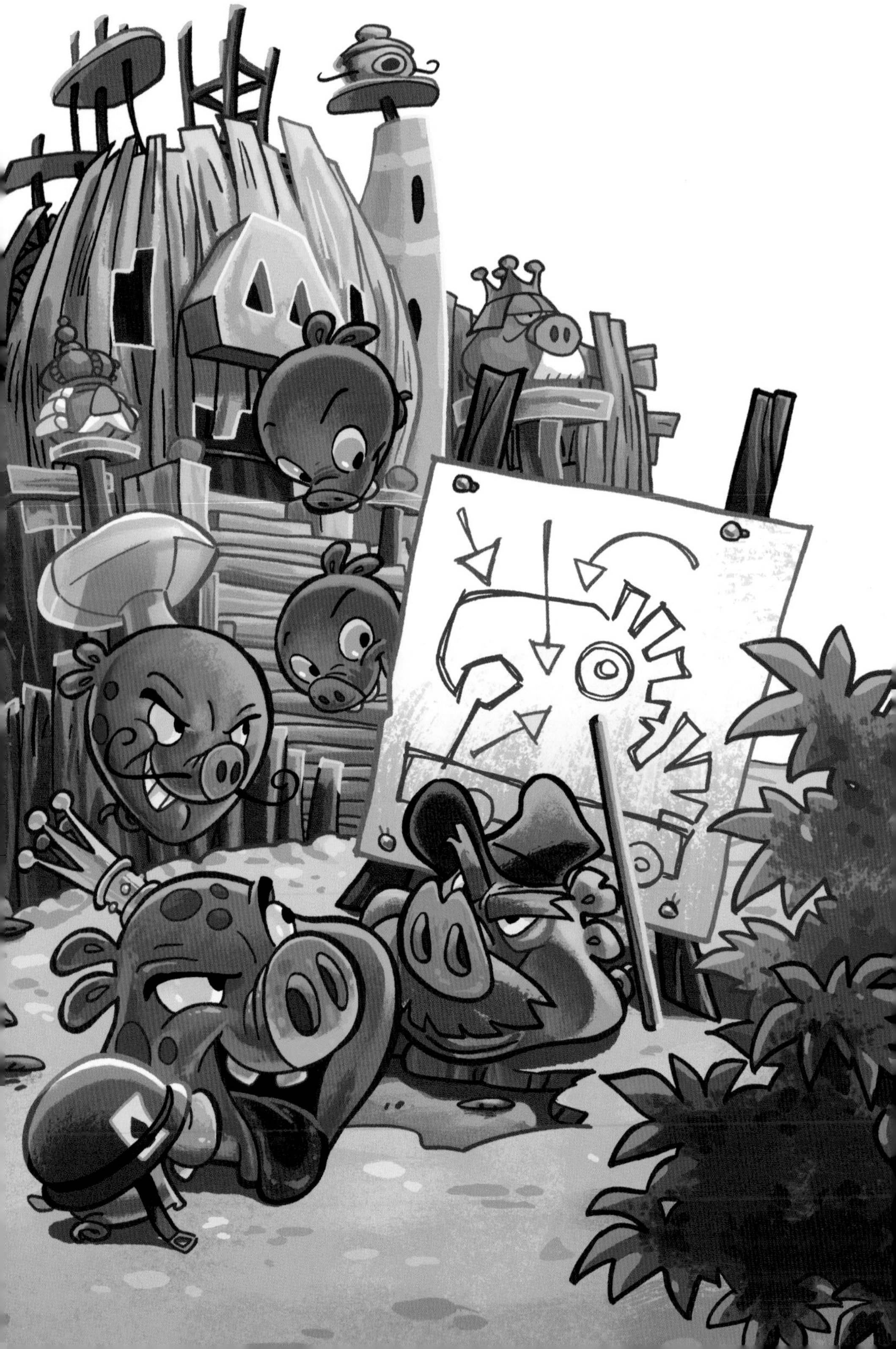

Artwork by Giorgio Cavazzano
Colors by Digikore Studios

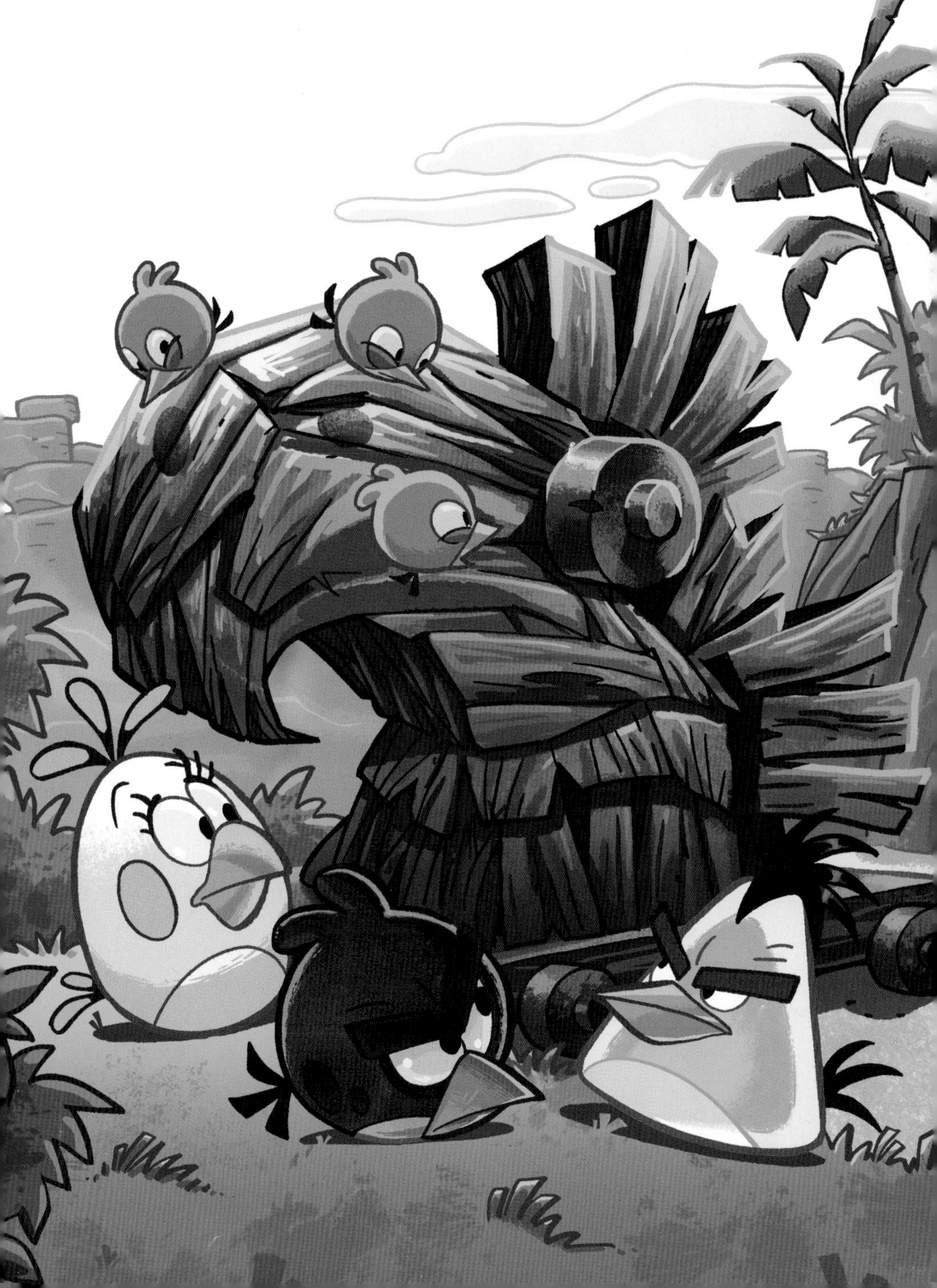

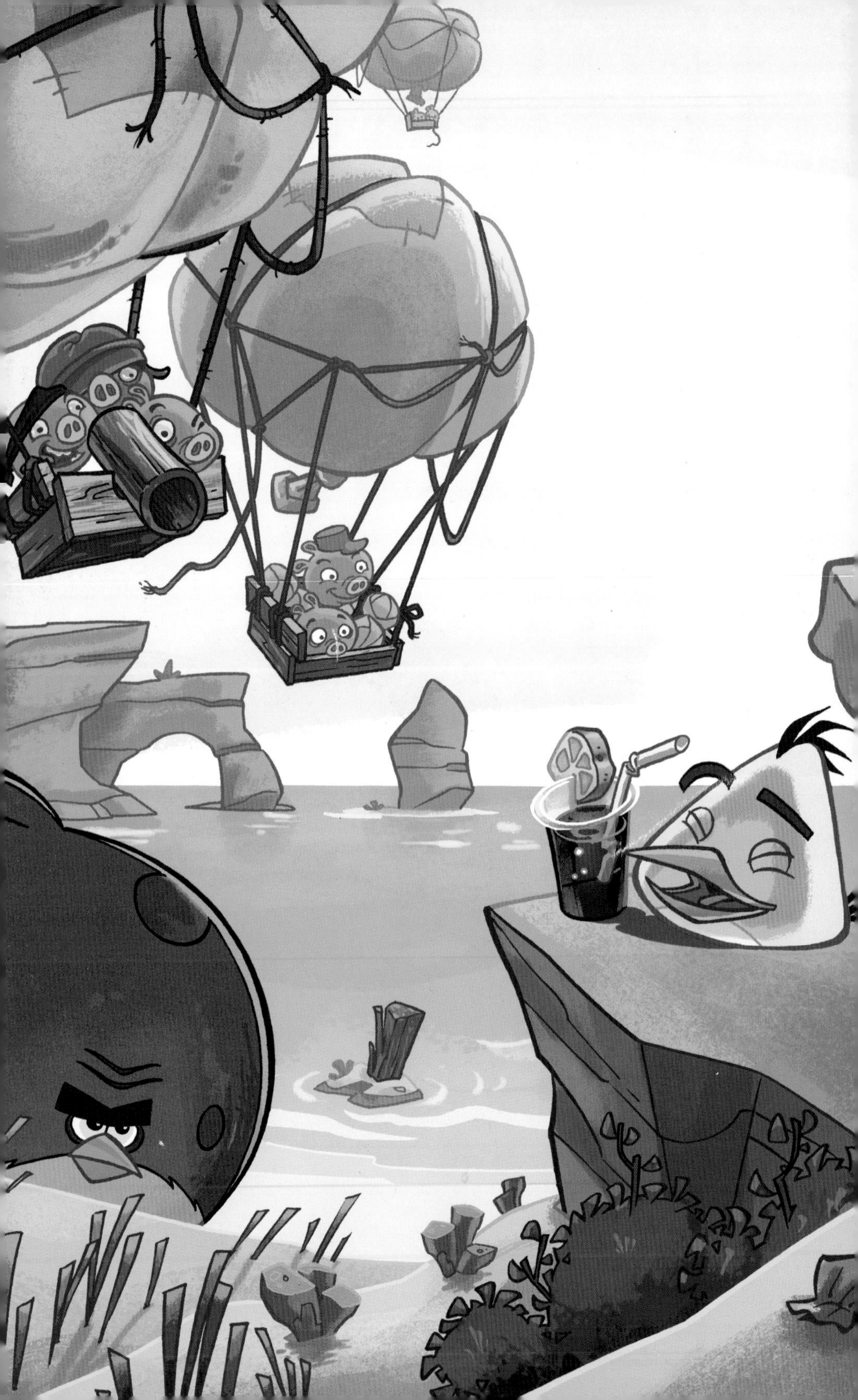

Artwork by Cēsar Ferioli
Colors by Digikore Studios

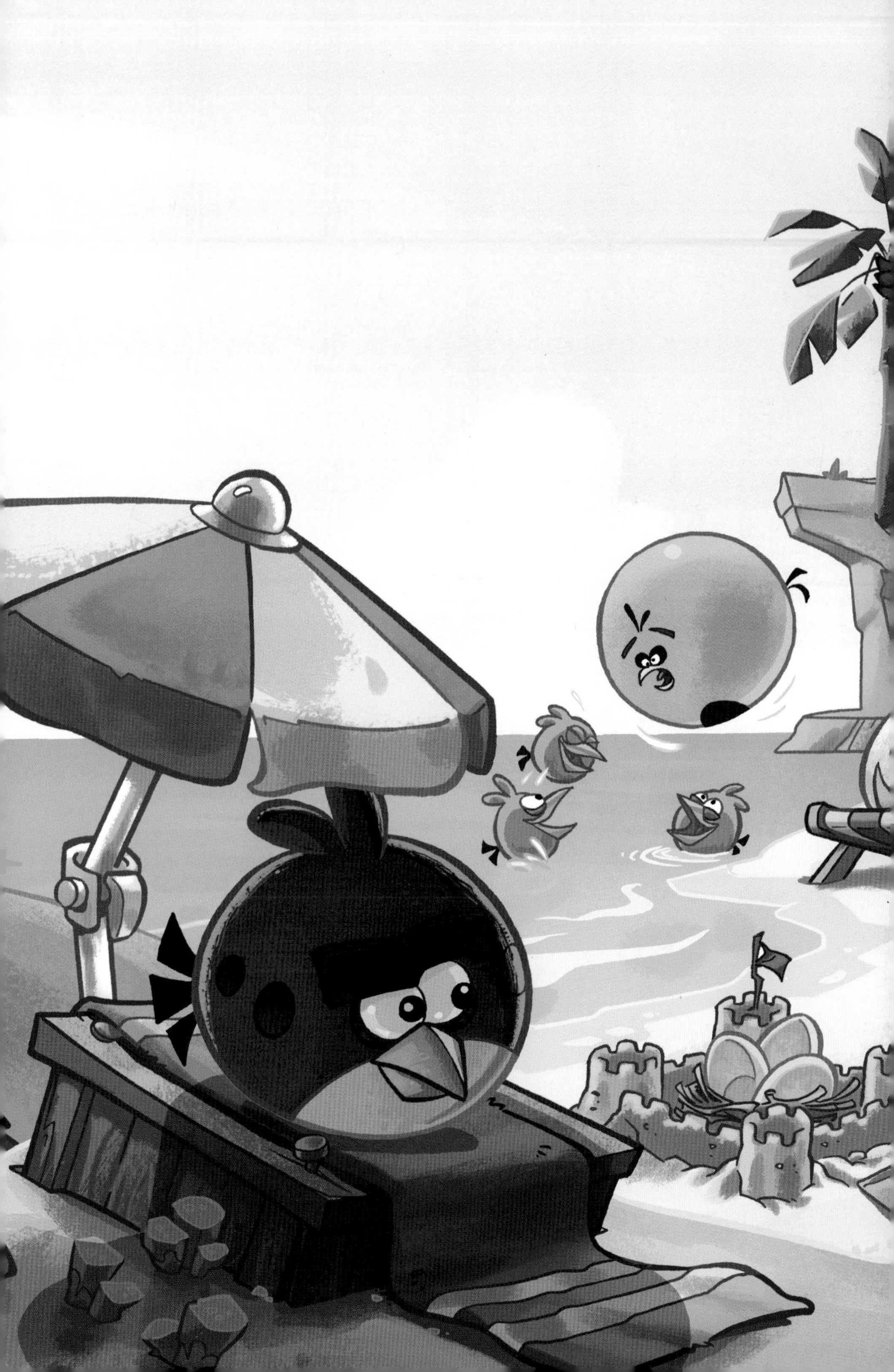

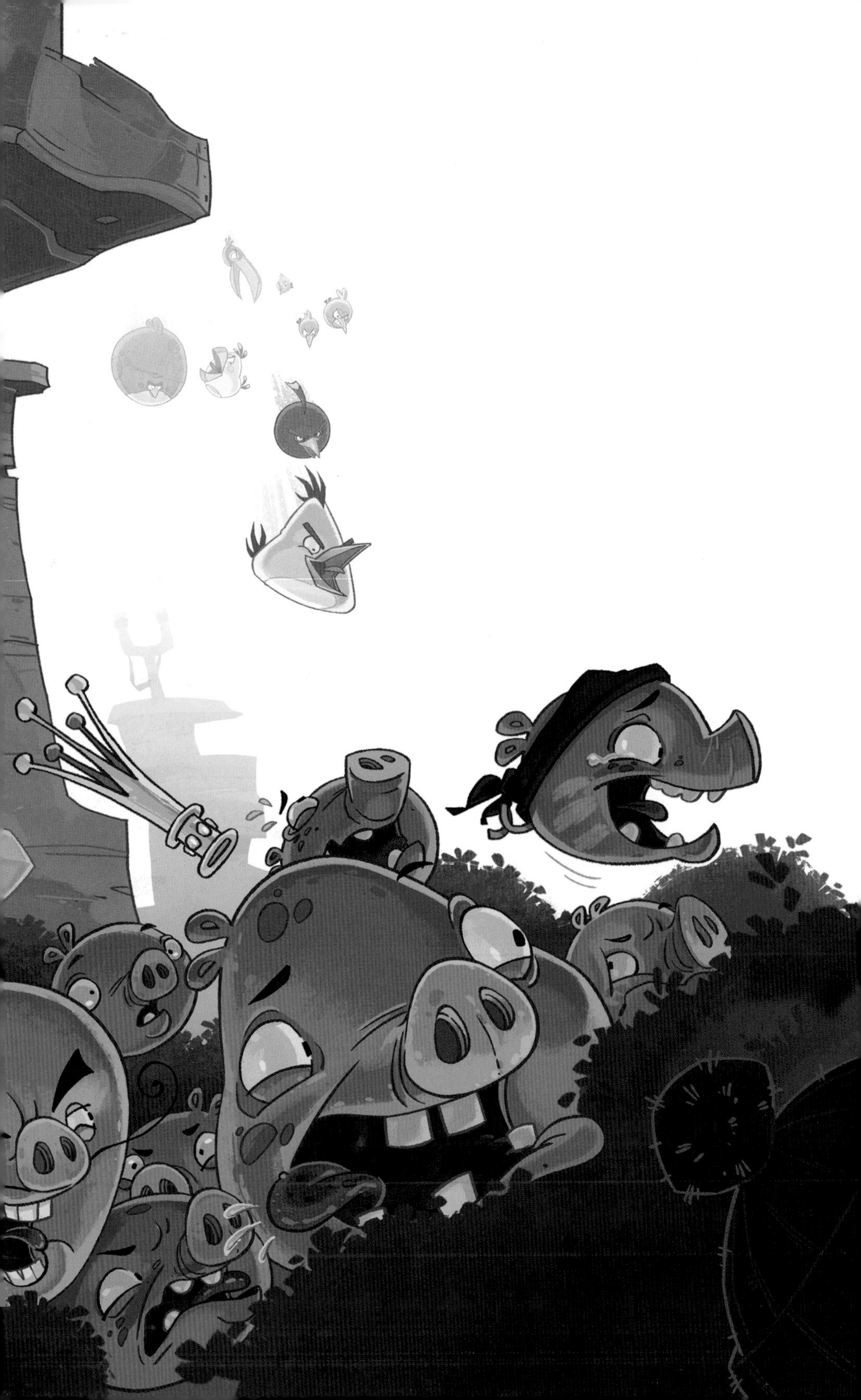

Artwork by Jean-Michel Boesch

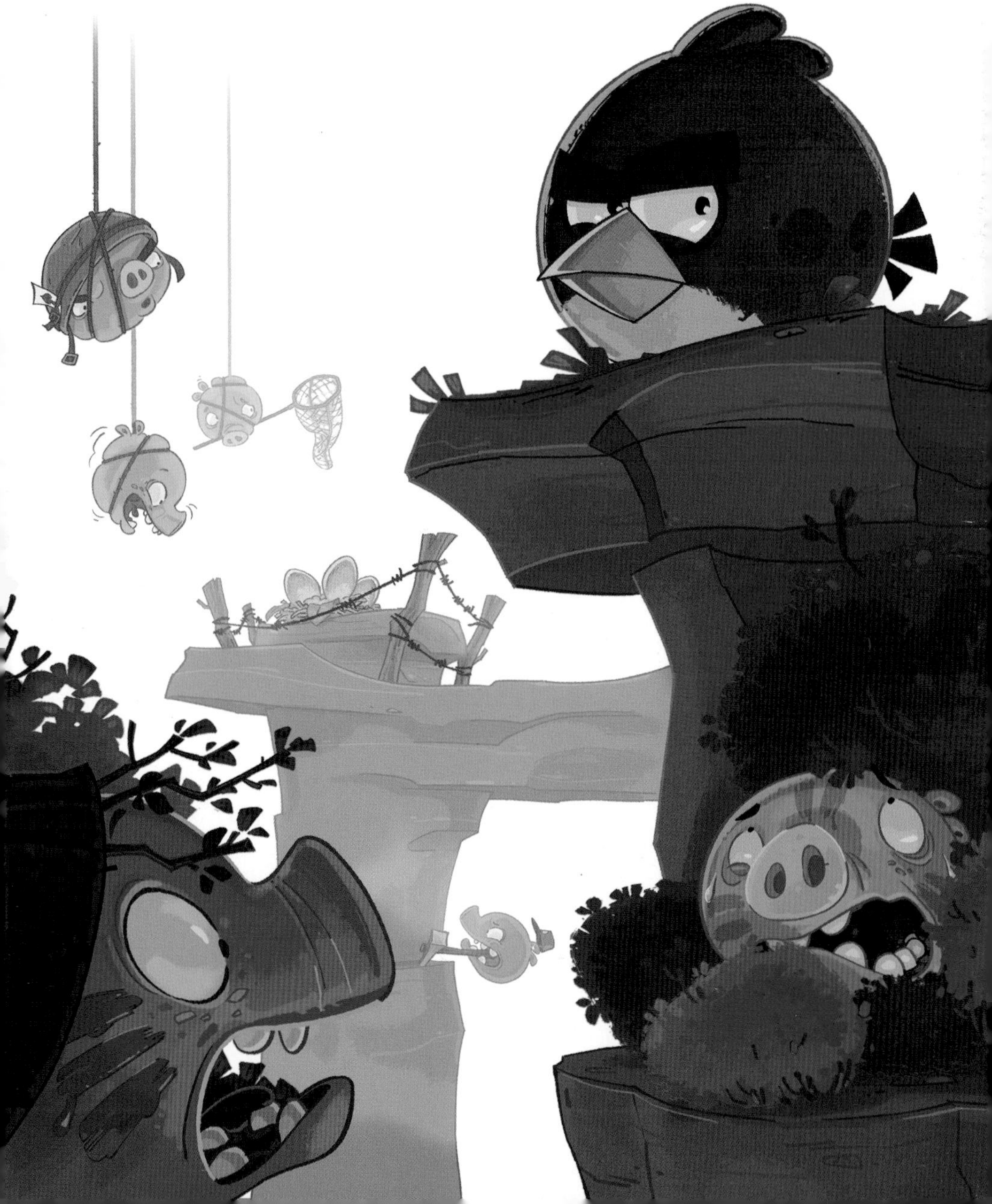

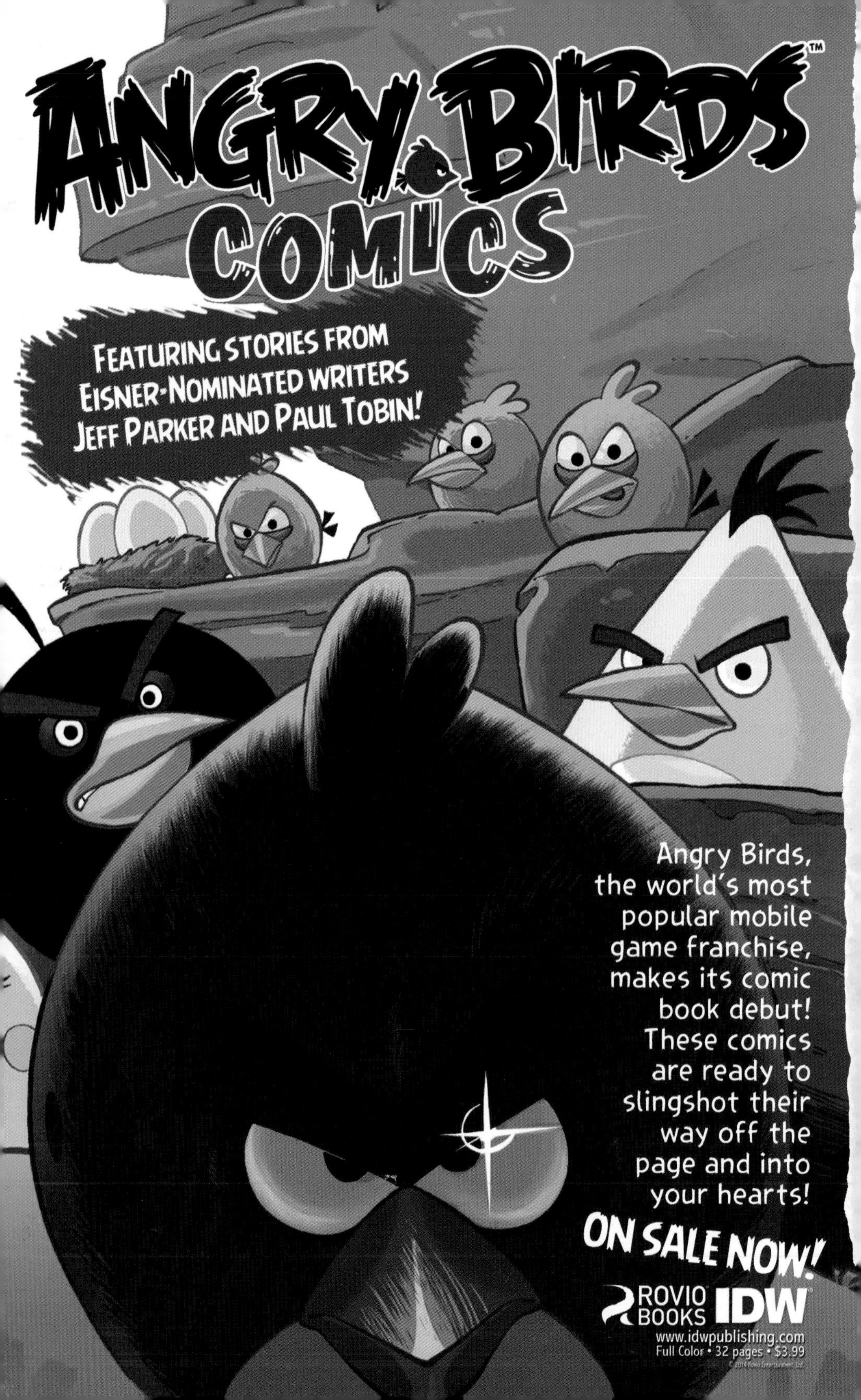
ANGRY BIRDS™
COMICS
FEATURING STORIES FROM EISNER-NOMINATED WRITERS JEFF PARKER AND PAUL TOBIN!
Angry Birds, the world's most popular mobile game franchise, makes its comic book debut! These comics are ready to slingshot their way off the page and into your hearts!
ON SALE NOW!
ROVIO BOOKS IDW
www.idwpublishing.com
Full Color • 32 pages • $3.99
© 2014 Rovio Entertainment, Ltd.